"Emily Brightwell continues to brighten the well-being of her fans with ENTERTAINING MYSTERIES."
—*Midwest Book Review*

"[A] WINNING COMBINATION IN WITHERSPOON AND JEFFRIES. It's murder most English all the way!"
—*The Literary Times*

INSPECTOR WITHERSPOON ALWAYS TRIUMPHS . . . HOW DOES HE DO IT?

Even the Inspector himself doesn't know—because his secret weapon is as ladylike as she is clever. She's Mrs. Jeffries—the determined, delightful detective who stars in this unique Victorian mystery series. Be sure to read them all . . .

The Inspector and Mrs. Jeffries
A doctor is found dead in his own office—and Mrs. Jeffries must scour the premises to find the prescription for murder.

Mrs. Jeffries Dusts for Clues
One case is solved and another is opened when the Inspector finds a missing brooch—pinned to a dead woman's gown. But Mrs. Jeffries never cleans a room without dusting under the bed—and never gives up on a case before every loose end is tightly tied . . .

The Ghost and Mrs. Jeffries
Death is unpredictable . . . but the murder of Mrs. Hodges was foreseen at a spooky séance. The practical-minded housekeeper may not be able to see the future—but she can look into the past and put things in order to solve this haunting crime.

Mrs. Jeffries Takes Stock
A businessman has been murdered—and it could be because he cheated his stockholders. The housekeeper's interest is piqued . . . and when it comes to catching killers, the smart money's on Mrs. Jeffries.

continued . . .

Mrs. Jeffries Takes the Cake
The evidence was all there: a dead body, two dessert plates, and a gun. As if Mr. Ashbury had been sharing cake with his own killer. Now Mrs. Jeffries will have to dish up clues . . .

Mrs. Jeffries Rocks the Boat
Mirabelle had traveled by boat all the way from Australia to visit her sister—only to wind up murdered. Now Mrs. Jeffries must solve the case—and it's sink or swim . . .

Mrs. Jeffries Weeds the Plot
Three attempts have been made on Annabeth Gentry's life. Is it due to her recent inheritance, or was it because her blood-hound dug up the body of a murdered thief? Mrs. Jeffries will have to investigate . . .

Mrs. Jeffries Pinches the Post
Harrison Nye may have been involved in some dubious business dealings, but no one ever expected him to be murdered. Now, Mrs. Jeffries and her staff must root through the sins of his past to discover which one caught up with him . . .

Mrs. Jeffries Pleads Her Case
Harlan Westover's death was deemed a suicide by the magistrate. But Inspector Witherspoon is willing to risk his career treading political waters to prove otherwise. And it's up to Mrs. Jeffries and her staff to ensure the good inspector remains afloat . . .

Mrs. Jeffries Sweeps the Chimney
A dead vicar has been found, propped against a church wall. And Inspector Witherspoon's only prayer is to seek the divine divinations of Mrs. Jeffries.

MRS. JEFFRIES
STALKS THE HUNTER

EMILY BRIGHTWELL

BERKLEY PRIME CRIME, NEW YORK

MRS. JEFFRIES STALKS THE HUNTER

A Berkley Prime Crime Book / published by arrangement with the author

PRINTING HISTORY
Berkley Prime Crime mass-market edition / October 2004

Copyright © 2004 by Cheryl Arguile.
Cover design by Jill Boltin.
Cover illustrations by David Stimson.

ISBN: 0-425-19885-5

Berkley Prime Crime Books are published by The Berkley Publishing Group, a division of Penguin Group (USA) Inc., 375 Hudson Street, New York, New York 10014.
The name BERKLEY PRIME CRIME and the BERKLEY PRIME CRIME design are trademarks belonging to Penguin Group (USA) Inc.

PRINTED IN THE UNITED STATES OF AMERICA

10 9 8 7 6 5 4

In loving memory:
Doris Annie Arguile and Robert Thomas Arguile

CHAPTER 1

"Blast," Sir Edmund Leggett swore softly as he pushed back the heavy curtains and peeked out the window at Thornton Square. "She's there again."

Roland Leggett walked up behind his cousin and peered over his shoulder through the glass pane. On the far side of the square, a young, red-haired woman wearing a straw bonnet, a gray jacket, and a pale lavender day dress stood staring at the house. He had a perfectly good view of her as she stood next to the lamppost beside the entrance to the garden. Roland had seen her a good half-dozen times in the last few days. "She's certainly persistent," he said softly. He glanced over his shoulder at the three people having tea in the huge drawing room. "Is Miss Parkington aware of her existence?" he whispered.

"I'm not that stupid," Sir Edmund hissed. He dropped

the curtain and stepped back. "She knows nothing about her, and I intend to keep it that way."

"What are you two whispering about?" asked Julia Parkington, a matron of fifty-five, who turned to look at the two men. She was a tall woman with graying blonde hair, pale blue eyes, and rather bland features.

"It's nothing, Madam," Sir Edmund gave his future mother-in-law a wide smile. "I merely wanted to ascertain that you'd have fair weather for your journey home."

"How very kind of you," Mrs. Parkington replied. "You're so very considerate."

"Excellent character," Mr. Osgood Parkington beamed at his future son-in-law and wished his daughter, Miss Beatrice Parkington, who was sitting next to her mother on the settee, would make a complimentary comment about her future husband. For God's sake, what did the girl want? He'd gone to a lot of time, trouble, and expense to get the chit a titled and handsome husband, and all she could do was glare sullenly at the carpet.

Beatrice Parkington was a lovely, dark-haired young lady of twenty-two. She stared at the lap of her elegant, emerald-green day dress and said nothing.

Sir Edmund glanced at his intended and wondered if beneath that calm façade, there was any personality whatsoever. Then he shrugged mentally and decided it didn't matter what went on in that empty head of hers, as long as she married him. Quickly. His creditors were beginning to be most unpleasant in their threats. "May I offer you more tea, Miss Beatrice?" he asked politely.

"No thank you," she replied in such a low voice he could barely hear her.

"Speak up, girl," her father, Osgood Parkington, snapped. "Sir Edmund doesn't want to marry a mouse."

She looked up sharply and opened her mouth; then she clamped it shut.

"Now, Osgood, do be kind," Julia Parkington said

quickly. "We don't want Sir Edmund thinking we're the sort of family that speaks harshly to one another."

Osgood shot his wife a quick frown. He was a tall, balding man with a few tufts of graying hair left here and there on his scalp. He had thin lips, watery brown eyes, and a large nose. He was dressed in an expensive black suit, which despite its expensive cut, couldn't quite hide his potbelly.

"It's quite all right," said Edmund, who'd moved to the settee and was standing directly in back of Beatrice, patting her on the shoulder. "My lady is just shy." He felt her cringe away from him.

"She'll get over it once she's married," Osgood blustered. He glared at Beatrice, furious at the way she was embarrassing him in front of a nobleman.

"Now dearest," Mrs. Parkington soothed. "Don't be hard on the girl. She's simply not used to such imposing company."

"Her inexperience is your fault, Julia. You've let her grow up with her nose in a book instead of learning the proper way for a young woman to conduct oneself in society."

"I can speak for myself," Beatrice said. She looked directly at her father. "If I have something worth saying."

"And I'm sure you have much that is not only worth saying, but definitely worth hearing." Roland laughed lightly and sat down on the settee next to Mrs. Parkington. "Let's do talk about something pleasant. When is the engagement to be announced?"

Sir Edmund sat down in the wing chair next to Mr. Parkington. "Yes, madam, now that all the legal matters have been settled, we must move ahead with the wedding plans."

Now that he knew how much the Parkingtons were willing to settle on him for making their daughter a lady of the land, he was eager to get on with it. The girl was nice and malleable, so being wed to her shouldn't be any great inconvenience. Once he got an heir from her, he'd send her to the country and continue his life as it had always been. But it had to be done quickly. Some of the more aggressive of his creditors were actually threatening him. He needed that settlement money soon.

"Oh, it'll take at least a year to plan the wedding," Mrs. Parkington replied airily. "These things take a great deal of thought and preparation."

Sir Edmund contorted his face into what he hoped was a besotted-with-love expression and looked at his intended. "I can't wait that long for us to be together."

"Perhaps it can be done in six months," Mr. Parkington suggested eagerly.

"That's quite impossible," Mrs. Parkington announced. "One simply can't plan a wedding in such a short period of time."

"Let's at least announce the engagement quickly," Sir Edmund said. If his creditors knew he were marrying an heiress, they might give him a bit of leeway. "Let's do it tonight at Lord Keighley's. We're all going to be there and we've got to make it public."

"Jolly good," Roland exclaimed. "That's the perfect place to do it."

"That's a splendid idea," Osgood Parkington declared. "Absolutely splendid."

"You'll be the center of things, my dear," Mrs. Parkington said to Beatrice with a laugh. "It'll be so very exciting."

But Beatrice didn't look in the least excited. Roland Leggett watched the girl's face. He decided that she looked positively sickened by the news that her engagement was going to be announced.

Mrs. Hepzibah Jeffries, housekeeper for Inspector Gerald Witherspoon, reached for the big brown teapot and poured herself a second cup. She and the rest of the staff were gathered around the kitchen table for their morning tea.

"I'll finish up them top windows as soon as we're done 'ere," Wiggins, the footman, said. He was a handsome lad with round apple cheeks, brown hair, and a ready smile.

Mrs. Jeffries was glad to see him in such good spirits. The lad had gone through a difficult time lately but seemed to be coming out of it nicely. "You be very careful, Wiggins. I don't want you falling over the railing and into the street."

"Humph," Mrs. Goodge, the cook, snorted delicately. She was a portly, elderly woman who'd worked in some of the finest houses in all of England. She'd ended up working for Inspector Gerald Witherspoon when her last employer had let her go because she'd gotten old. At the time, she'd been quite dismayed at how she'd had to come down in the world. But now, she wouldn't trade her place here for anything, not even if she were offered a position at Buckingham Palace. "As far as I'm concerned, those windows can stay dirty. No one looks out of them. You shouldn't be going up there, it's dangerous."

"Not to worry," he replied. "I know what I'm about."

"'Course you do, lad," Smythe, the coachman, said. "But why don't you wait until later today to finish up them attic ones. I'll be free in a couple of 'ours and I'd rather you didn't climb out there on your own." Smythe was a big, muscular man with dark hair, harsh features, and kind brown eyes.

"Why can't you go up with him straight after tea?" Betsy, the maid, asked. She was a young woman in her twenties with big blue eyes and a beautiful smile. She and the coachman were engaged.

"Because I want to nip over to one of my sources and see if there's any word about her."

The "her" he was referring to was Edith Durant. She

was wanted for murder, and as the entire household of Inspector Witherspoon secretly helped him with his cases, they were on the hunt for her, so to speak.

Smythe, who had various underworld acquaintances, had crossed a few palms with silver to find any information on Edith Durant's whereabouts. Smythe was also very, very wealthy. But only a few people in the household were privy to that knowledge.

He'd made a fortune in Australia and then returned to England. He'd gone to see his old friend and previous employer, Euphemia Witherspoon, the inspector's aunt, who had asked him to stay on and look after her nephew. As she was dying, Smythe had agreed. By the time everything was settled, the household was investigating murders and he was in love with Betsy.

Gerald Witherspoon had inherited Euphemia's house and fortune. He'd also inherited Smythe and Wiggins. As the inspector had been brought up in very modest circumstances, he'd no idea how to run such a big house. So he'd hired Mrs. Jeffries as his housekeeper, Mrs. Goodge as his cook, and ended up with Betsy when she'd collapsed half-starved on his doorstep. When she had recovered, she'd been hired as a maid.

"I can't believe the police can't get their hands on the woman," the cook shook her head in disgust. "She can't have disappeared off the face of the earth."

"She's a very clever woman," Wiggins said. "She's probably gotten clean away."

"Let's hope not," Mrs. Jeffries said quickly. "Smythe, is your source reliable?"

"He's not failed me yet," Smythe replied. "If she's in England, he'd be the one to know it."

"I don't think she's still here," Betsy murmured. "Like Wiggins said, she's clever. She'd know that the police were looking for her and she'd get out of the country."

"She's probably in America or Canada," Mrs. Goodge

suggested. "It's easy to get lost in those big countries. There's lots of places to hide."

"It's a good thing we don't 'ave us a murder now," Wiggins said. "We'd be 'ard-pressed to do much investigatin' with us still on the 'unt for our last one."

"We got the murderer on our last case," Mrs. Goodge said defensively. "Leastways, we got one of them. His trial starts next week and he's sure to be found guilty." Edith Durant and her lover had committed two very ugly murders. She'd gotten away before she could be arrested and left him to face the music.

"That's true," Mrs. Jeffries interjected. "We did catch one of the killers. But Wiggins is correct as well, it is nice that things are a bit quiet now. Trying to find Edith Durant and work on another case would be a bit much."

"I wouldn't mind," Betsy mused. "I love our cases. It makes life ever so exciting and it feels like we're doing something really important."

"We are, dear," Mrs. Goodge assured her. "But it's nice to have a bit of a rest."

Little did they know that they had less than twenty-four hours before another case landed squarely on their doorstep.

Beatrice Parkington took her father's hand as she alighted from the carriage. "If you muck this up, girl," Osgood hissed at her, "I'll have you thrashed. You're going to marry Sir Edmund if it's the last thing you do."

Beatrice stared stonily at her father. She had no intention of marrying that stupid fool. But she'd learned years ago that it was pointless to try and reason with her father. "I won't muck up anything."

"I do wish you'd have let your maid tighten those corset strings," Mrs. Parkington frowned at Beatrice's pale pink gown. "You look quite plump."

"The dress fits fine," Beatrice replied, "and I refuse to

be trussed up like some ridiculous bird for the sake of idiotic fashion."

"Come on, then," Osgood snapped at the two women, "we don't want to keep Sir Edmund or the Keighley's waiting."

The three of them entered the Grecian-style Belgravia mansion and were greeted by their hosts, Lord and Lady Keighley. But before Beatrice could escape into the crowded party, Sir Edmund and Roland Leggett arrived.

"You look lovely, my dear," Sir Edmund swooped down for a kiss, but Beatrice turned her face quickly enough so that he only bussed her cheek.

"Thank you," she replied. From the corner of her eye, she could see her father frowning at her, but she didn't care.

Sir Edmund, who pretended he hadn't noticed her avoidance of his lips, offered her his arm. "Shall we go inside?"

Beatrice gave him a tight smile, took his arm, and let him lead her into the festivities. The rooms were crowded and before too many minutes had passed, Beatrice managed to evade her parents and her fiancé. As unobtrusively as possible, she slipped over to a window that faced the street and slowly drew the curtain back. She smiled in satisfaction. The woman was there. She'd followed Sir Edmund.

Beatrice probably wouldn't have noticed that her fiancé had an admirer had he not started acting so peculiar. He'd started hovering around windows all the time. A few days ago, when she'd seen him peeking out the front window of his own drawing room for the tenth time that afternoon, she'd had a look herself and spotted the woman. She'd been standing by a lamppost and staring at Sir Edmund's front door. Since then, Beatrice had seen the woman several times. Good, she thought, the girl was an integral part of her plan to avoid marriage to this dolt. He might be titled and handsome, but she had no intention of spending her life saddled with a cruel man like Edmund Leggett.

She'd rather be dead than stuck with a monster like him. No, better yet, she'd rather he was dead. There were far too many things she still wanted to do in her life.

"Come along, girl," her father's harsh voice intruded on her thoughts. "Get into the drawing room, Sir Edmund is getting ready to make the announcement."

"Coming, Father," she murmured. She trudged after him and hoped this wouldn't take too long. She had a lot of plans to make.

Sir Edmund Leggett weaved his way down Pont Street. A light mist had begun to form pockets of fog, but the air wasn't moist enough to sober him up. All in all, he thought the announcement had gone well tonight. He burped lightly and stepped around a postbox that had inexplicably jumped out in front of him. Too bad his fiancée didn't seem overly enthusiastic about the match, it had been a bit embarrassing tonight with her walking off only seconds after the champagne glasses had been raised, but she'd come around before the wedding.

He looked down the deserted street and sighed in relief. At least that other witch wasn't bothering him. He'd been half afraid that she'd be outside waiting for him when he escorted the Parkingtons to their carriage, but she'd gone. Thank God for that, he thought. Old man Parkington was desperate to sell his daughter to the nobility, but even he'd balk at a really ugly scandal sullying the family name. A few of his acquaintances and friends had spotted the girl hanging about everyplace he went, but he'd managed to let them think she was one of his cast-off mistresses. In truth, he was getting worried. The girl should have gotten tired of her silly game by now, but she hadn't. The woman loathed him. When he'd confronted her the second time she'd stood outside his home, she'd never said a word, merely stared at him with such utter contempt that a chill had literally crawled up his spine.

But she wasn't here now and he wasn't going to let the witch ruin his plans. As of today, he was officially engaged to Miss Beatrice Parkington, heiress. His financial troubles were over. Now, if he could just get rid of that troublesome woman who'd been following him, life would be perfect. He fully intended for his life to be perfect.

Edmund turned the corner into a narrow street and stumbled to a halt as a heavily cloaked figure appeared out of nowhere. "I say, you'd better watch where you're going." He broke off as he recognized the face beneath the hood. "Good Lord, what on earth are you doing here . . ."

The figure raised a gloved hand, leveled a gun at Edmund Leggett's heart, and fired three shots in rapid succession. Edmund gaped at his assailant for a split second and then toppled over onto a heap. The cloaked figure knelt down and made sure the victim was dead, then looked up and down the narrow, fog-enshrouded street. It was still deserted. The figure rose quickly, took one last look up and down the street, then hurried off into the night.

Less than fifteen minutes later, a constable who was patrolling the area found Sir Edmund's body. At first he thought the fellow was simply drunk and passed out on the street. Such things happened, even in good neighborhoods. But then he saw the blood and knew that murder had been done.

The knocking came at half past three. Mrs. Jeffries, who was a light sleeper, heard it first. She put on her robe, lighted the small lamp she kept at her bedside, picked it up, and went downstairs.

The inspector called out to her just as she reached the front hall. "I'm on my way down, Mrs. Jeffries, let me open the door. You don't know who's out there."

"It's Constable Cooperman, sir," a voice called through the door. "We've had a murder and I've been sent to fetch you."

By this time, the inspector, wearing a dark maroon dressing gown, reached the front door. He unlocked it and yanked it open. "It really is a constable," he muttered to Mrs. Jeffries. "Do come in lad," he invited, as he stepped back and gestured for the officer to step into the hall.

"I'll put the kettle on, sir." Mrs. Jeffries said quickly. She knew that something important was happening. Despite his having solved more homicides than anyone else on the force, it was rare that they sent a constable around to get Inspector Witherspoon at this time of night.

"Thank you, Mrs. Jeffries," he said. He was such a lucky man to have such a devoted staff. "Come along, Constable. Let's go down to the kitchen and have a cup of tea while you tell me what this is all about."

"Yes sir," Constable Cooperman replied. "I could do with something hot. It might be spring, but it's very chilly outside tonight." He was a tall, gangly young man with curly brown hair, deep-set hazel eyes, and a large mouth.

Mrs. Jeffries was pouring the boiling water into the teapot when the two men reached the kitchen. "It'll be ready in a moment, sir."

"Take a chair, Constable," Witherspoon directed as he sat down at the head of the table. "Now, what's this all about?"

Mrs. Jeffries fussed over the tea tray. She wanted to hear what the constable had to say.

"There's been a murder, sir," Constable Cooperman said. "In Belgravia. Sir Edmund Leggett was shot in the chest tonight."

"Are there any witnesses?" Witherspoon kept his voice calm. He hated working on murders that involved the nobility or the upper classes. They were always such a bother. Getting any decent information about the deceased was generally as difficult as dodging raindrops during a thunderstorm.

"No, sir, nary a one."

Mrs. Jeffries slowly picked up the teapot and the strainer. She poured the tea into the inspector's favorite mug.

"Where's the body been taken?"

"They've left it alone, sir," Cooperman replied. "That's why they sent me along to fetch you. Chief Inspector Barrows happened to be at the station when the news came in, sir. He sent along instructions that the body wasn't to be moved until you'd had a chance to look at it. Your methods are becoming quite well known, sir. We all know not to muck up the evidence until you've had a good look."

Mrs. Jeffries handed the inspector his tea and then handed the constable the cup she'd poured for him. She took her time getting the sugar bowl.

"I suppose I'd best get cracking then," Witherspoon said. "If you'll wait here, Constable, I'll pop upstairs and get dressed. I shouldn't be more than a few minutes." He glanced at the housekeeper. "I'll take my tea with me."

"Yes sir." She waited until the inspector had disappeared and then she turned to the constable. "Would you care for a bun or perhaps a scone?"

Cooperman brightened. "I wouldn't mind a bit of a nibble. I missed my dinner hour."

"Of course." She fairly flew to the cupboard where she knew Mrs. Goodge kept the baked goods and pulled down a cloth covered bowl. She took the bowl over to the dish cupboard. "You must be very hungry."

"I am a bit peckish," he admitted. "Mind you, I'm surprised I've got any appetite at all. Considering what someone had done to that poor fellow."

"Murder is dreadful, isn't it." Lifting the clean towel, she pulled out one of Mrs. Goodge's excellent scones and laid it on a dessert plate. "Did you find the body?"

"No, but I was the one that answered the police whistle. Thank you, ma'am," he said as she put the scone in front of him. "I don't mind tellin' ya, I've not much stomach for what happened tonight. Grisly, it was."

"I take it there was a lot of blood?"

"From what I could see, the man probably bled to death. It was everywhere, all over his shirt and on the pavement, as well."

"How very clever that you were able to identify the body so quickly." She took a sip from the cup of tea she'd poured for herself.

He gave her a lopsided grin. "Cleverness had nothing to do with it, he had his calling cards on the inside pocket of his coat. 'Sir Edmund Leggett, Number 14, Thornton Square, Belgravia.' Mind you, that was a bit of luck. These days it's rare to find anyone, even people of that class that still use calling cards. They're a bit old-fashioned."

"He was an older gentleman, then?" she pressed.

"No, ma'am, he wasn't young, but he wasn't older either. I'd put him in his mid-thirties."

"Mrs. Jeffries?" Smythe, who'd obviously dressed in a hurry as his shirt buttons were undone and he was barefoot, came into the kitchen, his gaze fixed on the constable. "Is everything all right?"

"It's fine, Smythe." She smiled. "Constable Cooperman has come to fetch our inspector. There's been a murder in Belgravia."

"Murder? Must be someone important for 'em to fetch the Inspector out at this time of night," Smythe murmured softly.

"Officially, he's no more important than any other victim." Cooperman grinned. "But unofficially, we'd best get crackin' on this one or they'll be questions asked."

Inspector Witherspoon came into the kitchen with Fred, their mongrel dog, at his heels. "Gracious, Smythe we must have been making quite a racket to wake you up. But not to worry, everything is fine."

"Yes, sir, but I wanted to make sure. I expect that's how Fred got out, I must have left the door to our room open. Come on, boy, let's get you back upstairs."

"Go on, old fellow." Witherspoon patted the dog on the head. "You need your rest. Up you go."

Smythe shot the housekeeper a meaningful glance and then herded the reluctant dog toward the back steps. Mrs. Jeffries knew that the coachman was going upstairs to finish dressing. He'd be back down and following the inspector in two shakes of a lambs tail. The inspector would be none the wiser, of course.

"Do you have time for another cup of tea, sir?" she asked Witherspoon. "It's very chilly out there, and you'll not get anything else until sunrise." She wanted to delay him long enough for the coachman to get his shoes on and his shirt buttoned.

"Just a quick sip, Mrs. Jeffries," Witherspoon replied. "Then we must be off."

She refilled his mug and handed it to him.

The Inspector turned his attention back to Constable Cooperman. "Has the police surgeon been summoned?"

"Yes sir." Cooperman drained his own cup.

"Do you know who the surgeon for that district might be?"

"It's Doctor Grayson, sir."

"Right then, I expect he'll be there by the time we get back. How did you get here? Surely you didn't find a hansom this time of night?"

"We did find one, sir. He was dropping off a late fare around the corner. I had him wait, sir. I hope that's all right."

"That's fine, Constable." He drained his cup. "Let's be off then."

Mrs. Jeffries escorted them to the front door. As soon as she'd closed it behind them, Smythe charged down the staircase. "Did you manage to hear the actual address. If they're in a hansom and I'm on foot, I might not be able to keep up with them."

"It's just off Pont Street," she replied. "In Belgravia. You should spot it easily."

"Good, I ought to be back with something by breakfast."

Mrs. Jeffries closed the door behind him and then went back to the kitchen. She glanced at the clock on the pine sideboard. It was past four in the morning. There was no point in going back to bed. She'd never get to sleep. She might as well do a few chores. As it appeared they had a murder, she might as well get a bit ahead on the housework. She could have the drawing room swept and polished by the time the others got up.

Three constables and the police surgeon were standing around the body when Witherspoon and Constable Cooperman reached Carlotta Street in Belgravia.

"Good evening," Witherspoon said politely. He didn't look at the corpse. He was rather squeamish in that regard, but he knew his duty. He'd look at it when he had to and not a moment sooner.

"Are you Inspector Witherspoon?" A man wearing a dark overcoat and holding a medical bag stepped forward and extended his hand. "I'm Dr. Grayson, the police surgeon. I'll have a look as soon as you're finished. Though I must say, it's rather odd being told not to touch the body until you've had a chance to look at the fellow."

"How do you do, Doctor." Witherspoon shook the man's hand. "I'll be as quick as I can. I know my methods are a bit different, but there are things one can learn about the murder by having a good study of the victim before he's been moved too much." The inspector had no idea when that particular habit had become part of his method for solving homicides or why the method had seemed to have spread through the police force. He wasn't even certain what he hoped to find when he looked at an untouched murder scene, but he knew that it helped. He glanced at the constables. "Do any of you have a hand lantern?"

"We all do, sir," Cooperman said quickly.

"Good, shine them on the body then." He steeled himself and knelt down next to the victim. The man was lying on his side. His eyes were wide open and he was staring straight ahead. He wore formal evening dress but no overcoat. Blood had stained the front of his white silk shirt and pooled beneath him enough to soak through to the pavement. An ebony walking stick lay on the ground next to the body. Witherspoon picked up the stick and examined it closely. "He must have been murdered quickly," the inspector said. "He obviously didn't have time to use his stick as a defensive weapon."

"How can you tell that, sir?" one of the constables asked eagerly.

"Because there's nothing on it. This is a heavy stick, and if he'd struck someone with it, there'd be blood or skin or some sort of mark to show it had been used. It's not got a mark on it anywhere." He handed the stick to a constable. "Book this into evidence, please. I might have someone take a look at it with a magnifying glass."

Cooperman pointed to the victim's right hand. "It wasn't a robbery, sir. No thief would leave a ring like that one." The ring was a heavy gold filigree band with a large, black stone in the center. "It's valuable."

"You're right," the inspector frowned thoughtfully. "A thief would have taken that straight away. Check his pockets and see if he's any money."

The constable checked the inner coat pocket first. "Nothing there." Then he examined the trouser pockets. He pulled out a wad of pound notes and counted them. "There's four pounds here. No thief would have left this untouched."

Witherspoon winced. He'd been hoping it was a simple

robbery gone awry. Drat. "Then I suppose we can discount robbery as a motive."

"Looks that way, sir."

Witherspoon finished his examination of the body and then got up and said to Dr. Grayson, "I'm through. He's all yours now. Where will you be taking the body for the postmortem?"

"St. Thomas's," Grayson replied. "I ought to be finished with him by noon. I'll send the report over straight away."

"Thank you, sir." Witherspoon turned to the constables. "As soon as it's light, search the area and then get some lads to do a house-to-house along this street."

"What are we looking for, sir?" one of the constables asked.

"Anything that strikes you as odd or out of place," Witherspoon replied. "It appears our victim was shot more than once and the shots must have been quite loud. Ask everyone if they saw or heard anything unusual tonight. If anyone did, make sure you ask them if they noted the time."

The police van trundled around the corner and for the next few minutes the inspector supervised the loading of the body onto the gurney and into the van proper.

He then borrowed a hand lantern from Constable Cooperman and used it to search the immediate area where the body had lain. He found nothing. But he and the other constables stayed in the area searching for clues with hand lanterns and oil lamps until the sun came up.

Constable Barnes arrived at Carlotta Street a few minutes past eight. "You should have sent for me, sir," he said to the Inspector. The constable was a tall man with a craggy face and a headful of gray hair under his policeman's helmet. He'd worked with Inspector Witherspoon on all his cases and was somewhat put out that the inspector hadn't sent for him straight away.

"It was the middle of the night, Constable, and I didn't

want to disturb your good wife. She's just getting over that nasty bout of influenza and I knew she needed her rest."

"That's very thoughtful of you, sir," Barnes replied. He was somewhat mollified. But he was fiercely protective of his inspector and knew that Witherspoon, for all his brilliance in solving murders, didn't know how to watch his back. A rich nobleman had been murdered and that always brought trouble. But now that Barnes was here, he could keep an eye on things.

"Not at all, Constable." He told him everything that had been done thus far. "I think we'd best get to Sir Edmund's home and have a word with his family." He sighed and started toward the Brompton Road. "Let's find a hansom cab."

"It's never nice to deliver this kind of bad news, is it, sir?" Barnes fell into step with the inspector.

"To be truthful, Constable, it's the absolute worst thing I have to do in this job."

The household of Upper Edmonton Gardens was gathered around the kitchen table and eagerly waiting for Smythe to return. Two others had been added to their numbers. Luty Belle Crookshank, an elderly American woman with white hair, dark eyes, and a love of bright clothes, sat next to a tall, distinguished-looking man. He was her butler and he'd worked for Luty Belle for years. Though his hair was as white as his employer's he was a good many years younger than she.

They'd become involved with the inspector's household in one of the very first cases that the staff had helped solved. Once Luty figured out what was going on, she'd come to them for help with a problem of her own. One thing had lead to another and before long, Luty and Hatchet were firmly entrenched in the inspector's homicide investigations.

"What's takin' him so long?" Luty asked.

"Patience, madam," Hatchet replied. "I'm sure Smythe is doing an exemplary job of learning as much as he can about the victim. He'll be here shortly."

"If 'e don't come quick, maybe I ought to go after 'im and see what's what," Wiggins offered.

"We don't need both of you out and about," Mrs. Goodge said quickly. "Sure as you set a foot outside the house, Smythe will turn up and then we'll be delayed even more waitin' for you to get back."

"He's here." Betsy got up and hurried to the back hall.

They heard the back door open and the murmur of low voices. A moment later they returned. Smythe was holding Betsy's hand. "Sorry it took so long," he said as they took their places. He nodded at Luty and Hatchet. "But I wanted to find out as much as I could."

"Let me pour you some tea." Mrs. Jeffries picked up the pot and poured it into his mug.

"I'll get his breakfast plate," Betsy said. "I can listen while I'm fixing it." She got up and went to the stove where his breakfast had been kept hot in the warming oven.

"The victim is Sir Edmund Leggett and he doesn't live very far from where he was murdered. I went along and had a look at his house and found out a few things the police don't know yet, but I'll get to that part in a bit." He took a quick sip of tea. "According to the police surgeon, it looks like he was shot more than once but he won't know for sure until he digs the bullets out of the fellow."

"You spoke to the police surgeon?" Hatchet asked.

"No, but I eavesdropped on a couple of coppers," he replied.

"I don't suppose you managed to find out where the body is being taken for the post mortem?" Mrs. Jeffries asked.

Smythe grinned. "We're in luck. It's St. Thomas's."

The household had a good friend, Dr. Bosworth, who was a physician at St. Thomas's. He frequently helped them in their investigations.

"Good. I'll go along and have a word with Dr. Bosworth this afternoon," Mrs. Jeffries replied. "Do go on, Smythe."

Betsy put a plate of food in front of him. "Here, you can eat while you talk."

"Ta, love." he picked up his fork. "Anyway, like I was sayin', I went along and had a gander at Leggett's house. Grand it was, too, but showing a bit of wear on the outside if you know what I mean. But that's neither here nor there. What is important is that I found out from a servant that Sir Edmund got engaged last night. He was murdered while he was walking home from the dinner party where the engagement was announced."

"Cor blimey, that's a bit of bad luck," Wiggins exclaimed.

"Poor fellow," Betsy clucked sympathetically.

"How sad for his fiancée." Mrs. Goodge shook her head.

"Life simply isn't fair, is it," Hatchet said somberly.

"Not so fast." Smythe held up his hand. "Accordin' to what I found out, his fiancée is probably doin' a jig this mornin'."

"Doing a jig?" Betsy repeated. "You mean she didn't want to marry him?"

"That's right," Smythe replied. "She didn't want to marry the fellow. Her parents were forcin' her into it. Apparently, he's got a bit of a problem with women in his life. 'Cause there was another one who'd been houndin' 'im."

"Hounding him?" Mrs. Goodge repeated. "How?"

"Well . . . " Smythe wasn't certain how to explain it. "She sort of stalked him like. Spent her days standing outside his house and glaring at his front door, and then she'd show up everywhere he went. Followed him about and made a nuisance of herself."

"Cor blimey, the murder's just happened and we've already got two suspects." Wiggins grinned broadly.

"And both of them are female," Luty murmured. "Don't that just take the cake."

CHAPTER 2

"This is always the worst part, isn't it, Constable?" the inspector said to Barnes as they stood in the drawing room of the late Sir Edmund Leggett's home. He'd apparently forgotten he'd already told the constable how much he hated this part of his job.

"Yes, sir, it's never pleasant to tell someone a loved one has been murdered," Barnes replied dutifully. As was his habit, he studied the room as they waited. You could tell a lot about people by studying the objects with which they surrounded themselves.

On first glance, the house appeared to be the home of a rich nobleman. It was three stories high and made of pale gray brick with a tiny bit of garden in the front. But Barnes had noticed that the black paint on the window frames was peeling, the stone on the steps was lined with cracks, and the brass door lamps were dulled with neglect.

21

In the drawing room, he could see worn patches in the woven oriental carpet and there were bare spots along the walls where paintings had been removed. Barnes would bet his police pension that Sir Edmund routinely told people the paintings were being cleaned, while in truth, he'd probably sold them off. "But then again, sir, it's often the loved one that's done the killing in the first place.

"Still, that's not always the case, is it?" Witherspoon replied. He did hate to be cynical about life, but Constable Barnes made a valid point. It was frequently one's nearest and dearest that did the evilest of deeds.

He turned as the door opened and a neatly dressed man in a gray suit stepped into the room. His shirt was open at the throat and his cravat hung around his neck untied. He'd obviously hurried downstairs when the butler had told him the police were here. "I understand you wish to speak with someone from the household." He looked at Constable Barnes as he spoke. "I'm afraid you'll have to make do with me. Do forgive me if I seem a bit muddled. Your presence gives me some cause for alarm. My cousin, who is the master of the house hasn't returned home from last evening's engagement."

"I take it your cousin is Sir Edmund Leggett," Witherspoon said."

"That's correct. I'm Roland Leggett." He advanced toward the inspector with his hand outstretched. He was a tall, handsome man with thick brown hair, blue eyes, a full mouth, and high cheekbones.

"Inspector Gerald Witherspoon." The two men shook hands. "And this is Constable Barnes." Leggett turned and shook hands with the constable, who looked a bit surprised by the gesture. Generally, people of this class only acknowledged a uniformed man with a nod of their head.

"What's this all about, sir?" Roland Leggett asked the inspector. "Oh, do forgive me, I've forgotten my manners.

Please sit down." He gestured toward the settee and two wing chairs near the fireplace.

The three of them took a seat and then Constable Barnes took out his little brown notebook.

"I'm afraid I have some bad news," the inspector began. "Your cousin didn't come home last night for a very good reason . . ."

"Oh God, he's been hurt," Roland interrupted. He shook his head. "I told him he oughtn't to walk home on his own. But he insisted. Once he's made up his mind, he's not the sort to listen to anyone."

"He's not been hurt, sir," Witherspoon said quickly. "I only wish that were the case. I'm afraid your cousin is dead."

Roland Leggett's mouth dropped open. "Dead?" he repeated the word like he'd never heard it before. "But that's impossible. He was perfectly all right last night, a bit drunk, perhaps, but not enough to have done him any harm. How did it happen? Was he struck by a carriage . . . or did he fall . . ."

"He was shot, sir," Barnes replied. "In the chest. He probably died instantly."

"Shot? But how can that be? Who would do such a thing . . ."

"That's what we want to find out, sir," Witherspoon replied. "I know this must be difficult for you, but do you feel up to answering some questions."

"Just give me a moment, Inspector," Roland said, his expression dazed. "I can't seem to take it in. Edmund. Dead. Murdered."

"Take as much time as you need, sir," the inspector said softly. He looked away, wanting to give the poor man some privacy for his grief.

Constable Barnes, on the other hand, watched Leggett carefully but unobtrusively. He could see nothing but genuine grief and shock on the man's face. But he knew that meant nothing, he'd seen a good many murderers in his day who were also very fine actors.

"When did it happen?" Roland finally asked.

"We don't know the exact time, but we do know it was late last night," Witherspoon replied. "It would be very helpful if you could give us an idea of Sir Edmund's movements yesterday evening."

"We went to Lord Keighley's for a supper party," Roland replied. "But of course, it was really much more than that. My cousin announced his engagement last night. Oh my God, I must get to the Parkingtons. I don't want Beatrice to read about it in the papers."

"Don't worry, sir. It shouldn't have made the morning papers," Barnes said. "There wouldn't have been time."

"But I must see her before she hears it from someone else," Roland insisted.

"I take it Miss Parkington was Sir Edmund's new fiancée?" Witherspoon clarified. "In that case, sir, please don't trouble yourself. If you'll give us the address, we'll go there next, and I assure you, we'll break the terrible news to the lady as gently as possible. Now, if you'll just finish with your statement."

Roland hesitated a moment, as though he wanted to argue the point. Then he shrugged and said, "The Parkingtons live at number ten Clively Street. It's only half a mile or so from here."

"Thank you, sir," Witherspoon said softly. He glanced over and noted that Barnes had written down the address. "Now, if you'll continue with your narrative."

"As I've said, we were at the Keighley's and my cousin used the occasion to announce his engagement."

"What time did you arrive at the Keighleys?" Barnes asked.

Roland thought for a moment. "Oh, it must have been close to eight o'clock. It was quite a gala evening, that's why Edmund chose the occasion to make the announcement. There was champagne and congratulations, of course, and then some dancing."

"Was Sir Edmund enjoying himself?" Witherspoon asked. "Or did he appear to be agitated in any way?"

"He seemed to be having a good time," Roland replied, his expression thoughtful. "He was drinking quite a bit and accepting the congratulations of all his friends. Why do you ask?"

The inspector shrugged. "Because how he behaved might be an indication of his state of mind. What I'm trying to find out is if he appeared to be upset or worried about anything."

Roland waved his hand impatiently. "No, no, he was pleased to be engaged."

"We didn't wish to imply anything untoward," Witherspoon said softly. "But we must ask the question. Do please carry on."

"The party was over relatively early," he continued. "The Parkington's left about half past eleven as did most of the other guests. Lady Keighley and her sister retired a bit past midnight."

"What time did Sir Edmund leave?" Barnes asked.

"I don't know exactly," Roland replied. "But it was late. After the ladies went upstairs, we went into Lord Keighley's study for a whiskey."

"Who is 'we', sir?" Barnes looked up from his notebook.

"There was Edmund, of course, and Lord Keighley. Let me see, Alex Drummond was still there, and myself. We had several rounds of drinks, sir. After that, things get a bit vague. I remember that Edmund was the first to leave. I tried to talk him into riding with Alex as he'd brought his carriage, but Edmund was adamant that he preferred to walk."

"When he left, did anyone see him to the door?" Barnes asked.

"Only the butler." Roland smiled sheepishly. "I'm afraid the rest of us had another whiskey. To be frank, Inspector, we were all quite drunk."

"What time did you leave, sir?" Witherspoon asked.

"I don't know exactly. But it was good hour or two after Edmund had gone," he replied. "I'd fallen asleep, you see. As I'd no wish to embarrass myself further in front of my host. When I woke up, I saw that Drummond and Lord Keighley were both asleep on the settee so I slipped out the front door."

The inspector leaned forward. "Was the butler still on duty when you left?"

"No, by that time, even the servants had gone to bed. None of Edmund's household was awake when I arrived home, either. The old customs have died out, sir. Servants no longer stay up all hours of the night to await the master's return."

"Do you know what time you actually arrived home, sir?" Barnes looked up from his notebook.

"It was still dark outside," Roland replied. "But I didn't check the time. I'd no reason to, you see. The walk home had sobered me up a bit and my head was beginning to ache. All I wanted to do was go to bed."

"How did you get in, sir?" Witherspoon asked.

"I have my own key," he replied. "Edmund insisted on giving me one whenever I'm in London."

Barnes looked up from his notebook. "You don't live in London, sir?"

"No, I live in Bristol, but I'm here quite often on business. I always stay with my cousin when I'm in town." His voice broke and he looked away. After a moment, he said, "Forgive me, please. I don't usually lose control, but Edmund was more of a brother than a cousin. We're the only ones left in the family."

"I'm dreadfully sorry, sir," Witherspoon said gently. "I

assure you, we'll do our best to find whoever did this terrible thing and bring them to justice."

Roland nodded and then straighted up and looked at the two policemen. "Thank you, Inspector. Please continue with your questions."

"Did your cousin have any enemies?" Witherspoon sighed inwardly. That was always a silly sort of question, but one he had to ask anyway. Of course Sir Edmund had an enemy, he had a chestful of bullets to prove it.

"What do you mean?" Roland's expression clouded into confusion. "What sort of enemies? Surely this was a robbery or some such thing."

"We don't think it was a robbery, sir," Witherspoon said softly. "It appears your cousin was deliberately murdered."

"But surely he was just at the wrong place at the wrong time," Roland protested. "These things happen all the time."

Witherspoon shook his head slowly. "Murder does happen, sir, but not as often and not as randomly as one might think."

"I can't believe it. Who would want to kill Sir Edmund? Ye gods, he was just engaged this evening . . . oh my Lord, of course. It has to be her . . . it must be. She must have heard the news and gone mad . . . absolutely mad to have done such a thing."

Witherspoon looked sharply at Barnes and then cut back to Roland Leggett. "Who is 'she', sir?"

"I don't know her name," Roland replied excitedly. "But she's been following him about for the last two weeks or so. Edmund tried to ignore her, but she was there, just outside the house, day after day. She must have killed him, Inspector. She must have done it. He would never have admitted it, but he was terrified of her."

"What do we do now?" Wiggins asked eagerly. He'd missed much of the last investigation because his grandfa-

ther had become ill. Wiggins, though somewhat estranged
from his relatives, had dutifully gone to visit the elderly
man. The visit hadn't been successful and he'd returned to
London, but his conscience had forced him to go back even
though he knew his relations weren't overly fond of him.
That visit had been far more successful and, even better, his
grandfather hadn't died after all. But Wiggins was eager to
get on the hunt, so to speak.

Mrs. Jeffries thought for a moment. "I think we ought to
do what we always do. Find out everything we can about
our victim." She glanced at Smythe. "The police are sure it
wasn't a robbery?"

"They're sure. They found money in his pockets." He
nodded. "And a big, fat gold ring on his finger. Besides,
most robbers don't shoot their victim. They might cosh 'im
over the 'ead, but they don't fill 'em with lead."

"So we now have to assume it was a premeditated, pur-
poseful murder." Mrs. Jeffries turned to Luty. "Can you
use your sources to find out about Sir Edmund's financial
situation?"

" 'Course I can," Luty replied with a grin. "Just because
he's a 'Sir' don't mean he ain't as broke as a drunken sailor
on a Saturday night."

"Really, madam, I hardly think comparing an English
gentleman to an inebriated seaman is appropriate." Hatchet
sniffed disapprovingly. "However, you do have a valid
point." He turned his attention to the housekeeper. "Would
you like me to ask a few questions about the gentleman? I
do have some rather useful sources."

"We've all got useful sources," Mrs. Goodge put in. "If
it's all the same to everyone, I'll do my usual bit." The
cook did all her investigating from the kitchen.

She had a vast network of former colleagues, tradesmen, delivery men, chimney sweeps, rag-and-bones men,
tinkers, and laundry boys that she used for information.
She lured them into her kitchen with tempting treats and

then plied them with tea until she'd wrung every morsel of gossip there was to be had. She could find out anything about anyone who was someone in the whole of England. The more important they were, the more there was to know. She had less success finding out information about ordinary people, but she didn't let that stop her. Gossip was a universal currency and she had plenty of money in her account.

"That would be very helpful," Mrs. Jeffries replied, nodding at both Hatchet and the cook.

"I expect you want me to try and make contact with one of his servants," Wiggins said eagerly.

"Correct." Mrs. Jeffries picked up her teacup.

"And I'll have a go at the local merchants," Betsy added. Then she frowned. "Or maybe I ought to see what I can find out about his fiancée?"

"Find out what you can about Sir Edmund," Mrs. Jeffries said quickly. "We'll worry about the fiancée later." She glanced at Smythe. "Did you manage to find out her name?"

"No, the footman I was speaking to wasn't sure of her name. He worked next door to the Leggett house." Smythe didn't tell them that he'd bribed the lad for this information. "But what about this other woman? What do we do about her?"

"How did you find out about her?" Luty asked.

He shrugged. "From the footman. Apparently the whole neighborhood was gossipin' about the girl. They call her Sir Edmund's shadow."

"I'll bet she's one of Sir Edmund's cast-off ladies," Mrs. Goodge said darkly. "He ought to be ashamed of himself. Well, I suppose he ought to if he wasn't dead but now that he is, I'm sure God will have a sharp word or two for him."

"But Mrs. Goodge, we don't know anything about the woman," Hatchet protested. "Why do women always assume the worst when they hear of this sort of situation?"

"Because we're smart," Luty retorted. "If some woman was following him around, you can bet your ebony walking stick that it wasn't because she liked lookin' at his back. He did her wrong and that was her way of getting' at him."

"Why don't we find out as much information as we can before we make any more assumptions," Mrs. Jeffries interjected. She didn't want a battle erupting between the men and the women. They'd done that before and that kind of competitiveness wasn't really very nice, though it had been quite effective in helping to solve that case. "We'll meet back here for a late tea this afternoon and compare notes."

Constable Barnes studied the Parkington drawing room as he and the inspector waited for the family to appear. This house was only a half a mile from the Leggett home but it was bigger, brighter, and in better condition.

The walls were papered in blue-and-white stripes and the carpet was a brand-new, hand-woven, brightly colored Persian. The windows were artfully draped with pale blue taffeta fringed curtains and every furniture surface was covered with crystal, silver, or china knickknacks. This was a rich man's house and he'd gone to great lengths to let the world know it.

Suddenly, the door burst open and a man dashed into the room. "What is the meaning of this?" he demanded, glaring at Constable Barnes.

This was not a neighborhood that welcomed visits from the police.

"I'm Inspector Gerald Witherspoon," the inspector replied calmly, "and this is Constable Barnes. We'd like to speak to Miss Beatrice Parkington."

"I'm her father," he snapped. "So you can talk to me."

"No, I'm afraid I can't," Witherspoon said, staring directly at the man. "I need to speak with your daughter.

"What is it, Osgood." A middle-aged woman hurried

into the room, her expression annoyed. Directly behind her came a young woman. "The entire household's a flutter."

"Father, is it true there are police here?" The girl's voice trailed off as she saw Barnes.

Witherspoon took the initiative. "Are you Miss Beatrice Parkington?" he asked the girl.

"I am, sir," she replied.

"Now, see here," Osgood Parkington interrupted.

The inspector ignored him. "Then I'm afraid I've some very bad news for you. Your fiancé is dead."

"Sir Edmund is dead?" she repeated, her voice dazed.

"Osgood," the older woman wailed. "What's he saying? Sir Edmund can't be dead. He was going to marry Beatrice."

"Is this true, sir?" Osgood Parkington demanded.

"I assure you, it's quite true," Witherspoon replied. He was glad to see the girl wasn't going to become hysterical. "I'm sorry for your loss, miss. This must be horrid for you."

"I didn't love him, sir," she replied. "But I am sorry he's dead. Was it an accident?

"Oh, do be quiet, girl," Osgood snapped at his daughter.

"Osgood." Julia Parkington burst into tears. "This isn't fair. It simply isn't fair. How dare he die before he married Beatrice. Now she won't get the title. It's not fair, it's simply not fair."

"I'm sure he didn't mean to die, mother," Beatrice said softly. She put her arm around the sobbing woman. "Don't upset yourself so."

"Oh, stop your blubbering, Julia," Osgood yelled. He glared at the policemen. "When did this happen?"

"As near as we can tell, it was after he left Lord Keighley's residence late last night," Barnes replied.

Witherspoon stared at Beatrice Parkington. "In reply to your question, miss, Sir Edmund's death wasn't an accident. He was murdered."

Mrs. Parkington squealed even louder. "Oh my stars, it simply gets worse and worse. We can't have anything to do with someone who was murdered!"

"Mother, why don't you go and rest," Beatrice said soothingly. She led the distraught woman toward the door.

"Yes, that's a good idea," Julia Parkington replied. "I simply can't think. This is terrible, terrible news. What will people say?"

As soon as the double oak doors closed behind her mother, Beatrice turned to the two policemen. "I suppose you have some questions for me."

"Be quiet, girl," Osgood shouted again. "I'll deal with this matter."

Beatrice ignored her father. "If you'd prefer that I come to the police station, I'll be happy to do so."

"It's Miss Parkington we'd like to question first," Witherspoon said to the now furious man. "But do rest assured we've a number of questions for you, as well."

Osgood Parkington's mouth dropped open, but before he could say anything, Beatrice Parkington said, "Please father, do go and see that mother is resting. She's had a dreadful shock. I'm quite capable of answering a few questions. I don't need you here."

Osgood recoiled slightly, then got hold of himself. "Fine. When I've seen to your mother, I'll be in my study." He turned on his heel and stomped out.

"Do sit down, Inspector, Constable." She waved them toward the settee and chairs near the fireplace.

"Thank you, Miss Parkington," Witherspoon said as he took the wing chair next to the settee. Barnes took the one opposite him and then pulled out his notebook.

"Ask whatever you like," she smiled sadly. "As I said, I didn't love my fiancé, but I'd no wish to see him dead."

"Can you tell us what happened last night," the inspector asked.

"I'm not certain what it is you want to hear?"

"Just tell us what happened from the time you arrived at Lord Keighley's," Witherspoon replied.

She swallowed heavily and nodded. "That sounds simple enough, I suppose. We arrived at Lord Keighley's about eight o'clock. We must have been one of the last guests to arrive because the festivities were already quite well along." She smiled suddenly. "My father has a horror of breaching etiquette, sir. We generally are the last people to arrive at any social occasion. I believe a viscount once told him it was bad form to arrive early or even on time for a function."

"Was Sir Edmund there when you arrived?" Barnes asked.

"No, he arrived right after we did. He and Mr. Roland Leggett came in as we were being greeted by the Keighleys. We greeted one another and then went inside."

Witherspoon nodded encouragingly. "And he escorted you into dinner?"

"It was actually a buffet supper," she said. "But yes, he took my arm and escorted me inside."

"Did he appear to be his usual self? Was he upset? In short, Miss Parkington, was there anything unusual about his behavior?"

"Not that I recall," she replied. "He seemed perfectly ordinary. We chatted amicably enough and then he made the announcement about our engagement. Everyone congratulated us and Lord Keighley sent for more champagne."

"What happened after supper?" Barnes asked.

"Nothing, really, just the usual dancing and chatting and milling about the place. It was a typical London social engagement. I was bored to tears . . ." she broke off. "Wait, there was one moment that was odd. I saw Sir Edmund go to the front window. He pulled the curtain back and looked out."

Witherspoon watched her carefully. "Do you know what he was looking at?"

"I expect he wanted to see if the young woman who has been following him about for the past few weeks was there," she replied.

"Was she?"

"Oh yes." Beatrice smiled slyly. "She was standing just across the road. With the torches and the lamps outside, you could see her quite clearly."

"Was this the first time you'd seen this young woman?"

"Oh no, I'd seen her several times. Edmund thought I didn't know about her, but I did. I was delighted she was there. I was going to use the poor girl, you see. That's how I was planning on getting out of my marriage. I'd already decided I wasn't going to spend my life stuck with an idiot like Sir Edmund Leggett."

Betsy walked into the grocer's shop on the Brompton Road. It was the closest shopping district to Sir Edmund's house and she hoped to find out something about the household. She stood near the door and studied the interior. It was like any other grocer's, except it was a bit more posh and she suspected the prices in this neighborhood were a bit dearer.

Behind the counter, there was a plump middle-aged matron packing an order into a carrying basket for a maid. Several other customers milled about waiting their turn to be served.

Betsy sighed. This was certainly less than ideal. Deciding she ought to come back later, she heard one of the waiting customers say, "Isn't it awful about that murder."

"It was Sir Edmund Leggett that got murdered," said the woman behind the counter. "Terrible, isn't it."

"I'll bet it was that Ripper feller," another customer ventured.

"Sir Edmund was shot," the first customer said quickly. "The Ripper always used a knife."

"It must have been one of them lunatics," the second customer put in.

"Lunatic?" the woman behind the counter snorted. "It was probably one of his cast-off women. I don't care if he had a 'Sir' attached to his name, from what I hear, he wasn't a gentleman in the least." She put the last item in the basket. "There you go, dear. I'll add this to their account."

"Thanks, Letty. My master thinks Sir Edmund was shot by an outraged husband or father." The girl reached for the basket and then stepped aside. "Leastways, that's what he said to the mistress this morning at breakfast."

Even though the murder hadn't been reported in the press, the news had obviously made it around the neighborhood. Betsy realized that she'd walked into the perfect place. She stepped to the back of the line, her ear cocked at the ready when a tall, gray-haired woman came out from behind a striped curtain at the end of the counter. She frowned at the clerk. "Letty, do get on with it. We've got customers lined up."

"Sorry, ma'am, it's just this murder's happened and everyone wants to talk about it."

The woman, who was obviously the owner, ignored her. She directed her attention to the next person in line. "May I help you?" she asked. Her tone and manner effectively ended any more gossip about the murder of the late Sir Edmund Leggett.

Well, drat, thought Betsy, the old woman had certainly put a stop to the talk. Fat lot of good it would do to ask any questions here. She gave her a quick glare, turned and headed for the door. There were bound to be other shops nearby and it was obvious that the whole neighborhood was gossiping about Sir Edmund's murder. Finding someone to chat with was probably going to be as easy as drinking a cup of tea.

* * *

Wiggins leaned against the lamppost and stared at Sir Edmund Leggett's big house. So far, he'd not seen hide nor hair of a servant. They were probably too busy taking care of all the people making condolence calls. There'd been plenty of carriages and hansoms coming and going, but none of them were letting out or picking up the sort of people who'd talk to him. That was the trouble with the upper class. They couldn't be relied upon as a decent source of information.

"Are you a friend of that girl's then?" The voice came from behind him.

Wiggins whirled about and came face-to-face with an old man dressed in a footman's livery. He was holding a tin of brass polish and a rag. His uniform hung limply on his skinny frame and there were two buttons missing from jacket. "What if I am?" Wiggins replied carefully.

"Then you're out of luck, lad. She's done a scarper. Haven't seen her about today, not now that Sir Edmund's been murdered."

"You saw her last night?" Wiggins asked.

"Sure did." He grinned broadly. Several of his front teeth were missing. "Saw her standing right where you are, staring hard at the house and glaring at Sir Edmund when he come out."

"Did he see her as well?"

The man laughed. "He pretended to ignore her, but I could tell he was scared of the lass. He walked down the street with his back ramrod straight, like she wasn't worth the dirt under his feet, but as soon as he got to the corner, he turned back to see if she was following."

"Was she following?" Wiggins couldn't believe his good luck.

"'Course she was. She waited till he and his cousin were fifty yards or so up the street before she took off after him." He shrugged. "Most of us wondered why Sir Edmund didn't call a policeman when the girl started her shenanigans. But there's some that think it's because he wouldn't dare. Some say he didn't want the police to hear what the girl might have to say 'Course now she'll not say anything. She's done a scarper."

"You haven't seen her at all?"

He shook his head. "No and I miss her. She was a pretty thing and friendly, too, if you took the trouble to smile at her and say hello properly." He sighed heavily. "Not many will bother with the likes of me. Even in the house, I'm pretty much at the bottom of the staircase. But she was sweet. She'd give me a nice smile and spend a few minutes passing the time. 'Course she never took her eyes off his house while we talked."

"Did she ever tell you her name?" Wiggins asked eagerly.

"I never asked, lad. I'm an old man and I know a troubled soul when I see one. No, I was glad just to have a few minutes of her company. I never asked her any questions, but wherever she is, I hope she's all right."

"Even if she's a murderess?" he replied. "They say she killed Sir Edmund."

"I expect there's plenty that had good reason to want Sir Edmund dead but I've no doubt it's her the police will waste their time trying to find." He shrugged again and started to walk away. "Who are we to judge. Maybe he deserved to die."

Wiggins started after him. "Just a minute, sir, do you have any idea where I can find 'er?"

The old man started up the short walkway of the house just as the front door opened and a butler with a very annoyed expression stepped out. "Where have you been, Jasper. You were supposed to have gotten these lamps polished hours ago."

"Sorry, sir," Jasper hurried his steps. "I forgot where I'd left the tin."

"Well get on with it, man," the butler snapped.

Wiggins, not wanting to get the old gentleman in any more trouble, kept on walking past the house. He thought the old fellow probably knew more than he was letting on, but now wasn't the time to try and find out any more. He made up his mind to come back later.

But he'd learned something very important. He'd found out their mysterious girl had followed Sir Edmund to his engagement party.

He'd also found out that Sir Edmund wasn't particularly well liked by his neighbors.

"Here is a guest list, Inspector." Lord Robert Keighley handed a sheet of paper across the desk to Witherspoon. "I had my secretary draw it up as soon as I heard about poor Edmund."

"Thank you, sir." Witherspoon was rather taken aback. He hadn't expected a peer of the realm to be so very cooperative. Generally people of Keighley's class would barely condescend to even speak to a policeman. But from the moment he and Constable Barnes had stepped into Lord Keighley's book-lined study, the man had been both courteous and helpful. "We'll do our best not to trouble your guests unnecessarily, but we must speak to anyone who might have information for us. Someone may have seen or heard something very important."

"Of course, Inspector." Lord Keighley nodded. He was a middle-aged man of medium height with dark hair liberally threaded with gray, blue eyes, and sharp, hawklike features.

"Do you recall what time Sir Edmund left?" Barnes asked. He wanted to confirm Roland Leggett's account of the evening.

"I'm afraid I can't, sir. Once most of the guests had left and the ladies had retired for the evening, I'm afraid a small group of us did some additional celebrating. In short, gentleman, I passed out. When I woke up, both Edmund and Roland had gone."

"What time was that sir?" Witherspoon asked. "I mean, what time was it that you woke up?"

Lord Keighley thought for a moment. "It was very late, I know that, past two in the morning."

"So when you woke up, both Sir Edmund and his cousin were gone?" Barnes pressed.

"That's correct. Drummond was gone as well. He was one of the other celebrants." He smiled wryly. "I'm generally far too sensible to indulge like that. I don't know what came over me. Usually I can hold my whiskey and Alex Drummond can certainly hold his. Oh well, I expect we all had more champagne than we should have and it's never a good idea to mix spirits and wine."

Witherspoon nodded in understanding. Actually, he didn't understand in the least. He occasionally enjoyed a sherry or a beer but he never over-indulged in either. Frankly, he was always a bit mystified by those that did. Surely they knew that if they drank too much, they'd either pass out or be sick. Oh well, it wasn't his place to pass judgment on a lord of the realm and his drinking habits. "Can you tell me, sir, if Sir Edmund was his usual self?"

Lord Keighley frowned. "I'm not sure I understand what you mean, sir? He'd announced his engagement so I expect he was perhaps a bit more excited than usual."

"Was he happy to be getting married?" Barnes asked quickly.

"He seemed quite pleased by the prospect," Keighley replied. "You must understand, Constable. People of our class generally marry for very pragmatic reasons. Sir Edmund's marriage was going to alleviate a great deal of financial difficulty. He may have had a title and an estate but the estate's drained him dry, and these days the only thing a title will get you is a bride with money."

Witherspoon nodded. "So he wasn't in love with his bride to be?"

"No, and I don't think she was in love with him." He stopped and looked down at his desk. "I overheard something and it's not very pleasant. But it may have something to do with his murder. A few moments after Edmund made the announcement, I went towards Miss Parkington to offer her my best wishes. Just as I reached her, I overheard her turn to her mother and say quite clearly that she'd rather be dead than married to Edmund Leggett."

"We know, sir," Witherspoon replied. "Miss Parkington told us herself that she didn't wish to marry the gentleman. As a matter of fact, she was rather annoyed that a young woman who'd been following Sir Edmund about for the past few weeks wasn't anywhere to be seen."

"So she knew about the girl?" He frowned. "That must have been humiliating for her."

"On the contrary, sir," Witherspoon replied. "She was going to use the girl as an excuse to break off her engagement."

"Only now she won't have to, will she?" Lord Keighley said. "Her problem seems to have resolved itself now that Edmund's dead."

"Can you verify the time that the Parkingtons left?" Barnes asked. He made a mental note to speak to the servants. They frequently heard more, saw more, and were willing to talk more than the gentry.

"They called for their carriage after it had gone eleven o'clock. Sir Edmund escorted them to the front door."

"Excuse me, sir, but you said you overheard Miss Parkington tell her mother she'd rather be dead than married to Sir Edmund. What did Mrs. Parkington say in response?"

"She said Miss Beatrice wasn't to worry her head about marriage. She said that women had been managing men for hundreds of years and that Miss Beatrice would just have to cope." He smiled wryly. "I daresay, she's right.

Everyone knows that despite how Osgood Parkington likes to bluster in public, it's Julia Parkington that really runs that household." He shrugged. "But you can probably say the same for every household in London. My wife certainly knows how to manage me."

CHAPTER 3

Everyone arrived on time for their afternoon meeting and took their usual seats. Mrs. Jeffries poured the tea into cups, handed them around, and then sat back in her chair. "Who would like to go first?"

"I've nothing to report," Mrs. Goodge said, as she handed a plate of scones to Wiggins. "I spent the day baking and getting ready for my sources. I ought to be hearin' plenty in a day or two, though. I've a goodly number of people comin' through the kitchen tomorrow and I've been in touch with some of my old associates."

"That's excellent," Mrs. Jeffries murmured. She took a quick sip of tea. "Your sources are always so good at giving us a general background for most of our suspects."

"Let's hope they don't let us down this time," the cook replied. But she looked pleased with the compliment.

"I found out that the woman that's been shadowin' Sir

Edmund followed him to the engagement party," Wiggins said. He took a bite from his scone. "But that's about all I learned. I wasn't able to talk to anyone from the Leggett household. All the servants was too busy today to so much as stick their noses outside."

"Then how'd you find out about the girl followin' Leggett?" Luty asked.

"An old gent who lives across the way told me about her," he replied. "'E says the girl was real sweet, 'e liked 'er."

"I don't suppose he knew her name?" Mrs. Jeffries asked.

"He claimed 'e never asked." Wiggins shrugged. "Claimed 'e could tell a troubled soul when he saw one, but he did say somethin' else interestin'. He said everyone wondered why Sir Edmund didn't call a policeman when the girl started 'angin' about and then 'e said he thought it might be because Sir Edmund didn't want a policeman 'earin' what the girl might have to say."

"That is very interesting," Mrs. Jeffries said. She rather thought Wiggins informant had a point. "Obviously, the people in the neighborhood had noticed the girl and were discussing it openly."

"And Sir Edmund never took any action against the girl," Wiggins continued. "According to the old man, he never tried to talk to her or run her off or anything. He just acted like he was scared of her. Leastways, that's what old Jasper claimed."

"Scared of her," Mrs. Goodge repeated. "How could he possibly know such a thing? Did the girl tell him that?"

"He claimed he could tell by the way Sir Edmund walked." Wiggins told them the rest of the conversation he'd had with the elderly footman.

"I must admit I've often formed opinions based on ob-servations of how people behaved," Mrs. Jeffries said thoughtfully. "So we mustn't dismiss the footman's opin-ion out of hand."

"But why would someone like Sir Edmund Leggett be frightened of a young chit of a girl?" Mrs. Goodge demanded.

"I think that's one of the things we ought to find out," the housekeeper replied. "Why don't you see if any of your sources can help? Surely, there's a great deal of gossip about the girl and Sir Edmund. Someone must know something."

"With my sources, it's hard to say what will turn up once people start talking." The cook shrugged philosophically. "But I'll do my best to see what I can find out about the girl."

"Can I go next?" Luty asked. "I found out something right interestin'."

"I've got nothing else to say," Wiggins said.

"Good, then it's my turn." Luty grinned broadly. "I had a chat with several of my friends and I got an earful about Sir Edmund Leggett. Seems I was right earlier, he's broke and that's why he was getting married."

"That's hardly a revelation madam," Hatchet interjected. "A good many noble houses are in reduced circumstances of late. It's simply the way of the modern world."

She ignored him and kept on talking. "His fiancée's name is Beatrice Parkington. She's an heiress. Her father was supposedly going to settle twenty-five thousand pounds on Sir Edmund when they married."

"Twenty-five thousand pounds!" Hatchet exclaimed. "I heard it was fifteen thousand."

"Then your sources don't know what they're talkin' about," she snickered, delighted to have bested her butler. "Take my word for it, it's twenty-five and not a pound less!"

"Either amount is a fortune," Mrs. Goodge said.

"So Mr. Parkington was buying his daughter a title." Mrs. Jeffries mused. "That's not particularly unusual."

"But if he was broke, how was he managing to pay his bills?" Betsy asked.

"He wasn't," Luty replied. "According to the gossip, he was being hounded something fierce by his creditors."

"And maybe someone got tired of waiting," Smythe suggested.

"That's what I thought," Luty agreed. "Sometimes people aren't particular about who they borrow money from, if you get my meaning."

"You mean, he might have been murdered because he'd borrowed money and not paid it back," Mrs. Goodge said. "But that doesn't make sense. If he was dead, he'd never repay a debt he owed."

"Maybe he was killed as a warning to others," Betsy suggested softly. She'd grown up in the worst part of London and had seen firsthand how brutal life could be. "That happens. I remember when I was a little girl, the man who owned the newsagent's shop borrowed money from one of the thugs that ran our part of London. He kept trying to pay it back, but things kept happening to the poor fellow. One night when he didn't come home for dinner, his daughter found him beaten to death in his shop. They'd done it as a warning to the other locals that owed them money. No one was ever arrested for the crime."

Under the table, Smythe grabbed Betsy's hand. He'd give ten years off his life if it would take away the horrible memories from her childhood in the east end of London. "It happened a long time ago, lass," he said softly. "Don't think about it."

She gave his hand a quick squeeze. "I'm all right. I was just mentioning it because we can't afford to ignore any possible motive for Sir Edmund's murder. Thugs don't care if their victims are knights or tinkers. If he owed and wasn't paying, it's possible he was killed by professional criminals."

"Betsy has a good point," Mrs. Jeffries said.

"I'll 'ave a look into it, then," Smythe said. He knew exactly who he was going to ask.

"I wish we knew who this other woman is," Hatchet mused. "That would be very helpful."

"Does that mean you didn't find out anything?" Luty asked gleefully.

Hatchet gave her a crafty smile, delighted that she'd walked into his trap. "On the contrary, madam, despite your assertion that my sources are unreliable, I trust them implicitly and furthermore, I found out quite a bit. Sir Edmund Leggett wasn't just in dire straits financially; he also had a reputation as a bit of a rake."

"Which probably explains why he's bein' 'ounded." Wiggins nodded wisely.

"According to my information," Hatchet continued, "Sir Edmund has made the rounds of the ladies. He's left a trail of broken hearts from here to the Scottish border. One of them has supposedly threatened to kill him."

"Who?" Luty demanded, annoyed that he'd stolen her thunder. "You got a name?"

"Of course," Hatchet replied with another smile. "Her name is Harriet Wyndham-Jones and she's a widow. Supposedly, she's been Sir Edmund's uh . . ." he glanced at Wiggins who was watching him eagerly.

"Mistress," Mrs. Jeffries supplied the word that Hatchet was too gentlemanly to use. "She was his mistress?"

Hatchet smiled in relief. "Precisely."

"Where does she live?" Betsy asked.

"She lives in Mayfair."

"'Ow long were she and Sir Edmund together?" Smythe took a sip of tea.

"Three years." Hatchet shot Luty another devilish grin. She glared right back at him. "And my informant says she fully expected Sir Edmund to marry her. Apparently, she's quite wealthy."

"If she's got money, then why didn't he marry her if he was broke?" Wiggins asked.

Hatchet shrugged. "I don't know. I expect there could be any number of reasons."

"I think it's important to find out," Mrs. Jeffries said. As the meeting had become more of a discussion than straight reporting, she looked around the table and then asked, "Has anyone else got anything to report?"

"I didn't do so well today," Betsy said. She told them about the grocer's shop. "I didn't have much luck anyplace else, either. The only gossip going about was what we've already learned. He was a bit of a rake and had more than one irate father or brother after him."

"I think that's an inquiry worth pursuing," Mrs. Jeffries said. "See if you can find out any names. Ruining a young woman's reputation is the sort of thing that can cause blood feuds. Especially if there was someone he'd seduced who expected him to make an honest woman of her. Hearing about his engagement could easily have pushed someone to commit murder."

Betsy looked surprised. "All right, then. I'll have a go at that. But I'm going to see what else I can pick up from the shopkeepers in the area, as well."

"We'll all keep at it," Mrs. Jeffries said. She looked at Luty and Hatchet. "I'll see what we can learn from the inspector tonight. If I hear of anything that might be useful for either of you, I'll send Wiggins over with a message tomorrow morning. Otherwise, let's just keep on with what we're doing and we'll meet again tomorrow afternoon."

"What about this Harriet Wyndham-Jones?" Smythe asked. "Shouldn't one of us find out a bit about 'er?"

"I can do that," Luty volunteered eagerly. "If she's been Sir Edmund's lady friend for the past three years, I know plenty of women that can supply me with the details."

* * *

Inspector Witherspoon was back at the Leggett household. Roland Leggett was making funeral arrangements for his cousin but he'd given the staff instructions to answer all of the inspector's questions.

Witherspoon pulled out one of the mismatched chairs at the rickety table in the long, narrow servants hall. The shelves on the green painted walls were filled with mismatched crockery, china, and old pots and pans. A gray curtain hung limply at the small window at the far end of the room, blocking what little sunlight that managed to filter into the lower rooms of the house. The door opened and a middle-aged man with blue eyes, thinning light brown hair, and a receding chin stepped inside. "You wanted to see me, sir?"

"I take it you're the butler?"

"That is correct, sir."

The inspector waved at the chair next to him. "Please sit down. I've a few questions for you. We'll be speaking with everyone in the household."

"So Mr. Leggett told us, sir." He sat down and stared at the inspector warily.

"First of all, let me say I'm sure this must be a very difficult time for you and the rest of the staff. I'll make this as brief as possible. What is your name, please?"

The butler nodded somberly. "It's Hamilton, sir. John Hamilton."

"How long have you been in the household?" The inspector always thought that getting a bit of background was useful.

"Five years, sir."

"Can you tell me if anything unusual happened yesterday?" Witherspoon watched the man carefully. He knew that servants frequently saw and heard many things that their masters assumed was private. But butlers could be odd, sometimes they were quite willing to talk and sometimes they felt it necessary to keep their masters' secrets. He'd no idea which way Hamilton might go.

"Unusual?" Hamilton seemed surprised by the question. "I'm not aware of anything, sir. It was a perfectly ordinary day. Sir Edmund arose at his regular time, had breakfast, saw to his correspondence, went to see his solicitor, and then had tea with the Parkingtons."

Witherspoon leaned forward. "Do you know why he saw his solicitor yesterday?

"I've no idea, sir," Hamilton replied. He sniffed disapprovingly. "It was hardly my place to ask."

Drat, the inspector thought, this butler wasn't going to give up his secrets easily. "What time did Sir Edmund return home?"

"Just after three o'clock, sir. As I said, The Parkingtons were coming for tea."

"What time did they arrive?" Witherspoon had often found having a timeline of people's movements very useful.

"At four o'clock, sir."

"Thank you, Hamilton." Witherspoon rose to his feet. "That will be all. Ask the housekeeper to come in, please."

Hamilton looked a bit surprised by the abrupt dismissal, but he quickly masked his reaction and got up. "As you wish, sir."

Witherspoon sighed inwardly as the man left. He hoped the housekeeper would be a bit more forthcoming. In the next room, he could hear the low murmur of voices and wondered how Barnes was faring. He was questioning the maids and footmen.

"Good day, sir." A tall, austere-looking woman with white hair and a beautiful complexion stepped into the room. "I understand you wish to speak to me. I'm Abigail Kaylor, the housekeeper."

"Good day, ma'am, please have a seat. I'll be as brief as

possible but as I'm sure you understand we do have to question the staff."

"Of course you do, sir." She smiled politely and took the chair the butler had just vacated. "What would you like to know?"

Witherspoon decided to get right to the heart of the matter. "Did anything unusual happen yesterday?"

She thought for a moment. "Well, that depends on what you'd call unusual."

"We're looking for any information you might have for us," he replied quickly.

"The young woman was outside again, sir, but then that's hardly unusual as she'd been there for over two weeks."

"You're talking about the young woman who'd taken to following Sir Edmund."

"That's right, sir. We first saw her about two weeks ago. I remember it well, sir. We were having a dinner party that evening to welcome Mr. Roland to London. The household was in a bit of an uproar, sir." She glanced at the door. "That's why I remember it all so well."

"Mr. Roland's return caused an uproar?"

She waved her hand dismissively. "Oh no, sir, it wasn't that at all. It was because the butcher refused to deliver the meat, sir. Cook was having a fit, Sir Edmund was furious and the scullery maids were so frightened they were hiding in the larder. By the time we got it all sorted out, dinner was late and that's why I was in the dining room helping to put things right. Hamilton was in the foyer, taking the guests cloaks and such so I was lending a hand in the dining room. That's how I happened to be coming down the front hall and saw Sir Edmund. He looked out the drawing room window, probably wanting to see who was arriving, when all of a sudden he gasped and leapt back like he'd just seen the devil."

"Did you ask him what was wrong?"

She shook her head vehemently. "Oh no, sir, perhaps Hamilton could have asked such a question, but unless the master had actually fallen onto his backside, I'd not be able to step out of my place. Sir Edmund wasn't one to let us take liberties."

Witherspoon didn't see how showing concern for one's employer could be construed as a "liberty," but he wisely said nothing. "Do go on, ma'am."

"I was very curious, sir, but of course I didn't want Sir Edmund to see me being a nosy Parker, so I went on into the parlor. I was taking some fresh flowers in, sir. For the ladies, you see. They always used the front parlor while the men had their cigars. As soon as I got inside, I hurried to the window and looked out. But there was nothing there but this young woman standing next to the lamppost and staring at the house. I thought nothing of it at the time, but when she was there the next day, I realized that she must have been what Sir Edmund was looking at when he was so startled."

"Do you have any idea why he was startled by her appearance?"

"I don't." She smiled apologetically. "But she must have had a good reason for being his shadow, she certainly worked hard enough at it. She spent hours watching the house and following him about."

"Did you ever hear him speak about her?" Witherspoon had found it was best to ask very specific questions.

"No sir, never."

"The butler has said that Sir Edmund went to visit his solicitor yesterday morning. Was that common knowledge amongst the household?" Witherspoon had no idea why he asked this question, but it had popped into his head and as his housekeeper was always telling him, he must learn to rely on his "inner voice."

She frowned slightly. "He never told us directly where

he was going, but everyone knew. It wasn't a secret. He spoke about it openly."

"Spoke about what?"

"About the settlement, sir," she exclaimed. "That's why he was at the lawyer's. He met Mr. Parkington there and they signed the marriage settlement papers. I heard him tellin' Mr. Roland that once the papers were signed and the engagement announced, all his problems would be over."

"Would you like a sherry before dinner?" Mrs. Jeffries asked the inspector as she hung his bowler on the coat tree.

"That would be lovely," he replied. "It's been a very long day."

"I expect you're tired." She led him toward the drawing room.

"Very, I'm going to retire directly after I have my supper." He sank down in his favorite chair and closed his eyes for a brief moment. When he opened them, she handed him a glass of Harveys. "Thank you, do pour one for yourself, Mrs. Jeffries," he insisted. "I could use some company."

"Thank you, sir." She went back to the sideboard and helped herself to a glass. The inspector frequently asked her to share a glass with him, especially when he was in the midst of a case. She was always glad to do it, too, not just because it gave her access to information, but because she was genuinely fond of her employer.

She suspected he was missing their neighbor, Lady Cannonberry, a great deal more than he'd expected. The two of them had begun a relationship that never seemed to move forward because Lady Cannonberry, or Ruth, as the household called her, was always being called out of town to take care of her late husband's relatives. They were a sickly lot and she was a woman of conscience. She didn't know how to tell them "no" when they imposed upon her. Unfortunately, they imposed upon her a great deal.

Mrs. Jeffries decided she was going to hint to the inspector that he ought to be a tad more forceful. Perhaps if Ruth understood how lonely he was, she'd tell the next uncle or cousin or aunt to hire a nurse. The Cannonberrys were a wealthy family, they could easily afford to pay for proper care. "Was it a particularly nasty corpse, sir?" she asked as she took the chair across from him.

"Well, it wasn't very nice." He grimaced. "There was a great deal of blood. But the constables had done the right thing and not moved him about much. I think he was shot at very close range."

"Why do you think so?" she asked curiously.

"Because it was dark and most people aren't very good at shooting a gun," he replied. "What's really odd is that no one heard the shots. Mind you, it's a very wealthy area, and there appeared to be a number of people having social functions in the neighborhood. But you'd have thought someone would have heard the noise of a gun being fired. They're not exactly quiet."

"And you've done a house-to-house, sir?" she asked.

"As much as we could," he replied. "But it's only been a few hours so we've more ground to cover, so to speak. The poor man had just announced his engagement, as well."

"How very sad, sir," she murmured. "I expect his fiancée is most distressed."

"She's upset, but she certainly isn't inconsolable," he replied. He told Mrs. Jeffries about his visit to the Parkington household. She listened carefully, occasionally asking a question or making a comment which she hoped would get him thinking in a specific direction. By the time he'd finished his second sherry, he'd told her every single detail of his day. Then he yawned.

"Oh dear, you must be exhausted," she said. "You've been up for hours."

"I'm afraid I'll have to agree with you." He put his glass down and stood up. "I must eat my supper before I fall asleep on my feet."

"If you'll go to the dining room, sir, I'll bring up your tray."

Witherspoon was as good as his word. He went up to bed as soon as he'd finished his meal. He didn't even take Fred out for his usual evening walk. "Do ask Wiggins to see Fred," he'd instructed Mrs. Jeffries. "I'm simply too tired to take another step."

"Of course, sir," she'd replied. When she got down to the kitchen, she'd sent Wiggins and the dog off for their walk while the others tidied the place up. Then they took their usual seats around the table and waited for the footman to get back. None of them were going to bed without hearing what the inspector had said about the case.

"It's not really fair, is it," Smythe mused as he slipped into the chair next to Betsy. "Luty and Hatchet never get a chance at hearing what the inspector's learned until the next day."

"I don't think they mind," Betsy said. "I think they're just happy to be included."

"Where's that boy gone?" Mrs. Goodge demanded. "He should have been back by now. It's been ages."

"Perhaps he's giving Fred a bit of romp," Smythe suggested. "The poor dog's been shut up in the house today."

Just then they heard the back door open but instead of the click of dog nails and the thump of Wiggins feet on the hallway floor, they heard a murmur of low voices.

Smythe reacted first. He got to his feet and started toward the hallway. "Who's there?" he called.

"Don't worry," Wiggins yelled. "It's just me. But I've brought someone. We're coming right in."

They were all mindful that they worked for a police inspector who'd solved more murders than anyone in living memory. They were also aware that many of the people Witherspoon had arrested had powerful friends and family. Some of them might want vengeance.

Smythe didn't like the situation. He continued standing,

his body tensed. He wanted to make sure that someone wasn't holding a pistol into the footman's back.

But Wiggins was all smiles when he appeared and Fred's tail was wagging a mile a minute. A young woman with red hair trailed behind them. Her straw hat was slightly askew, the hem of her lavender dress was caked with mud, her jacket had dirt on the sleeves, and there was a streak of soot across her nose.

There was a short, stunned silence. Finally, Mrs. Jeffries said, "Wiggins, would you like to introduce us to your friend?" Her instincts had gone on full alert. Something very important was about to happen.

"This 'ere is Miss Camden. I found her out in the garden. I think she might need a bit of 'elp," Wiggins explained.

"How do you do, Miss Camden." Mrs. Jeffries said as she rose to her feet.

The girl gave a quick curtsy. Her brown eyes were wide and frightened, her complexion was pale as a sheet, and her hands were shaking. "How do you do?" she replied.

"You have a Devonshire accent," the housekeeper said softly. "I take it you're not from London."

"That's right," the girl said. She drew a deep breath. "I'm sorry to be botherin' you so late, but I heard that you might be able to help me."

"Help you how?" the housekeeper asked.

"Go on, then," Wiggins encouraged, "tell them what you told me."

"Help me avoid being arrested for murder," she blurted. "I was only trying to scare Sir Edmund into doing what was right, I didn't want him to die. Him bein' dead isn't going to do me or little Katie any good at all. We needed him alive, but the police aren't likely to believe me."

"She's the girl that's been 'oundin' Sir Edmund," Wiggins added. "And she's right scared."

"Thank you, Wiggins, I'd guessed as much." Mrs. Jef-

fries mind worked furiously. There were a number of is-
sues she had to consider very carefully. "Miss Camden,
please sit down. Would you care for some tea?"

"Oh yes, ma'am." She sagged in relief. "I'd love a cup.
I'm ever so thirsty."

"Take this chair." Betsy pointed to the empty spot next
to her. "I'll put the kettle on."

"Thanks ever so much," she replied as she hurried over
to the table and sat down. "My feet are dead tired. I've
been on the go since late last night. Please call me Sarah.
I'm not used to being called Miss."

"Are you hungry, girl?" Mrs. Goodge asked.

"I don't want to put anyone to any trouble," Sarah admitted, "but I've not had a bite since yesterday evening."

Mrs. Goodge got up and headed toward the dry larder.
"We'll fix you up, girl. We've plenty."

Mrs. Jeffries smiled at Sarah. She wanted to proceed
carefully here. She wanted to hear the girl's story but at the
same time, it was important that she find out how the girl
had known to come here. To come to them. "Would you
like to tell us what happened?"

Sarah looked down at the table. "I've been following Sir
Edmund Leggett for two weeks. But like I said, I didn't want
him dead, even though my family's got reason to hate him."

Mrs. Goodge returned from the dry larder with a loaf of
bread, a butter pot, and a plate of sliced beef. She sat the
tray on the counter and began putting the food onto a plate.
She listened to the girl's story as she worked.

"Why don't you tell us everything from the beginning,"
Mrs. Jeffries instructed. "How did you or your family come
to know Sir Edmund?"

"We didn't, but my sister Emma did." She paused and
took a deep breath. "My father's got a small ironmonger's
shop in Bristol. One of the hinges on Sir Edmund's carriage came off and he brought it into the shop to have it

fixed. I don't know why he came instead of his coachman, but he did and that's how he met Emma. We're twins, you see. But we didn't look that much alike. It just made us closer, like. We shared everything. Then all of a sudden, she was sneaking out on her own. Before long it was obvious she was meeting someone. Someone she didn't want me or my parents to know about. It was him, Sir Edmund. He'd been meeting her at a cottage on his estate." She bit her lip and looked away. "The blackguard seduced her and then when he got her with child, he tossed a few coins her way and threw her into the street. My parents couldn't bear the shame of it. My mother died of a broken heart and father's been drinking so much that his business is all but ruined. Emma died giving birth to Sir Edmund's child. That's when I decided to come here and force him to do what's right."

"What did you want him to do?" Wiggins asked.

"Provide for Katie," Sarah said. "We've very little money and she deserves a decent life. It's not her fault she's a foundling." She broke off as Mrs. Goodge set a plate of food in front of her. "Thank you."

"Do rest a moment and have something to eat," Mrs. Jeffries said. Sarah smiled gratefully and picked up a piece of buttered bread. She slapped a slice of beef on it and eagerly took a huge bite. She nodded her thanks as Betsy put a cup of tea down next to her plate.

They waited for a few moments, letting the girl satisfy her hunger and thirst. Finally, Sarah put her cup down. "You must think me an awful pig, but I was so starved. This is wonderful. Thank you so much."

"Go on with your story, then," Wiggins encouraged. "Tell 'em the rest of it."

"I decided to come to London and see Sir Edumnd. When I got here, I marched right up to his front door and demanded a word with the man. He wouldn't see me."

"When was this?" Mrs. Jeffries asked.

"Two weeks ago," Sarah replied. "When he wouldn't see me, I decided to hound him until he gave me what was right. I knew as long as I wasn't on his property or bothering his person that the police couldn't touch me. So I just started standing by the lamppost and staring at the house."

"Is that all you did?" Smythe asked softly.

"No, I followed him when he went out, as well," She grinned. "At first, he pretended not to notice me. But after a few days of this, he was really upset. I knew that much."

"What were you hoping to accomplish?" Mrs. Goodge asked.

"I wanted him to get so fed up with me, that he'd take care of Katie just to be rid of me. He tried coming out and scaring me right after I started hanging about his house. But I stared him right down, I did. He broke first and went scurrying back to his house like a scared rat."

"So you were hopin' that he'd do the right thing just to be rid of you?" Smythe said. "Is that right?"

"That's right." She nodded eagerly. "If that didn't work, I wanted to hang about long enough to start some nasty gossip and rumours about him. I knew he was wantin' to get married, and I know that having a bit of scandal is the best way there is to run off money. That's what he needed, you see. Money."

"Did you kill him?" Mrs. Jeffries asked.

She shook her head. "No. I wanted him alive, not dead."

"Did you follow him that night?" Betsy asked.

"Yes," she admitted. "I followed him to the house and I heard the cheers when the engagement was announced. The footmen and the coachmen were all talking about it, so I knew what was going on inside. It was real disheartenin'. I started to think that whoever was marryin' him probably didn't care if there was a bit of scandal attached to him. I was afraid he was never goin' to do right by little Katie. So

I just sort of stood there for what seemed hours, staring at the bright lights of the big house and wonderin' what to do next. By then, the party was ending and people were startin' to leave. I watched for a while until I saw his fiancée and her family come out and get into their carriage. I almost tried to speak to them, but the carriage moved off too fast." She stopped and took a quick sip of tea. "So I decided to follow them. I wanted her to know what kind of man he was, you see."

"You followed the Parkingtons' carriage?" Mrs. Jeffries clarified. "Wasn't that difficult if you were on foot?"

"No. I knew where they lived, you see. It wasn't far from Sir Edmund's. It's only a mile or so from where the party was bein' held and there was a lot of traffic on the Brompton Road." She grinned. "London's a funny place. Sometimes you can get around faster on foot than in a carriage."

"You beat them back to their home?" Wiggins asked.

"I was waiting for them when the carriage pulled up in front of their house," she replied.

"And did you get a chance to speak to Miss Parkington?" Mrs. Goodge asked.

"No, I couldn't."

"Mr. Parkington wouldn't let you?" Smythe guessed.

"That wasn't it at all," she replied. "I couldn't speak to her because she never got out of the carriage. She didn't come home with her parents."

"What?" Mrs. Goodge yelped. "What do you mean?"

"I mean she wasn't in the carriage."

"Had you actually seen her get in the carriage earlier?" Betsy asked. She'd learned it was never good to make assumptions.

"Oh yes, saw her as plain as day. Even though it was dark, there was plenty of light to see. The outside lamps were lighted and all the footmen had torches. She got into that carriage all right, her father was jawin' at her a mile a minute. He pushed her inside and slammed the door shut."

"Could she have gotten out the other side?" Smythe asked.

"No, there wasn't time. Her father yelled at the driver to go the second they were inside."

Mrs. Goodge leaned toward the girl. "Where was Mrs. Parkington?"

"She'd gotten in first." Sarah looked around in confusion. "I don't see what's so important. Miss Parkington is a bit of an independent sort, at least that's what I've heard. She might have just made her father stop the carriage before they got home so she could get some fresh air and have a look at the sky."

Mrs. Jeffries glanced at the others, cautioning them with her expression to hold their tongues. Obviously, Sarah didn't know that Beatrice Parkington hadn't wanted to marry Sir Edmund; if she had realized it, she'd have understood. "Yes, I'm sure that's it. She probably just wanted a chance to enjoy the beauty of the evening."

Sarah shrugged and took another bite. "I don't know if it was beauty she was after or not. She liked to watch the sky because she's interested in . . . in . . . oh, I can't recall the proper name, but it's when people like to know when the moon is going to rise and what star belongs where."

"Astronomy?" Smythe said. "She's an amateur astronomer?"

"That's it." Sarah smiled broadly. "She's always playing about with her little instrument. When I used to follow Sir Edmund to her house, you could sometimes see her slip out onto the roof and put it up to her eye."

"Put what up to her eye?" Mrs. Goodge demanded in confusion. She didn't like not understanding things.

"I think she means a telescope," Wiggins said. "They're nice. I saw one in a shop window on Bond Street. Mind you, they cost the earth."

"Right, it is a telescope. I know because her American

friend has one just like hers and that's what he called it."

"Her American friend?" Mrs. Jeffries prodded. She looked at the others and then back at Sarah Camden. This case was beginning to get very complicated. "Miss Parkington has an American friend?"

"Oh yes, he's ever such a nice person, handsome, too. I've met him several times." She laughed. "You see, I'm not the only one who was watching a house here in London."

CHAPTER 4

"Do you think we did the right thing?" Betsy asked as she glanced at the carriage clock on the sideboard. "For all we know, we might be sending a murderess over to Luty's."

"I don't think she killed him," Mrs. Jeffries replied, "and we really had no choice as to where to send her. We couldn't keep her here."

Sarah had told them everything she knew and then had asked for their help. She was terrified she was going to be arrested and needed someplace to hide until the police could catch the real killer.

They'd sent her along to Luty's house. Wiggins and Smythe were taking her there at this very moment, which explained why Betsy was anxiously watching the clock. Though she knew her beloved could take care of himself, she always worried when he was out late at night.

"Do you believe her story about how she came to be here?" Mrs. Goodge asked.

"I'm not sure," Mrs. Jeffries mused. "Her explanation is certainly possible."

Sarah claimed she'd taken refuge in a pub down by the river. She'd been terrified and alone. But when she'd noticed some men staring at her, she'd gone outside, intending to slip away and find a place to hide until morning. But the men had followed her, accosted her and then, wonder of wonders, she'd been saved by a middle-aged ginger-haired fellow wearing a porkpie hat. A tall, middle-aged woman with a no-nonsense manner and a ready hand with a club, had been with him. They'd taken her to a back room in the pub, let her wash her face and then, when she'd admitted she was running from the police, had told her to come here. They'd even put her in a hansom and paid for it, as well!

"I don't know." The cook frowned. "It sounds like a pretty tall tale to me."

"It's those kind that are often true," Mrs. Jeffries commented. "But true or not, we must decide if we believe the girl."

"I do," Betsy said. "To begin with, if she was guilty, the minute she'd murdered him, she'd have left town. Look at Edith Durant. Once she knew the police were on to her, she didn't let the dust settle about her feet."

"That's true," Mrs. Goodge agreed. "And the girl seems intelligent and resourceful. If she'd done it, I don't think she'd have come here. This is a policeman's house. What do you think, Mrs. Jeffries?"

"I think you're both right," she replied. "But I do wonder why she didn't go home."

"She's probably scared that that's the first place the police will look once they figure out her identity," Betsy said.

"That's true," Mrs. Jeffries said. "Eventually they'd discover who she is and where she comes from. The only true protection for the girl is finding the real killer. Otherwise, the police are sure to arrest her." She sighed. "I just wish everything wasn't happening so fast. All of a sudden, we're up to our elbows in suspects and we know absolutely nothing about any of them. There's Sir Edmund's mistress, Harriet Wyndham-Jones, Sarah Camden, Miss Parkington, and now this mysterious man who's been seen standing outside the Parkington house. I'm afraid we're going to become very, very muddled if we're not careful."

"Then we'll be careful," Mrs. Goodge said bluntly. She yawned. She was dead tired but she wasn't going to go to bed until the men returned. She'd been feeling her age lately but that didn't mean she had to coddle herself.

"And we'll be clever in the way we go about learning our facts," Betsy added. "You should keep a list of who is who," she suggested to the housekeeper. "That way we'd not be forgetting anything important."

"That's a very good idea," Mrs. Jeffries replied. She'd often thought she ought to start taking notes on their investigations. Perhaps one day she'd want to write about their cases in a memoir or something.

"They should be back by now," Betsy muttered. "What's taking them so long."

"They've only been gone an hour," Mrs. Goodge said, "and remember, they've got to tell Luty and Hatchet what's happened and explain who the girl is and how she came to be here."

Betsy slumped back in her chair. "I'm being silly, I know. But I do worry when they're out this time of night."

"I do wish we knew the man's name," Mrs. Jeffries murmured absently. "It would be so very helpful."

"We'll find out tomorrow," the cook said confidently. "We always do."

"His name is William Carter," Wiggins said as they sat down for their morning meeting. "He's an American and he's been corresponding regularly with Miss Parkington."

Luty and Hatchet, who'd just arrived, exchanged a glance. "Ye gods, Wiggins," Luty said. "How in the dickens did you find that out?"

"It was dead easy." Wiggins grinned. "I couldn't sleep so I went out early and nipped over to the Parkington neighborhood. There's a workingman's café right off the Brompton Road so I went in and had a word. They knew all about the fellow. He's been eatin' his lunch there every day for the past week."

Everyone stared at the lad. Finally, Mrs. Jeffries said, "How did you know to go to this particular café?"

Wiggins shrugged. "That was dead easy, too. Americans are always real friendly like, so I knew if I could find the café where he took his meals, we'd find out all about him. This one was the nearest place to the Parkington house. Sarah told us he were a big man, so I knew he needed his food. The waiter at the café knew all about him. Quite likes the bloke, too, says he's real nice, very considerate, and always leaves a decent tip."

"I don't suppose your waiter happened to know why William Carter was watching Miss Parkington's house?" Mrs. Jeffries queried.

Wiggins sighed disappointedly. "Nah, they didn't know that. But I did find out where he's staying. It's a small house near Victoria Station. Mr. William Carter is decently dressed and all, but from the impression I got of the fellow, 'e's watchin' his pennies pretty carefully."

"You've done an excellent job, Wiggins," Mrs. Jeffries said. "Why don't you see if you can find our mysterious Mr. Carter today."

Wiggins grinned. "Yes ma'am."

"How is Sarah doing this morning?" Mrs. Jeffries asked Luty.

"She seems to be settling in some," Luty replied. "I introduced her to everyone as a new housemaid."

"I'm sorry we had to impose upon you at such short notice," Mrs. Jeffries began.

Luty cut her off with an impatient wave of her hand. "Don't be silly, of course you should have brought her to my house. The girl's no killer and frankly, if the police get their hands on her, they'll throw her in jail."

"You believe her then?" Smythe asked.

"I do," Luty replied.

"As do I," Hatchet interjected. "But, of course, I've set Jon to keep an eye on the girl while we're gone during the day."

Jon was a young boy Luty had taken in after he'd become involved in one of their earlier cases. He was streetwise, cheeky, and utterly devoted to Luty and Hatchet. He'd make sure Sarah Camden wasn't a danger to anyone.

"That's a good idea," Mrs. Jeffries replied. "We may think Sarah Camden is innocent, but until this case is solved and the real killer caught, we best be on our guard."

"Have you had a chance to speak to Dr. Bosworth?" Hatchet asked Mrs. Jeffries.

"I've been trying to see him," she replied. "I've sent notes twice and both times he's sent back word that he's very busy. I'm going to try again today. He may be able to find out if the postmortem has any useful information for us."

"I thought I'd have another go at finding out what the local merchants might know about the Leggett household," Betsy said. "But as the Parkington's are so close, I might as well do them, and I'll keep my ears for anything else about Sir Edmund."

"And I think I'll see what I can learn about Roland Leggett," Smythe said. "Seems to me that as Sir Edmund died without a wife or children, it's likely that Roland Leggett inherits from him."

"I'll try to verify that information for you today,"

Hatchet volunteered, then he grinned at Luty, "You're not the only one with resources madam."

Witherspoon sighed and settled back in the hansom. They were on their way to the home of Sir Edmund Leggett's alleged mistress. "This is probably going to be a very awkward interview, Constable. Especially as the only information we have about Mrs. Wyndham-Jones is hearsay." At breakfast this morning, Mrs. Jeffries had shared some gossip she'd heard about Sir Edmund Leggett.

"I know it's only talk, sir," she'd said apologetically. "But I also know how very thorough you are in your investigations and how you've often said it was a tidbit of gossip or talk that sent you in the right direction. Well, when I overheard those women in the chemist's shop talking about Sir Edmund's murder and about how this woman had been his uh . . . mistress for a number of years, I knew you'd want to know about it."

He'd assured her she was correct, though, in truth, he couldn't recall ever making any comments about the value of gossip. But, then again, people were always telling him about brilliant observations he'd made about investigating murders, none of which he could ever remember. He really must start writing things down, he simply couldn't remember anything these days.

"Gossip is often very true," Barnes replied. "And the truth of the matter is that Sir Edmund's servants confirmed the information when I interviewed them. I meant to bring it up yesterday evening, but we got sidetracked, sir, and it simply slipped my mind. It's in my report."

"Not to worry, Constable, we frequently get 'sidetracked' as you call it but we end up coming through in the end." The hansom hit a deep pothole and the inspector bounced hard against the seat.

Barnes grabbed the handhold to steady himself. "By the

way, sir, we've still got to interview the Parkington household. I don't like the way Mr. Parkington rushed us out of
the house."

Witherspoon patted his bowler to make sure it hadn't
gone crooked. "Be sure and ask the footmen if the entire
Parkington family arrived home in the carriage together on
the night of the murder."

Barnes, who'd glanced out the window, swung around,
and stared at Witherspoon. "I'll do that, sir. That's a very
interesting observation. Do you think that one of them may
have gotten out of the carriage on the way home?"

"We know they left the Keighley's together, but it never
hurts to find out if they all arrived home together."

"Right, sir, I'll be sure to ask." Barnes suspected that
Mrs. Jeffries was putting ideas in the inspector's head. That
was just fine with him, he was well aware that the Witherspoon household did a lot more than just gather gossip
about their employer's murder cases. "What time is the funeral today, sir?"

"Not until half past ten, so we ought to have enough
time to do the interview with Mrs. Wyndham-Jones."

"Do you think she'll be going to his funeral, sir? If she
is, she might not want to see us?" Barnes asked.

"I've no idea if she's going or not but it's certainly possible. People do all manner of odd things these days."
Witherspoon shrugged haplessly. He'd never understood
the complexities of London society and he'd no idea if it
was socially acceptable for one's mistress to show up at
one's funeral.

They discussed the case as the hansom weaved through
the crowded London streets. The carriage finally pulled up
in front of a large, red brick townhouse in the middle of the
block. Barnes paid the driver and they walked up the short
path to the front door.

Barnes lifted the heavy brass door knocker and let it
drop against the wood. A few moments later, the door

opened and a housekeeper wearing a black bombazine dress peered out at them. "Yes, what is it?"

"We'd like to speak to Mrs. Wyndham-Jones," the inspector replied. "It's rather urgent."

She hesitated, then stepped back and opened the door wider. "You'd better come in, sir. I'll see if Mrs. Wyndham-Jones is receiving."

"If she isn't," Barnes said softly, "we'll be having some nice long chats with her neighbors."

The housekeeper looked surprised for a moment and then inclined her head briefly to show that she understood his meaning. She closed the door and left them standing in the foyer as she disappeared down a long, dark paneled hallway.

"Well done, Constable," Witherspoon said softly. "I'll warrant the lady condescends to see us."

"I hope so, sir," he sighed. He was aware he'd taken quite a liberty and if he'd been with any other police inspector he'd have kept his mouth shut, but Witherspoon was different. He really did believe the police were supposed to serve the public interest and not just enforce the property rights of the rich. "I just get so tired of a certain class of people thinking they don't have to take any notice of the police. It's not right, sir. No one is exempt from justice."

"I agree, Constable," Witherspoon replied.

The housekeeper reappeared and gestured for them to follow her. "Mrs. Wyndham-Jones will see you. This way, please."

She led them to a room at the far end of the hall and opened the door. "The police are here, ma'am."

"Show them in, Helga." The voice came from the depths of the darkened room.

Witherspoon and Barnes stepped across the threshold and then stopped just inside the doorway to let their eyes adjust to the dim light. The windows were covered with black curtains that had been tightly shut and the only light came from one small black candle that sat on a table. Witherspoon could barely make out the shape of a woman sitting on the settee.

"Please come in," she ordered. "Helga, light another candle."

The housekeeper pulled some matches out of her pocket and lit a candle on the table by the door. It didn't help very much, but it did give the two policemen enough light to move farther into the room.

Witherspoon squinted in the direction of the settee. He wasn't certain, but he thought she might have a black veil over her face. "Mrs. Wyndham-Jones?"

"That's correct," the woman replied. "I know who you are. You're the police and you're here about Edmund's murder."

"We are indeed, madam," the inspector replied. "I'm Inspector Witherspoon and this is Constable Barnes. I'm very sorry for your loss, madam. But we'd like to ask you some questions." His eyes began to adjust to the dim light and he could now see the outlines of furniture.

"What good will that do, Inspector? It won't bring Edmund back." She sniffed and dabbed under her veil with a dark-colored handkerchief.

"Of course it won't bring him back," he replied gently. "But your answers to our questions may help us to find his killer. You do want to find out who murdered him, don't you?"

She sighed, lifted a languid hand and gestured at the loveseat sitting at a right angle to the settee. "Please sit down. I'll answer your questions, Inspector."

They made their way carefully to the spot she'd indicated and sat down as quickly as possible. Barnes didn't bother with his notebook as there was no point, in this light he couldn't see well enough to write anyway.

"Mrs. Wyndham-Jones," Witherspoon began, "when was the last time you saw Sir Edmund?"

"Tuesday afternoon. He came to tell me he'd gotten engaged to that twit, Beatrice Parkington." She tossed the veil off her face and leaned toward the inspector. "He had the nerve to ask me if I minded. Can you believe the stupidity of some men? He asked me if I minded!"

Without the veil, they could see she was a woman of some beauty. Her hair was a deep, rich dark color and her bone structure was excellent.

The inspector wasn't sure how to respond to her. She still seemed rather angry about the whole situation. "I'm sure he meant well," he began.

"Sounds to me like he was bit of a cad," Barnes interrupted. Honestly, there were moments when he wanted to smack his superior in the head. "No doubt he'd been leading you on with a merry dance, hadn't he?"

She nodded eagerly and shifted her attention to the constable. "He'd promised to marry me. Oh, I knew he was seeing the chit, I knew he'd been in negotiations with her father for some time. But I honestly didn't expect him to go through with it. I thought it was merely for show. I didn't think he actually meant to do it. He was supposed to marry me!" She began to sob. "It's not my fault all my money is tied up in that wretched trust. I've got my lawyers working on it. They'd have broken it eventually. But he was in such a hurry." Her sobs turned into wails and she threw herself to one side and began pounding on the settee.

Alarmed, Witherspoon leapt to his feet. "Madam, please, you'll make yourself ill."

The door flew open and the housekeeper rushed inside. "There's no point in going on, sir," she said to Witherspoon as she dashed toward the now screaming woman "she'll not be rational to answer anything. This has been going on for two days now. You'd best come back later."

Barnes, who was less alarmed than his superior, watched Mrs. Wyndham-Jones as he got to his feet. He wanted to see if her hysterics were real, or just an act to get rid of them. But in the dim light, he couldn't see her face well enough to make any genuine assessment of the situation.

"He was supposed to marry me!" Mrs. Wyndham-Jones screamed. The housekeeper sat down next to her on the settee and pulled her into her arms. "You'd best come back later," she told them again.

"Ah yes, I suppose we must." Witherspoon moved for the door. Barnes followed.

As soon as they were out in the hallway, the inspector said. "Do you think she was faking?" He kept his voice low.

Barnes shrugged. "I couldn't tell, sir." He was rather surprised that Witherspoon was even thinking along those lines.

"Let's hang about out here for a moment or two and see if she goes quiet."

But she didn't. They stayed in the hallway for a good five minutes and if anything, the weeping and the wailing got worse. Finally, the inspector motioned for them to leave. "We'll come back later and have a word with the servants," he said softly. "I want to know what Mrs. Wyndham-Jones movements were the night her beloved was murdered."

Barnes looked at him sharply. "Do you suspect her?"

Witherspoon reached for the door handle and pulled it open. "I don't know. But if her grief is real, it may not be just grief. It may be guilt as well. She obviously hadn't expected Sir Edmund to carry through with his plan to marry Miss Parkington. When he actually went so far as to announce his engagement, it's possible she simply lost control of herself and decided to kill him. She could easily have lain in wait for him to leave Lord Keighley's."

"But how would she know he was walking that night?" Barnes queried as they stepped outside. "He might have taken his carriage."

"His carriage," Witherspoon muttered. "Yes, you're right. How could she have known? Did he use the carriage that evening?"

"He didn't, sir," Barnes replied. They were now out on the pavement and the constable looked both to his right and his left, hoping to spot a hansom. There were none about. "But he does have one. Let's go to the corner, sir, we'll do better getting a cab there. We'd best hurry if we want to get to Sir Edmund's funeral in time." They started up the road. Witherspoon was deep in thought. "Did he leave the carriage for Roland Leggett to use, then?"

"No sir, they walked to the Keighley's together. I don't know why he didn't use his carriage," Barnes replied. "I'll ask Mr. Roland Leggett. He ought to know."

Witherspoon nodded. "Have we had any reports of the young woman's whereabouts?"

There was no need to explain which young woman he meant. It was the one that had been seen lurking about the Leggett house for several weeks prior to the murder.

"Not as yet, sir." Barnes sighed. "It may take some time. Our description said the girl was dressed decently, but she doesn't appear to be wealthy so she may have actually been staying some miles away from Sir Edmund's home. Belgravia is a very expensive neighborhood. I doubt the girl could afford any lodgings in that or the surrounding areas."

"Have them try the area near Victoria Station," Witherspoon directed. "There's a number of cheap places that let rooms by the week around there."

"I've got a man on it, sir," Barnes replied. By this time they'd reached the end of the road. Barnes spotted a cab letting off a fare and waved the cabbie over.

"I think we ought to go and have another word with Miss Parkington," Witherspoon mused. "And I want to make sure we speak to the servants as well. I've got a specific question I'd like to ask Miss Parkington's maid."

"What question, sir?" Barnes asked. The hansom pulled

up and he waited for the inspector to step in and sit down. "St. Peter's Church in Mayfair," he called to the driver.

"I want to find out what time Miss Parkington retired on the night of the murder," Witherspoon said as he settled back in the seat. "She and her family left the party earlier than Sir Edmund. Now, if they all arrived home together, and you'll ask the footman about that, then it's quite possible that when she retired for the night, she slipped out a window and went back to try and deal with her unwanted fiancée in her own way."

"Would she have had time?" Barnes asked.

"Yes, the distance is very, very close, less than a mile," Witherspoon replied. "And she strikes me as a young woman who isn't frightened by the dark."

Smythe stopped just inside the door of the Dirty Duck Pub and surveyed the room. Even though it had only opened minutes earlier, the bar was crowded with dockworkers, day laborers, costermongers, and cab drivers. The benches along the walls were filled with men and women drinking gin and beer. The air was scented with cigar smoke, unwashed bodies, spilled drinks, and the sour scent of the river. He spotted his quarry sitting at the big table next to the fireplace.

Blimpey Groggins waved at Smythe and then said something to the bald-headed fellow sitting with him. The man nodded and got to his feet. "I didn't mean to chase you off," Smythe said apologetically as he reached Blimpey's table.

"No worries." The man gave him a big, toothless grin. "I wus done wif our fwend 'ere."

The man disappeared into the crowd and Smythe slipped onto his stool. "Hello, Blimpey, you got a few minutes? I've got some questions for ya."

Blimpey Groggins was a portly, ginger-haired man wearing a stained porkpie hat and an ancient checked jacket. A bright red scarf hung around his neck. "Questions is it? Then you'd best have at it. You be wantin' a drink?"

"I'll 'ave a beer." Smythe stared at him curiously. It wasn't like Blimpey to offer to pay for the drinks. Generally, it was Smythe that did the buying but then again, he was one of Blimpey's best customers.

Blimpey Groggins used to be a small-time thief. However, as he possessed a phenomenal memory, he'd soon learned that the advantages of using his mind to make a living far out weighed the disadvantages of thievery; mainly getting arrested or having a run in with a pistol-wielding householder.

Blimpey had become an information broker. He had a huge network of bank clerks, law clerks, con men, street arabs, and small-time crooks that fed him information constantly. All of them reported to him on a regular basis, and he knew everything that went on in London. If a bank was robbed, Blimpey might not know exactly who was behind it, but he'd have a pretty good idea; if a house was broken into, he'd know who was working that area. If a rich man was going on an extended holiday and leaving the family jewels behind, he'd know that, too. He sold his information to the highest bidder, but despite his occupation, he was a decent sort. He had principles. He didn't deal in death nor did he ever sell information that would hurt a woman, a child, or a preacher.

Blimpey caught the barman's eye, lifted his beer glass, and then held up two fingers. "So, what are you wantin' to know my friend."

Smythe hesitated. "Did you send a young woman 'round to the inspector's last night?"

"Of course, where else would I send the girl but to you lot," Blimpey admitted with a laugh. "The inspector's got the case and the girl's involved in it, so who better to send her to." He sat back and smiled as the barmaid brought them two frothy beers. "Thanks, luv. Put 'em on my account."

But Smythe had already pulled a coin from his pocket and was handing it to the girl. "These are on me, Blimpey." He waited till the woman was gone before continuing. "When Sarah told us about the man and woman who'd 'rescued' her, I knew it was you."

Blimpey laughed. "She musta done a good job describin' me."

"Quite a coincidence, her comin' to this pub and all," Smythe said casually.

"There weren't any coincidence about it," Blimpey replied. He took a quick sip of his beer. "I 'ad one of my street arabs send her here. The lad 'ad been keepin' an eye on the girl, he knew where she'd been stayin'. As soon as I heard about the murder, I sent 'im along to send the girl this way. I thought she'd be in a bit of a panic and she was. Come along like a duck to the water and thinking all along it was 'er idea."

"Did you set the toughs on her?"

Blimpey grinned. "Only to scare 'er a bit, Smythe. I wanted to get her along to you lot as soon as possible. The girl didn't kill Edmund Leggett. He was more use to her alive than dead. But I knew if the coppers got their 'ands on 'er, she'd be in the knick in two shakes of a lamb's tail. So I set it up so she'd be grateful for a bit of help and advice."

"Why were you interested in the girl?" Smythe asked curiously.

"When I get word that someone like Sir Edmund's got a woman shadowin' his every footstep, I want to know why. It's my job to know what's what in this town. One of my street arabs mentioned the girl 'angin' about Sir Edmund, and I knew there must be a reason." Blimpey shrugged. "It's knowin' those reasons that keep people like me gainfully employed and turnin' a decent profit."

"That makes sense," Smythe murmured. He knew it hadn't been coincidence that had sent the girl to the Dirty Duck Pub and Blimpey Groggins.

"'Course it does," Blimpey replied smugly. "Sarah Camden's not a killer. For starters, she were tucked up tight in Lorna McKay's roomin' house down on Firth Street. Lorna runs a decent house, and if you're stayin' there, you're not out and about at all 'ours of the night."

"You got the address of this roomin' 'ouse?"

"Is the Queen an Englishwoman," Blimpey shot back. "'Course I got the address. You 'irin' me on this one?"

"Of course," Smythe said smoothly. "I just 'avent 'ad time to get over 'ere and chat with you. But there's a few bits and pieces you can find for me. For starters, I want you to find out whatever you can about Roland Leggett."

"Sir Edmund's cousin." Blimpey nodded. "That'll be dead easy. Anything else?"

Smythe wasn't sure. This case already had such a huge number of people involved, he wasn't sure where to begin. "Well, you're already workin' on that other matter for me and I don't want to give you too much to do."

"Don't worry about that, I'll let you know when it gets to be too much for me." He grinned. "Besides, I can use the money now that I'm a married man. Nell's a treasure, that she is, but she does like her comforts and they don't come cheap."

Smythe laughed. He knew that Blimpey was devoted to his new wife and gave her anything she wanted. "I expect she's worth it."

"That she is," Blimpey replied. "And now that you're here, I suppose I ought to tell you that no one's seen 'ide nor 'air of Edith Durant. Not 'ere and not in France, either. She's done a scarper, Smythe, and she ain't comin' back."

"But you'll keep your people on it, won't you? I don't want us to miss her if she tries to slip back into the country."

"We'll not miss the woman," he said, "but I'd not hold my breath that she'll ever set foot in England again. Not if she's got any brains. So, who else do you need information about?"

Smythe thought for a moment. There was no shortage
of suspects in this murder, but on the other hand, he didn't
want to step on anyone else's toes and hog all the clues.
Betsy could get a bit testy if he was the only one coming up
with the clues. "For now, just find out what you can about
Roland Leggett. I'll be back tomorrow to see what you've
got for me."

Wiggins feet hurt and not only that, he was fairly sure it
was going to rain. Blast, he knew he ought to have grabbed
his umbrella before he left this morning. He ducked under
the awning of a grocer's shop as the first drop of water hit
him. What should he do now? He'd been to three lodging
houses already this morning and none of them had rented a
room to William Carter. He stared at the three-story house
across the road and hoped that his luck was changing. If
Carter wasn't here, Wiggins would have to go farther
afield, and in a city the size of London that meant the fellow could be staying anywhere.

Just then the front door opened and a tall, dark-haired
man wearing a black suit and a bowler hat stepped out onto
the pavement. He glanced up at the sky as the rain pelted
him, and then he opened a long, slim, black umbrella. He
started off down the road, and Wiggins hesitated. He didn't
know for certain whether or not this was William Carter,
but he certainly fit the description. He took off after the
man like a shot.

The man Wiggins thought of as Carter hurried through
the crowded streets as though he were late for an appoint-
ment. Wiggins stayed back far enough that he hoped the
man wouldn't notice him if he happened to glance over his
shoulder. The rain stopped, and the man closed the umbrella. Then he suddenly darted across Albermarle Street.
Wiggins ran after him, darting in front of a cooper's van
and ending up on the other side a bit too close to his quarry

for comfort. He slowed his steps as the man disappeared around the corner.

Wiggins followed and then skidded to a halt. The man was only a few feet in front of him. He was standing next to a lamppost and staring straight ahead at the front of St. Peter's Church.

"Blast a Spaniard," Wiggins murmured. He eased back, hoping that neither the man nor the familiar-looking fellows just across the street would turn their heads and spot him. It was Constable Barnes and Inspector Witherspoon. They were standing in front of the church watching the mourners arrive for the funeral of Sir Edmund Leggett.

Wiggins knew there was nothing he could say to Inspector Witherspoon to explain his presence here. He edged back around the corner and out of sight before either of the two policemen could see him. Then he slumped against the wall of a bank building in relief. Blast, he ought to have remembered the funeral was today. Mrs. Jeffries had told them that this morning at breakfast and she'd also mentioned that the inspector fully intended to be there. Witherspoon had told the housekeeper he wanted to have a look at the mourners and the bystanders who turned out to watch the funeral procession. He'd said one never knew what one would see until one bothered to look. All manner of odd things often happened at funerals. The inspector had once even caught a killer during a burial at a local cemetery.

Suddenly a police whistle blew and from down the road, he saw two mounted constables clearing traffic. Wiggins brightened up, it was the funeral procession and he had a front-row seat. He moved farther away from the corner just in case the inspector or Barnes should decide to move from their current spot. He stopped behind a postbox.

The hearse was pulled by four black horses, and it was a huge ebony affair with a set of eight black plumes on the top. A coffin with ornate gold handles was visible through the carriage window. Considering the procession was for a nobleman, Wiggins thought it odd there were no funeral mutes walking alongside the carriage nor were any feather-men with their trays of ostrich plumes anywhere to be seen. There was simply the hearse followed by the carriages of the mourners. There were six of them in all.

Wiggins watched the procession go past and then he hurried to the corner and had a quick look. His man was still there. Unlike the other onlookers, he hadn't bothered to remove his hat. He simply stood there staring at the carriages now lined up in front of the church.

The inspector and Barnes had moved to the other side of the road and up a bit, out of the way of the mourners, but still close enough to have a good look at things.

Wiggins was now sure that the man was Carter. He noticed that Carter paid no attention to the hearse or its contents as the pallbearers, in their black coats and top hats, lifted the heavy coffin out of the carriage.

Carter only had eyes for the first carriage, for the one now discharging a rather good-looking man, who Wiggins suspected was Roland Leggett, then an older man and woman and finally, another, much younger woman. All of them were dressed in black mourning clothes.

Wiggins was sure this was the Parkington family. The last person to emerge from the carriage was probably Beatrice.

Roland Leggett extended his hand to her and helped her down from the carriage. She wasn't wearing a long veil, merely an elaborate black hat and a black dress with a high collar and black lace at the throat and cuffs.

Leggett took her elbow and they fell in step behind the coffin. The elder Parkingtons, with Mrs. Parkington in full mourning regalia including a veil that almost touched her toes, followed Roland and Beatrice.

Roland leaned closer to Beatrice and spoke softly to her as they moved up the pavement and into the church.

Wiggins had positioned himself at an angle so that he wouldn't be seen by the inspector or Constable Barnes. From where he was now standing he had a full view of Carter's face. Wiggins was no expert on facial expression, but he knew what hatred looked like.

It looked just like William Carter's face as he watched Roland Leggett escort Beatrice Parkington into the church.

CHAPTER 5

Inspector Witherspoon felt rather awkward about watching what really should be a private moment, but this was a murder and, despite his misgivings, he knew that sometimes one could learn a great deal from watching the way people behaved at the victim's funeral. Besides, he'd no idea what to do next in this investigation. He still had people to interview, reports to read, and evidence to examine, but sometimes, none of it made any sense to him at all. He was always a bit mystified when things turned out well and he actually caught the guilty party. He hated to admit it, even to himself, but sometimes he felt less than adequate for his position. But Witherspoon wasn't one to wallow in his emotions and he knew he mustn't give in to these feelings. He was a police officer, sworn to uphold the law and he was duty bound to do his very best. He would keep on digging until he uncovered the truth, no matter how long it took.

"Do you see that man over there, sir?" Barnes flicked his eyes in the direction of a tall man dressed in a black coat and bowler. He was standing on the pavement opposite the church.

Witherspoon followed the constable's glance. "What about him? Oh, I see, he's not taken off his hat."

"And the coffin is still being carried into the church," Barnes replied. "Not very respectful, is it sir?"

"Perhaps he's a foreigner," Witherspoon suggested. "London has a lot of visitors. Perhaps removing one's hat in the presence of a coffin isn't done where he comes from."

Barnes didn't believe that for an instant. He was certain the man had come to the church for a reason. The constable had noticed him earlier. He had seen the fellow come around the corner and then station himself in a spot where he'd have a good view of the proceedings. "He's been glaring at Roland Leggett since the man got out of his carriage."

"Really? Are you certain, Constable?"

"I'm sure, sir. I think we ought to have a word with him. Ask him what he's doing here. He's more than just an interested onlooker, sir. I'd bet my copper's pension on it."

At just that moment, the man looked in their direction and saw that both policemen were staring at him. He hesitated for a brief moment, then turned on his heel and started toward the corner. With every step he took, his feet picked up speed.

"Oh dear, I do believe he's seen us." Without thinking, Witherspoon took off after the man. Barnes hurried after his inspector.

The man glanced over his shoulder just as he turned the corner, realized the police were after him and then turned his fast walk into an out-and-out run.

Wiggins had been watching the drama unfold and he reacted without thinking. He took off after the fleeing

William Carter before he realized the consequences of his actions. By this time, Barnes and Witherspoon had come running down the road and they'd been joined in the chase by two constables who'd been directing the funeral procession traffic.

Seconds after he'd taken off after Carter, Wiggins understood his folly. He knew he mustn't turn around, the inspector would recognize him for sure.

Barnes, on the other hand, did recognize the lad within a split second of turning the corner. He knew the jig would be up if they got close enough for the inspector to get a good look at Wiggins. Suddenly, a costermonger pushing a cart of fresh vegetables came out of an alley right in front of them and Barnes seized his chance. Carter and the lad had disappeared around the bend and the two police constables hadn't caught up with anyone as yet. Witherspoon dodged to the left of the cart, leaving enough room for Barnes to make it past, as well. The constable, though, deliberately banged into the handle, causing him to stumble badly. "Blast," he yelled as he tumbled forward onto his knees.

Witherspoon, concerned about his constable, skidded to a halt. "Are you all right?"

The costermonger began waving his arms and shouting in a thick Italian accent. "What's wrong with you English? Why you run? Where you come from? Why you hit my cart? Is public street, why you run into me?" He knelt down and began picking up the potatoes and carrots that had fallen onto the pavement.

"I'm fine, Inspector," Barnes replied. He saw that Wiggins had gotten far enough ahead to insure that he'd not be seen by the inspector. Of course, that meant that they'd lost their suspect. Barnes made a mental note to ask Mrs. Jeffries about his mysterious man. He was fairly sure she'd have a complete report on the matter. He brushed the dust off his trousers as he got to his feet. "My pride's hurt a bit but my bones are none the worse for wear."

"This not my fault." The costermonger tossed the vegetables back into their baskets. "It your fault you fall. I mind own business. Look what you do to my vegetables."

"Yes, yes, of course it isn't your fault." Witherspoon assured the fellow. "And we'll pay for any vegetables that are too badly bruised to sell."

"Is okay, I think." The costermonger picked up a stray carrot and tossed it back onto the basket on his cart.

By this time the two constables had arrived and they, too, stopped, their expressions a bit confused. "Is everything all right, sir?" one of them asked.

"I took a bit of a tumble, that's all," Barnes replied quickly. "And I banged into this poor fellow's cart. But no harm was done except that the man we wanted to speak to managed to get away."

"Should we keep after him, sir?" the younger of the two policemen asked Witherspoon.

Witherspoon shook his head. "No, he's managed to get away. But I expect we'll run into the chap sooner or later. Thank you for the assistance, lads, but you might as well go back to your posts."

"Right, sir." They nodded respectfully and went back to the church. The costermonger, muttering darkly under his breath, gave them one last glance and then pushed his cart on down the street.

"Sorry about that, sir." Barnes smiled sheepishly. "Silly of me to fall like that."

"Nonsense, Constable," Witherspoon replied. "It could have happened to anyone."

"It's a shame we lost him, sir," Barnes said as they started back toward the church. "He obviously knows something or he wouldn't have run."

"Not to worry, we'll find the fellow. Someone in London will know where he lives."

"Yes sir," Barnes replied. "I'm sure you're right." He silently prayed that Wiggins managed to stay on the man

until he found out something useful. If not, then Barnes
had banged his knees up for nothing and they might have
lost a good suspect.

Wiggins gulped air into his burning lungs and slumped in
relief as Carter slowed his pace to a fast walk. He'd kept
well behind him once he'd realized the police, and especially the inspector, had given up the chase. He didn't think
Carter had spotted him, but he was taking no chances.

His quarry turned the corner and then cut across the
road toward a café on the corner. Wiggins hesitated for a
brief moment and then followed him inside.

The café was crowded and noisy. Most of the tables
were full of working men and women having a midmorn-
ing cup of tea. Carter was at the counter.

Wiggins decided to be bold. He was certain Carter
didn't know him from Adam, so he moved toward the
empty counter space next to his prey.

"Tea will be fine." Carter gave his order to the counterman.

"And a bun, if you've got one."

"We've got some fresh in this morning." The counterman nodded at Wiggins. "You wantin' a cuppa?"

"Oh yes, I'm parched with thirst."

He laughed. "Fix you right up, then. Might as well pour
two cups as one. Hilda," he called over his shoulder to a
girl at the far end of the counter. "Get one of them buns for
the gentleman here."

Wiggins shoved his hand in his pocket, making sure he
had enough money for the tea. He had plenty. That was an
odd thing, too. No matter how often he took coins from the
small supply he kept in an old tobacco tin in his top drawer,
there was always plenty left. It was almost as if someone
was filling the tin up every time he took some out! He'd
mentioned it to Mrs. Jeffries once, and she'd laughed and
said it was just his imagination. But he was sure it wasn't.

"Why are you following me?" William Carter asked softly.

Wiggins started in surprise. "Following you?"

"I'm not stupid, sir," Carter continued, still keeping his voice pitched low enough so they'd not be overheard. "If you think to blackmail me or try to cause me any harm, I assure you, I'll not hesitate to call one of your policemen."

Wiggins knew it was stupid to lie. "I was only following you to talk to you. I'm not a criminal and I've never blackmailed anyone."

Carter's brows drew together. "Why do you want to talk to me?"

The counterman put their tea down and slid a plate with a small bun on it toward Carter. "That'll be a thruppence, sir," he said to Carter. "And a tuppence for you, young man," he said to Wiggins.

Wiggins handed him a coin, as did Carter. Neither of them said anything until the counterman moved away. Then Carter turned to Wiggins and stared at him expectantly.

"I wanted to ask you some questions about Sir Edmund Leggett," Wiggins said boldly. "And don't pretend you don't know what I'm on about, you were just at the man's funeral."

"Why is my relationship to Leggett any of your business?" Carter asked. "Look, that table is empty. Let's move over there and sit down. We could use a bit of privacy."

They took their tea and moved to the empty table near the window. Wiggins took the time to try and come up with a good answer as to why he was snooping about in someone else's business. As soon as they were seated, he took a quick sip of tea to give himself another second or two to come up with a decent story.

"Well?" Carter prodded. "Who are you and why are you asking me questions."

"My name's Wiggins and I work for someone that's investigating Leggett's murder," he replied. He'd decided to be as honest as possible, at least that way he didn't get himself tied into knots trying to remember what tales he'd told.

Carter stared at him and then his long, serious face broke into a grin. "You don't look like a private detective. You're much too young."

"I never said I was a private detective," Wiggins protested. Oh blast, this wasn't going well. He was used to wheedling information out of maids and footmen, not pushy Americans.

"That's true," Carter agreed. "I made a false assumption, that's a fatal error for a scientist."

"You're a scientist?" Wiggins asked eagerly. "Really?"

"Really," Carter replied. "I'm an astronomer."

"One of them people that looks at the stars all the time."

Carter's expression softened. "Not just the stars, but everything else that moves about up there," he gestured upward. "But let's not get off the subject."

"Oh, sorry," Wiggins apologized. "It's just excitin' meetin' someone like you, that's all. I've always wondered what made all the bits and pieces move about up there the way they do. It's right interestin', if you ask me. Anyway, you've still not answered my question."

"And you've still not told me why I should."

"Because it'd be best to talk to me rather than the police," Wiggins said. "If you didn't kill Edmund Leggett, you've nothing to worry about."

"I didn't kill him," Carter replied, "and I've plenty to worry about. I'm a foreigner, I hated Leggett and I have no one to verify my whereabouts for the time that Leggett was murdered. In short, sir, I'm the perfect suspect."

Wiggins gaped at him. He'd been hoping for some information, but this was a gold mine. "How do you know when Leggett was killed?"

"It was in the papers," Carter replied.

"The papers? Oh yes, it was, wasn't it." Wiggins took a

quick sip of tea to give him time to think. He wasn't quite sure what to do next. William Carter was obviously in a chatty mood and Wiggins didn't want to ruin it by asking the wrong question. Prior experience had taught him that saying the wrong thing could be disastrous. "Uh, and I guess from what you've said you weren't at home when it 'appened."

"Unfortunately for me, I'd gone out. Furthermore, because the landlady of the establishment where I'm temporarily residing has such ridiculous rules concerning the hours when her front door is open, I'd actually snuck out the window like a thief in the night." He grimaced. "The woman shuts that place up tighter than a tick at eight o'clock every evening. Well, for goodness sakes, man, I'm an astronomer. I do most of my work at night."

"Why didn't you move somewhere else?" Wiggins asked.

"Because it's cheap and I've not much money. Oh, for God's sake, why am I telling you all this?"

"I'm a good listener," Wiggins said quickly. "And when you've got troubles, it's good to talk to someone every now and again." He held his breath, hoping he was saying the right thing.

He must have been because Carter went right on talking. "I'm only here for a few weeks and I wanted to take some more astronomical measurements. I'd gone to Hyde Park, it's one of the few spots in London where you can get a clear view of the night sky. But, as usual in this godforsaken city, between the fog and filthy air I couldn't see a thing. How do you people stand all the smoke and soot and noxious fumes? It must be very hard on your lungs. Unfortunately, though, my landlady happened to bring me a telegram after I'd gone out. So she, along with the rest of the household, knows I wasn't in my room that night."

"Did anyone in Hyde Park see you?" Wiggins asked.

"No. It was very late and I didn't want to call attention to myself. When I realized I couldn't see a wretched thing in the sky, I went for a long walk. I had a lot of thinking to do."

"How do you know Miss Parkington?" Wiggins asked.

"That's none of your business," Carter snapped.

"The police will ask you the same question and if you don't answer them, they'll ask her." He was fairly sure that appealing to Carter's sense of chivalry would loosen his tongue. He'd noticed that Americans in particular tended to be very protective of women.

Carter sighed. "Miss Parkington and I have been corresponding for several years now. She is a very talented amateur astronomer. She read an article I wrote in the *Journal of American Astronomy* and contacted me with some questions. We've become very close friends as a result of our correspondence. When I found out I was coming to England, I took the opportunity to make her acquaintance."

"Why'd you come 'ere?"

"I beg your pardon?" Carter replied.

"I asked why'd you come to England? Was it to meet Miss Parkington?"

"Of course not," Carter snapped. "Not that it's any of your concern, but I came here to settle my great-uncle's estate. As I was here, I took the opportunity to meet Miss Parkington."

"You're in love with 'er, aren't you," Wiggins said. "Cor blimey, no wonder you hated Sir Edmund Leggett."

"Wouldn't you?" Carter shot back. "The man was a dolt, interested in nothing but drinking and gambling and trivialities. It's a sin that a woman like her was being sold into virtual slavery to a man like that just so her family could wallow in a title." He leaned closer to Wiggins, his eyes blazing fury. "I've never wished for the death of any human being, but I'll not shed any tears over Sir Edmund Leggett's death."

"Did you kill him?"

"Of course not." Carter sat back and sighed. "But as I said, I'm the perfect suspect so I'm going to have the devil of a time convincing the police I'm innocent."

Hatchet stepped inside the pub and stopped just inside the door. Despite the posh neighborhood, this was a working-man's place where all the butlers, footmen, cabbies, and the rest of those that kept the rich in comfort took a few minutes for themselves. Back in the old days, he'd spent many an hour drowning his sorrows here. He made his way to the crowded bar and wedged in between a plump frizzy-haired woman and a balding, middle-aged man dressed in a footman's livery.

"What'll you have, sir?" the barmaid asked.

Hatchet gave her his best smile. "Good day, ma'am, I was wondering if Mr. Fleming is available."

"He's in the back getting a cask of ale," she replied, jerking her chin toward a small door behind her. "Who's lookin' for him?"

"Would you please tell him that Hatchet would like to speak with him, if it's convenient."

Just then the door opened and a small, curly-haired man carrying a cask appeared. He looked over and spotted Hatchet. "Well, I'll be a dead man's ghost, look who the cat dragged in. What are doing here you old sod?"

"It's wonderful to see you too, Logan," Hatchet laughed. "Can you spare a few minutes? I need your help."

"Of course you do," Fleming replied. He put the cask on the counter behind the bar and set it upright. "This is ready," he said to the barmaid. He looked at Hatchet and then jerked his head. "Come on through to the back. We can talk in my office."

The barmaid lifted up the counter and waved Hatchet through. He followed his friend through a door that led to a short, dimly lighted hallway and into an office.

Fleming crossed the small room to a rickety desk and

flopped down on the chair behind it. He motioned for Hatchet to sit down on what looked like an old piano stool just to the left of the desk. It was the only other place to sit. The remaining space was taken up with wine racks, crates of gin and whiskey, beer kegs, and casks of ale. Hatchet lowered himself gingerly onto the piano stool. "It's good of you to see me, Logan," he said.

Logan shrugged. "Don't be daft, man, I'm glad you've come. You're always welcome here, you know that. Can I get you something to drink . . ." he broke off with an embarrassed grin. "Sorry, I forgot. You still not drinking?"

Hatchet smiled wryly. There were very few people who knew that he'd sworn off alcohol many years earlier. For a number of years after certain events in his life had taken place, Hatchet had crawled into a bottle and more or less stayed there for a good long while. When he'd decided to crawl out and see what the world was like, he'd been amazed to find that the world wasn't particularly interested in having him back.

He'd been unemployed, homeless, and more or less ready to pack it in. Then he'd met Luty Belle Crookshank and for some reason known only to her, she'd taken a chance on him and given him a job. He'd not touched a drop of liquor since. Logan Fleming was one of the few people who knew what he'd gone through and who'd helped him get back on his feet. "Sober as the proverbial judge," he replied.

Fleming snorted. "Most of the judges I've seen toss it back like it was water. How have you been? Still working for that crazy American woman?"

Hatchet laughed. "She likes to think of herself as colorfully eccentric." He looked around the office. "It appears that you're doing well."

"Can't complain," Logan replied. "I'm glad you stopped by, it's been far too long since we've seen each other. But

I know you, Hatchet, and I can tell by that look in your eye that you didn't come around to inquire after my health. What can I do for you?"

Logan was someone who Hatchet had tapped for information on several of their previous cases. He was an excellent source of information. Fleming was both a good friend and a discreet publican, so he didn't ask a lot of nosy questions. "You've heard about the murder of Sir Edmund Leggett?"

"Who in this town hasn't?" Logan replied. "From the gossip I've heard, the fellow wasn't very well liked."

"Really?"

Logan leaned back in his chair. "Leggett was known about town for being a bit of a cad, if you know what I mean. Especially with the ladies. He's probably got more than one blow-by out amongst his conquests if you get my meaning. He always had an eye for the pretty ones, especially from the lower classes. From what I've heard, he spread his seed both far and wide."

Hatchet pursed his lips in disgust. Of course, he already knew about Sarah Camden's sister but he couldn't tell Logan that. Sir Edmund Leggett wasn't the first aristocrat to seduce and abandon young women, and he would probably not be the last. "Do you know if he actually had any illegitimate children or was it just gossip?"

"Just gossip." Logan shrugged. "But fairly accurate gossip. I know he was being hounded by some woman from out of London. Word had it that Leggett couldn't set foot out his front door without the woman tagging along behind him. There's lots of my customers that had a good old laugh over that one. He wasn't well liked around these parts."

"Why?"

"Lots of reasons. He didn't pay his bills and when tradesmen would try collectin', he'd bully them." Logan shrugged again. "Mind you, that didn't work. Businessmen in London know that if they're going to survive, they've got to be tough. There was several from around the neighborhood that had taken legal action against the man. Dobson, the grocer, he had his solicitors preparing to take the man to court a couple of weeks back. But then, Sir Edmund's cousin come in and settled the account. Dobson was sure he was going to lose Leggett's business, but the household still kept buying their groceries from him."

Hatchet frowned. "Are you talking about Roland Leggett?" He remembered that he was supposed to be finding out what he could about Sir Edmund's cousin.

"That's the only cousin he's got," Logan replied. "The family is spread pretty thin over the ground. There's just Roland and Edmund left. Edmund got the title and the charm. But Roland got the brains."

"How so?"

"From what I've heard, Roland turned a fairly modest inheritance into a pretty good-size fortune. He's smart, is that one."

"Did he always pay his cousin's debts?"

Logan shook his head. "Not that I've heard. But perhaps once he found out that Sir Edmund was marrying an heiress, he figured he might as well keep the wolf from the door long enough to get Sir Edmund wed. Of course, now that Sir Edmund's dead, Roland gets it all."

"Are you sure?"

"I'm sure he'll get the title and the estate. The house in London is mortgaged to the hilt so the creditors will probably get that. But then, you never know. As I said, Roland's got plenty of money. He might pay off the creditors and keep the house for himself."

"He won't want to live on the estate?" Hatchet asked.

"He'll probably sell that off," Logan replied. "That's how he made a lot of his seed money. He sold off a piece of property he'd inherited from his mother to one of them developers for a new housing estate. He's a cunning bloke, is Roland."

"I see."

"He's supposedly a pretty decent sort, as well," Logan said. "There's no scandal attached to him, either here or in Bristol. That's where he lives when he's not in London. From what I hear, he works hard, handles his money wisely, and minds his own business. He supposedly treats Sir Edmund's servants well, which is more than you can say about the late Sir Edmund."

"We'll have tea and scones," Betsy told the waiter at the Lyon's Tea Shop.

"Yes, miss." The waiter hurried off to get their refreshments. Betsy smiled at the young woman sitting opposite her. The girl was quite pretty. She had blue eyes, brown hair, and very nice skin. Her name was Lucille Ryder and she worked at the Parkington household. Betsy hadn't been able to believe her luck this morning. She'd gone to the Leggett household this morning but the place had been empty. She'd not seen anyone so much as poke a nose outside, when she'd realized that all the servants had probably been forced to go to Sir Edmund's funeral.

So she'd gone to the Parkington house just as this young woman was coming out through the servant's entrance. She'd struck up a conversation and found, to her great joy, that it was Lucille's day out and that the girl wasn't going home to see her family. With very little prompting on her part, she'd managed to get the girl here for a bit of refreshment. "It's hard not seeing your family, isn't it?"

Lucille smiled shyly. "I miss them something terrible. I like to go home but it costs too much to take the train all the way to Leicester every week."

"I know what you mean," Betsy replied. "But when it's your day out, you want to get out and about even if you can't go home."

"Generally, one of the other maids and I go out to-gether," Lucille continued. "But they made her stay today to help Miss Beatrice get ready for her fiancé's funeral."

"Funeral? Someone died?" Betsy pretended ignorance. "That's terrible."

Lucille shrugged. "I suppose it's not very nice. But to tell you the truth, Miss Beatrice, she's the young mistress in our household, wasn't all that upset when Sir Edmund was killed. She wasn't in love with him. I don't think she even liked him."

"Then why was she marrying him?" Betsy asked. She nodded as the waiter put their food down in front of them. "Thank you."

"This looks really nice. Annabelle, she's the other girl that I share a room with, we're always a bit too shy to come into places like this. Sometimes London makes you feel like a right old country bumpkin."

"I know what you mean," Betsy replied. She wanted to get the conversation back to Beatrice Parkington. "It took me ages to get comfortable in the city. Now, why was your young mistress marrying this man if she wasn't overly fond of him."

"Why else?" Lucille picked up her scone. "Her parents were making her. They had a right old row about it. The old master, Mr. Parkington, threatened to toss her out on her ear if she didn't marry Sir Edmund. Mind you, she wasn't all that bothered about being tossed out into the street. She's well educated and could probably get quite a good position as a governess."

Betsy picked up her scone and took a delicate nibble. "She was going to run off, then?"

Lucille looked doubtful. "I don't think so. Mind you, she wasn't in the habit of confiding in us housemaids, but I've got eyes, you know. I don't know what she was actu-ally planning on doing about Sir Edmund, but I do know she had no intention of goin' through with the marriage."

She reached for her cup, blew gently on the surface of the hot liquid and then took a quick sip. "For all her quiet ways, Miss Beatrice is a strong one. She's not afraid of anything, even her old tartar of a father."

"Really." Betsy pressed. Lucille obviously had a high opinion of Beatrice Parkington's abilities.

"That's right." Lucille grinned. "Why should she be scared? She's like one of them American women you read about in stories. If she wants to do something, she does it. Mind you, everyone says she takes after her father. But I don't think so. I think she's much more like Mrs. Parkington. The mistress is one of them women who act like they're interested in nothing but parties and such, but if you ask me, she's plenty smart. When they think no one's about, the master is always askin' her advice on business matters. He has her look at his books, too, and not just the household ones, but the ones from his businesses and all his investments and such."

"Both the Parkington ladies sound like most capable persons," Betsy murmured. This was all very interesting, but she wanted more information about what Beatrice Parkington was doing the night of the murder. "How did Miss Parkington's fiancé die?"

"That's the horrible part." Lucille's voice dropped to a dramatic whisper. "He was murdered."

"Murdered?" Betsy pretended to be shocked. "Was he that man that was shot the other night? The one that was in the newspapers?"

"That's right, that's him." Lucille nodded eagerly and took a huge bite of her scone. "And what's more, Miss Parkington didn't come home with her parents that night. They'd all gone to some fancy party to announce her engagement to Sir Edmund, but something must have happened because when they got home, she weren't with them, and Mr. and Mrs. Parkington were having a right old screaming match."

"What were they screaming about?"

Lucille laughed. "Oh, you'll think me awful, what with that poor man dying, but it was funny. Annabelle and I sleep at the very top of the house and they was shouting so loud we could hear them all the way up there. When we heard the commotion, we opened the door and had a good listen. Well, it weren't the first time, you know, and we're both a bit curious. The other servants sleep at the back part of the top floors and they don't hear near as much as Annabelle and I. Anyways, like I was sayin', the Parkingtons were havin' a right old row. Mrs. Parkington was shoutin' that it was all Mr. Parkington's fault. That he was a beast and a monster for chuckin' his own daughter out on the street in the middle of the night. He was yelling back that he hadn't chucked the girl out, that she'd jumped out on her own." She paused and took a quick bite from her pastry.

"Then what happened?" Betsy asked.

"That's when it got really interesting," Lucille replied. "I heard Mrs. Parkington scream at the old master that if he didn't get off his arse and go find their daughter, she'd help the girl break off her engagement and the two of them would go off to Chester and live with her sister. He said he wasn't a monster, that of course he was going back out to find his daughter, and as far as he was concerned, once he got the chit home, the two of them could live with the devil as far as he was concerned. Then I heard a door slam and a few seconds later, Mrs. Parkington was pounding on the study door and asking him what he was doin'."

"You could hear all this up at the top of the house?"

Lucille laughed. "Oh no, by that time, I'd crept out of my room and come down to the landing. It was dark as sin there, so I wasn't scared of being caught. Anyway, Mr. Parkington come out and told Mrs. Parkington to shut up and quit her screaming. He'd gone to get his gun. He said the streets weren't safe and he wasn't going back out without protection."

Betsy held her breath. This could be very important. "He got a gun? Did you see it?"

Lucille shook her head. "Oh no, not from where I was, but he was shoutin' at Mrs. Parkington so loudly it's a wonder the Queen herself didn't hear the man. Then a minute later, I heard him leave and Mrs. Parkington stormed back into the study."

"Were there any other servants up? What about Mrs. Parkington's maid."

"Everyone had gone to bed. Things aren't like they used to be, you know." She sounded a bit defensive. "We're not slaves. Used to be someone had to wait up for them but they had such trouble hanging on to staff, that now they let us go to bed. Mrs. Parkington and Miss Parkington generally help each other with corsets and such. Why? What's it like in your household? Do you have to wait up at night when the master and mistress is out?"

"No." Betsy smiled. "Not really. We've only a master and he rarely goes out at night." She'd heard that in many households life had gotten better for servants. There were too many factories and offices needing staff these days for households to keep up their old ways. People worked hard, that was true, but they weren't slaves anymore and the old custom of having half the household wait up for the master and mistress just to help them take off a pair of boots or unbutton a corset had died out in all but the most grand of homes. "I don't suppose you were awake when Mr. Parkington returned, were you?"

"No, I went back to bed. But I know he didn't find Miss Parkington, because I overheard the three of them quarreling about it the next morning. Miss Beatrice told her father she wasn't going to marry Sir Edmund and there was nothing he could do to make her. Then I heard Mr. Parkington screamin' at Mrs. Parkington that this was all her fault, that she shouldn't ever have bought the chit that stupid telescope."

Inspector Witherspoon and Barnes waited until after all the mourners had left before they made their way out of the churchyard to the street. Sir Edmund Leggett had been laid to rest in the family vault with a minimum of pomp and circumstance.

"What now, sir?" Barnes asked. "Should we go back to the station and see if the lads have come up with something? The reports on the house-to-house ought to be in by now, and we can see if there's any word on the whereabouts of Edith Durant. We had a report last night that she might have been spotted in Rye."

Witherspoon thought for a moment. "Yes, let's go to the station. But first, let's pop around to my house, it's not far from here and we can have a spot of lunch. I'm sure Mrs. Goodge has something in the larder we can nibble on and I, for one, am very hungry."

Barnes turned his head to hide his smile, he was fairly certain that the cook did have quite a bit of food cooked and he was equally certain she wouldn't fancy wasting her goodies on the two of them when she could be feeding her "sources."

The constable was well aware of what each member of the Witherspoon household contributed to the inspector's cases, but as his own career had benefited greatly from their assistance, he was more than willing to keep their secret. Besides, they could get information that a copper couldn't and they didn't have to worry about judges' rules and the proper way to gather evidence. "I think that's a splendid idea, sir. Perhaps Mrs. Goodge will have some of her wonderful buns baked."

CHAPTER 6

"Are you alone, Mrs. Goodge?" Mrs. Jeffries called out as she came down the hall toward the kitchen. If the cook was chatting with one of her sources, Mrs. Jeffries didn't want to interrupt her.

"There's no one here but Fred and I," the cook replied. She was sitting at the end of the kitchen table. "It's been a very slow day. I've not seen anyone but the butcher's boy, who doesn't appear to know much of anything, and the man from the gas works, who knows even less. Honestly, Mrs. Jeffries, some people are only interested in themselves. I can understand the butcher's boy not having anything to say, he's just a lad, but the gas man hadn't even heard of the murder." She shook her head in disbelief. "What's this world coming to when people stop taking an interest in each other! But not to worry, I've invited several of my old acquaintances around for tea so I ought to be hearing something interesting in the next few days."

Mrs. Jeffries hung up her hat and coat. "I'm glad you're not down-hearted, Mrs. Goodge. Some days we simply don't learn very much."

"The kettle is on, would you like a nice cuppa?" the cook asked.

"That would be lovely, but don't get up, I'll make it myself. Can I get you one?" Mrs. Jeffries asked.

"No, I've had enough. I take it you haven't had much luck today?"

Mrs. Jeffries pulled her favorite mug down off the shelf. "I saw Dr. Bosworth, but he wasn't very helpful."

"Not helpful?" The cook frowned. "But he's always so good about telling us what he knows."

Mrs. Jeffries poured the boiling water into the teapot and then leaned against the counter, her expression thoughtful. "Oh, I don't mean he wasn't cooperative, he was. It's just that he wasn't able to add anything new to what we already know."

"Oh." Mrs. Goodge nodded sagely. "Well, that's all right, then. We wouldn't want to lose him as a source. I was afraid for a minute there that you meant he was getting stubborn and stupid. So many men get that way when they get a bit of power, and Dr. Bosworth did get appointed as a district police surgeon last month. I was afraid the new position might have gone to his head."

"Oh no, it's nothing like that." Mrs. Jeffries laughed as she poured out her tea. She came to the table and sat down beside the cook. "He simply wasn't able to add anything new to the case, that's all. He apologized for being unavailable to us earlier this week, but he's been saddled with overseeing some medical students and didn't have a moment to himself."

"So what do we do now?" the cook asked. "We've still got suspects all over the place and we've learned very little about any of them."

"We keep on snooping," Mrs. Jeffries replied. She took a sip of tea. "But I am going to take Betsy's advice. I'm going to make some notes on the case. Frankly, it's getting difficult to keep everything and everyone straight. I must be getting old."

Mrs. Goodge stared at her for a moment. "Making a few notes is a good idea, but not because you're getting old or forgetful. There's nothing wrong with your mind."

"But I am getting older and sometimes, elderly people do get a bit forgetful. Oh dear, excuse me, Mrs. Goodge, I wasn't talking about you, I was referring to myself."

"Neither of us is getting forgetful," Mrs. Goodge insisted. "And I, for one, think we're both doing very well in our investigations. We may not be young, but we still do our part, if you know what I mean."

"Of course we do," Mrs. Jeffries replied. "I didn't mean to imply we didn't do our fair share. But honestly, Mrs. Goodge, I'm completely at a loss in this case. I've not got a clue what to do next." She didn't often get discouraged about their cases, but this one wasn't going near as well as she'd hoped. There wasn't even the beginning of a pattern to this one.

In most of their other cases, after a few days of investigation, she'd generally begin to have some idea of how to proceed, either that or she'd develop a "feel" for what to do next. But in this one, she was completely at a loss.

"It's early days yet," the cook said stoutly. "And you are getting forgetful if you think that we ever know what's going on this quickly in a case. It's always a bit of a muddle until it gets sorted out and that never happens till right at the very end. For goodness sakes, Sir Edmund was only killed a couple of days ago and we've learned ever so much."

"I suppose you're right," Mrs. Jeffries said thoughtfully. "We have learned enough to keep going forward. Sir Edmund wasn't the most popular man in town."

"He was a bounder and a cad," the cook said bluntly, "and except for his mistress, I don't think there's going to be many tears shed at his funeral today."

"Do you think she'll attend?"

Mrs. Goodge shrugged. "It's possible. In these modern times, the old proprieties have broken down."

They heard the back door open and the sound of voices in the hallway. "Hello, hello," the inspector called. "Is anyone about?"

"We're in here, Inspector." Mrs. Jeffries leapt to her feet. The cook got up, as well.

Witherspoon and Barnes walked into the kitchen. The constable nodded respectfully at the two women.

The inspector smiled brightly. "We've come to have a bit to eat," he said. "I do hope it's not too much bother. I know you weren't expecting me home for lunch, but I happened to smell some delightful scents this morning and I knew that Mrs. Goodge was baking something special."

"It's no bother at all, sir," the cook replied. "I was making currant buns. I'll do up some lunch trays and send them on up."

"That won't be necessary," Witherspoon said as he pulled out the chair from the head of the table. "Constable Barnes and I will eat right here. There's no point in you ladies having to run up and down the stairs. Do have a seat, Constable," he said to Barnes.

Barnes took the spot next to the inspector. "Thank you, sir."

"I take it you'd like a cup of tea," Mrs. Jeffries asked as she went to the pine sideboard. She took down two plates and handed them to Mrs. Goodge.

"That would be very nice," Witherspoon replied. He sighed deeply. "I, for one, am simply happy to be off my feet. It's been a very tiring morning."

Mrs. Jeffries got two mugs out of the cupboard and poured the tea. "Did you go to Sir Edmund's funeral, sir?"

"Indeed we did. It wasn't as grand an affair as I'd have thought it would be. The procession was quite simple. There was just the hearse and the carriages of the mourners."

She brought their tea to the table. "A lot of the old ways are dying out, sir."

"Even noblemen don't like the expense of paying for feathermen and mutes," Mrs. Goodge added as she headed for the dry larder. "I'll be right back with your food."

"We did have a bit of excitement at the funeral," Constable Barnes said. "We spotted a suspicious-looking fellow watching the procession and we went over to have a word with him." He paused and took a quick sip of his tea, more to give his inspector a chance to continue the tale than because he was thirsty.

"But before we could get close enough to the fellow to ask him anything, he started running," Witherspoon said. "We took off after him, but I'm afraid he gave us the slip."

"That was my fault," Barnes said. "I went bashing into a costermonger's cart and took a tumble. That delay was long enough for the man to get clean away."

"Graciou re you all right, Constable?" Mrs. Jeffries asked as she ot their silverware out of the drawer.

"I'm fine. My pride's hurt more than anything else and I'm disappointed that we let the fellow get away. I know he could have told us something."

"What made you suspicious of him in the first place?" she asked. She opened a second drawer and got out their serviettes.

"It was Constable Barnes' quick eye that put us onto the fellow," Witherspoon replied. He told her the details about their mad dash after the mysterious man.

"How very resourceful of you, Constable," she said to Barnes as she put the salt cellar and the pepper pot on the table. She noticed that Constable Barnes kept watching her closely, as though he were trying to tell her something.

Barnes stared her straight in the eye. "The man's actions is what made him stand out. I'm only sorry he got away from us. But as the inspector said, we'll catch him eventually."

Mrs. Jeffries wished she were a mind reader. She knew the constable was trying to communicate something to her.

"Here's your lunch, sir," Mrs. Goodge said as she came out of the dry larder with their plates on a tray. "It's only cold roast chicken, pickled onions, and currant buns, but there's plenty of it."

"This looks lovely. Thank you, Mrs. Goodge," Witherspoon replied as the cook put their lunch in front of them. "Where is everyone?"

Mrs. Jeffries was ready for that question. "The house is in good order, sir, so I've sent everyone out on errands. Wiggins is out getting some brass polish, Betsy is at the draper's to see if they've any material to match those curtains in the dining room, and Smythe's gone to Howard's to see to the horses."

"Have you had any luck finding Edith Durant, sir?" Mrs. Goodge asked.

Witherspoon sighed. "Unfortunately, the woman seems to have disappeared off the face of the earth."

"You'll catch her sir, you always do," Mrs. Jeffries said calmly. "What are you going to do this afternoon, sir?"

Witherspoon hesitated. "Well, we're going to go back to the station and go over the house-to-house reports. But I'm not sure that's going to tell us much."

"Are we going back to the Parkington house, sir?" Barnes asked. "You mentioned earlier that you wanted to have a word with the servants. That you wanted to verify that Miss Parkington was home all night." He shot a quick glance at Mrs. Jeffries.

"That's an excellent idea," Witherspoon replied. He was suddenly feeling much better, much more confident in his abilities to solve this crime. "We'll pop along to the station and look at those reports to see if there's anything useful in them, then we'll go along to the Parkingtons. Perhaps, if we're very lucky, one of the lads will have found out something about our mysterious young woman."

Mrs. Jeffries winced inwardly. She felt so guilty. But she simply couldn't tell the inspector or Barnes about Sarah Camden. The girl had come to them in good faith and until they had evidence to the contrary, Mrs. Jeffries would keep that faith. She wouldn't turn her over to the police. Not even to her dear inspector. Sarah was one of the few people who didn't have a decent alibi for the murder, and despite Sarah's assertion that Sir Edmund had been more use to her alive than dead, it was obvious that the girl hated him.

Hatred was a powerful motive for murder.

"The lads will keep looking, sir," Barnes said as they rode in a hansom toward the Parkington house. "She'll turn up eventually."

Witherspoon sighed. "I was so hoping they would have found the young woman. But it seems as if she's disappeared into thin air."

"Not to worry, sir, she's got to be somewhere," Barnes replied.

"She might have left the city," Witherspoon said. "She might have gone back to wherever she came from. The impression we had of the girl was that she wasn't local."

"We'll keep on looking anyway, sir. I've a feeling that she's still in town." Barnes had no idea what made him say such a thing, but the moment the words were out of his mouth, he was quite certain he was correct.

"Let's hope so, Constable," Witherspoon replied. They talked about the case as the cab moved through the crowded streets toward Belgravia.

"Perhaps the Parkington servants will have some information that helps, sir," the constable said as they pulled up in front of the house. He paid off the hansom and they went to the front door. The constable banged hard on the brass knocker.

A tall, thin-faced butler answered. "Mr. and Mrs. Parkington are not at home," he said stiffly.

Barnes was having none of that. "We know. We're not here to see the Parkingtons. It's the staff we want to interview."

"The servants?" The butler repeated. "But, but what will Mr. Parkington say?" Yet he stepped back and opened the door wider to let them inside.

"Not to worry," Witherspoon said soothingly as he and Barnes stepped into the foyer. "We'll take care of Mr. Parkington. When he arrives home, I'll have a word with him. Take us down to the servants' hall, please, and summon your housekeeper."

Within a very short time, Barnes was seated at one end of the large kitchen talking to the maids and the inspector was in the servants' dining room. The inspector had elected to start his interviews with the butler.

The poor man kept glancing over his shoulder, as though he expected his employer to appear at any moment and start shouting.

"What is your name?" Witherspoon asked him.

"Elder, sir. John Elder."

"How long have you worked for the Parkingtons?"

"Two years, sir. Before that I worked for Lord Benford." Witherspoon's eyes widened in surprise.

"Mr. Parkington offered me substantially more wages to come work for him," Elder explained.

"You must be an excellent butler."

"I do my best, sir," the man replied. "But mainly, he just wanted a butler that had worked for an aristocrat. That sort of thing is very important to Mr. Parkington."

"And would having his daughter marry an aristocrat also be important to him?"

"Oh yes, sir," Elder said quickly. "He was set on getting the young mistress a titled husband."

Witherspoon was rather amazed at how easy it was to get the butler speaking so freely. Butlers were often even more snobbish than the people they served. "And Sir Edmund had a title, didn't he."

"He was only a knight," Elder sniffed. "That's not really much of a title if you ask me."

"It's my understanding that Miss Parkington wasn't very happy with the plans for her future."

"She didn't want to marry the man, and I don't blame the girl. He was a bounder. Everyone in London knew that." He leaned forward and lowered his voice. "Some say he even used laudanum to drug young women so he could have his way with them. But Mr. Parkington turned a deaf ear to all the gossip and went ahead with the marriage plans."

"What did Mrs. Parkington think?" Witherspoon asked.

Elder hesitated. "Mrs. Parkington went along with the idea. She always went along with Mr. Parkington's ideas. But that's all just a ruse on her part, she can generally make him come around to her way of thinking, eventually."

Witherspoon wasn't sure what the butler was trying to tell him. "You mean that she was opposed to Miss Parkington's engagement to Sir Edmund?"

"No, sir." He frowned. "I don't think she was opposed to the idea. At least I didn't . . . but something odd happened on the day of the party and I think she might have been having second thoughts."

"What happened?" Witherspoon leaned toward the butler. This might be very important.

"It was about half an hour before the family was to leave for Lord Keighley's, sir. I'd just set out Mr. Parkington's evening clothes and I was on my way back downstairs. Just as I passed Miss Parkington's room, I heard Mrs. Parkington tell the young mistress that she wasn't to worry, that she'd not have to go through with the marriage."

"You heard all this?"

"Oh yes, sir. I was so surprised that it stopped me dead in my tracks. The door was opened a crack, sir, and I could hear very clearly. Mrs. Parkington was most definitely telling her daughter that she'd not have to go through with it."

"Is that all you heard?"

"No, I stood there for a few minutes. As I said, sir, I was quite shocked. I was under the impression that Mrs. Parkington had been in favor of the marriage all along. Now here she was telling the girl that she had a plan to get her out of it."

Witherspoon wasn't sure what to ask next so he just blurted out the next thing that popped into his head. "Did she mention what the plan might be?"

Elder shook his head. "I don't know. One of the maid's came up the back stairs and I had to move along." He smiled slyly. "I'd have loved to hear what the woman had planned. She might act like a bit of a silly, but she's a very smart woman. That's where the young mistress gets her intelligence."

Downstairs, Barnes wasn't getting information as easily as his superior. Neither the cook nor the kitchen maid had seen or heard anything useful. They'd both been sound asleep when the Parkingtons had arrived home on the night of the murder.

Now he had the upstairs maid sitting across from him. "What's your name, miss?" he asked kindly.

"It's Lucille, sir. Lucille Ryder."

"Lucille, don't be nervous, but I'd like to ask you a few questions."

"About the night of the murder, sir?" she replied. "I know. The housekeeper told us to answer your questions." She smiled broadly. "I've been out this morning, and I must say, this is ever so exciting. I had tea with a new friend at Lyon's Tea house, and now I get to talk to the police."

Barnes was taken aback. "You made a new friend this morning, isn't that nice?"

"Oh yes, sir. A nice girl she was, too."

The constable would have loved to have asked a couple more questions concerning Lucille's new friend, but he didn't dare. He didn't want to call attention to the situation. But he was fairly sure he knew who the girl had met. "Did anything unusual happen on the night of Miss Parkington's engagement party."

Lucille thought for a moment. "What do you mean by unusual?"

"Anything odd or out of the ordinary."

"They had a right old row when they got home," Lucille replied. "But that wasn't all that unusual. There's generally a lot of cross words in this house. Mr. Parkington is always yelling at the young mistress about something or other. Poor Mrs. Parkington does her best to calm the two of them, but she's not always successful at keeping the old master from losing his temper. 'Course, he's generally more bark than bite, if you get my meanin', sir."

"Can you tell me about the row?" He persisted.

She shrugged. "They was screaming loud enough to wake the dead when they come in that night. But the rest of 'em—" she jerked her head toward the kitchen, indicating the other servants—"sleep at the back of the house. Maybe they didn't hear what was going on, but I did." She told Barnes everything that she'd overhead that night. He listened carefully, occasionally asking a question or making a comment. By the time she'd finished, he was fairly sure he'd gotten all the pertinent details out of the girl. But as she got up to leave, he thought of one last question. "Do you happen to know if Miss Parkington was aware that Sir Edmund was being followed?"

"She knew about it," Lucille replied with a grin. "We overheard her telling her friend about it."

"Which friend?" he asked.

"Her American friend, Mr. William Carter. He's an astronomer, just like Miss Parkington. That was another thing Mr. Parkington was angry about. He kept tellin' Mrs. Parkington it was all her fault that Miss Parkington wasn't interested in proper society."

"What did he mean by that?" Barnes asked.

She shrugged again. "I'm not sure. But he was always tellin' Mrs. Parkington she should never have bought Miss Parkington her telescope and paid for all her magazine subscriptions. 'Course he'd have been really livid if he knew that Mrs. Parkington knew all about Miss Parkington's friendship with Mr. Carter." She giggled. "But what he don't know won't hurt him, will it? I think Mr. Carter's in love with Miss Parkington. What's more, I think she's in love with him."

They had their meeting late that afternoon. Wiggins arrived home first. Fred, who had snuck upstairs to have a nice sleep on the soft rug in Inspector Witherspoon's room, bounded down the back stairs as soon as he heard the footman's voice. "Hello, old boy," Wiggins exclaimed as the dog rushed into the kitchen. "We've had us quite a day."

"Well, I'm glad you've had a good day," Mrs. Goodge said, "I've not found out a ruddy thing and we'd had the inspector and Barnes here for a late lunch."

"Cor blimey, did they say anything about me?" Wiggins asked.

Mrs. Jeffries looked at him sharply. "Not really. Why?"

Wiggins looked relieved. "I almost got caught today. I

was watching Sir Edmund's funeral and William Carter
made a run for it. When I ran after 'im, I almost got
caught . . . oh bother, I'll explain when the others get 'ere.
No point in explainin' it twice."

"That's a very good idea," Mrs. Jeffries replied. "The
others should be here soon."

Luty and Hatchet arrived next, followed by Betsy, and
then Smythe. They took their places at the table.

Mrs. Jeffries said, "If it's all the same to everyone, let's
let Wiggins begin. He seems to have had the most exciting
time today."

Wiggins told them about following Carter and how he'd
been almost caught by the inspector and Barnes. Then he
told them about his meeting with Carter.

"You came close on that one." Smythe shook his head.
"Lucky for you that Barnes took a tumble and slowed the
inspector down."

Mrs. Jeffries suspected that the constable had taken a
tumble to buy Wiggins time to escape. That was probably
what he'd been trying to communicate to her earlier. He
didn't generally stare at her quite so intently as he had today.

"I know," Wiggins admitted. "I think he might have
done it on purpose. I feel real bad about it, what with his
age and all . . ."

"He's not that old," Mrs. Goodge snapped. "And the
constable doesn't do anything he doesn't want to do. Now
let's get on with discussing the case. It appears that your
Mr. Carter wasn't tucked up snugly in his room when
Leggett was murdered."

"He were out and about that night, but he's an astronomer, that's when they do their work." Wiggins replied.

"It sounds as if you rather like Mr. Carter," Mrs. Jeffries
said.

"He seems a nice enough sort of fellow, but that doesn't
mean he's not our killer," he replied quickly.

"Does he have a gun?" Betsy asked.

"All Americans have guns," Hatchet said.

"That's not true," Luty snapped. "Some Americans don't have firearms. I knew a Quaker family once that didn't have weapons. Nice bunch they was, too."

"But I'll warrant that Mr. Carter has a gun," Hatchet argued. "He's traveling on his own in a foreign country."

"How can we find out?" Betsy asked. "That seems to me to be the sensible thing to do. He couldn't have murdered Sir Edmund unless he had a gun. Wiggins says the man is watching his pennies, so it's not likely he'd have bought one when he got here."

"He might have bought one if he wanted to commit murder," Smythe suggested.

"If he was going to do the murder, why not buy a knife?" Betsy argued. "They're much cheaper. You can pick one up at any ironmongers' or even at a street stall. Guns are expensive and they're not that easy to get your hands on without someone remembering. If I worked in a shop, I'd remember a big American man coming in and buying a firearm."

Mrs. Jeffries was afraid that this was going to degenerate into one of those arguments that get less and less useful to the task at hand. "So what we really need to do is to find out if Mr. Carter had a weapon with him," she said. "But that could be very dangerous. The only way to do it would be to search his room, and I don't think I want anyone taking that kind of a risk."

"I could do it," Wiggins said. "I'm right good at nippin' in and out of places."

"Don't be daft, lad," Smythe snapped. "If you got caught, there's no way this side of Hades you could talk your way out of the situation. There's other ways of handling the problem."

Alarmed, Betsy looked at Smythe. "I don't want you doing it," she exclaimed.

"No one has to do it," Mrs. Jeffries said firmly. "It'll only become necessary when and if Mr. Carter becomes our prime suspect. Besides, even if he is the killer, he could just as easily have tossed the gun in the river as keep it. Now, who would like to go next?"

"I made contact with a maid from the Parkington house," Betsy said, "and I got an earful." She told them about her meeting with Lucille Ryder. When she'd finished, she leaned back in her chair with a satisfied smile on her face. "So it seems like our prime suspect could be either Mr. or Miss Parkington. Both of them were out that night and Mr. Parkington did have a weapon with him."

"And he's the one person who really didn't want Sir Edmund dead," Mrs. Goodge muttered.

"As far as we know," Mrs. Jeffries countered. "Perhaps we ought to take a closer look at Mr. Parkington. Perhaps he, too, had a reason for wanting Sir Edmund dead."

"I think we can eliminate Beatrice Parkington as a suspect. Unless Miss Parkington took a gun to her engagement party, I don't think she could have done the deed," Hatchet said thoughtfully.

"Not unless she planned to meet up with William Carter, and he had a gun," Luty suggested. "Maybe they did it together."

"If that was the case, why kill Sir Edmund?" Betsy asked. "If the two of them had planned to meet that night, why not just run away together. She had plenty of jewels and things she could have sold. Why take the risk of committing murder?"

"Maybe Sir Edmund caught them," Wiggins said. "Maybe that's why he left the party right after the Parkingtons did."

Luty shook her head. "They couldn't have planned it. They had no idea that Sir Edmund would be walking home that night instead of taking his carriage."

"By that logic, the only person who could have murdered Sir Edmund was someone who was actually following the man, or someone who knew he'd not taken the carriage that night," Hatchet said softly. "Sarah Camden knew the Leggetts had gone on foot to Lord Keighley's."

"Sarah's no killer," Luty shot back. "And besides, considering how hard up Sir Edmund was, the whole town probably knew he couldn't use his carriage. It's too expensive."

"We're getting mired in details here," Mrs. Jeffries said softly. "But I think it's a detail worth knowing. Why didn't he take the carriage that night? Surely a little bit of expense could be justified on such an occasion."

"I think I can find out," Smythe volunteered. He felt like he'd not contributed very much. Even the bits and pieces he'd learned today about Sarah Camden was something they already knew.

"That would be very helpful, Smythe," Mrs. Jeffries said. "And frankly, we need all the help we can get on this case. I must admit, I've no idea who killed Sir Edmund Leggett."

"You'll figure it out," Wiggins said confidently. "You always do."

"Did you have any luck today?" Betsy asked the housekeeper.

Mrs. Jeffries sighed. "Not really. Dr. Bosworth simply verified what we already knew. Sir Edmund was shot in the chest three times at very close range." She shrugged. "Not much useful information there. Oh, and he also said the man was quite drunk. But we knew that, too."

"Did we?" Hatchet said softly. "Or did we simply start making assumptions because Sir Edmund was walking home from a party?"

Mrs. Jeffries stared at him thoughtfully. "What are you implying?"

"Well," he hesitated, not wanting to sound critical of the

others or the investigation. "I think we've gotten a bit ahead of ourselves. We've been very remiss in one very important aspect of this case, namely, none of us have concentrated on what happened at the engagement party."

"But Mrs. Jeffries told us what the inspector told 'er about the party," Wiggins began. "Cor blimey, you're right. We shoulda hot-footed it over there and found out what was what for ourselves. There's probably lots that happened that no one told the inspector about."

"Hatchet is right," Mrs. Jeffries murmured. "We have gotten ahead of ourselves."

"What should we do, then?" Wiggins asked curiously. He thought they'd been doing quite well.

She thought for a moment. "We should get more details about what happened at that party and we should make sure that Sarah Camden is telling the truth."

"You mean, find out if Sir Edmund really did seduce her sister?" Betsy shook her head. "But why would she lie about something like that?"

"Maybe she was the one that got seduced," Smythe said softly. "Hell hath no fury like a woman scorned."

"Exactly." Mrs. Jeffries nodded in satisfaction. "Just because we like the girl doesn't mean we ought to accept her story at face value. It should be easy enough for us to find out if she has a niece. That's something I can take care of tomorrow morning. Furthermore, we need to find out what we can about Osgood Parkington. He's the one person we know was out that night with a gun. Just because he appeared to fawn over Sir Edmund doesn't mean he didn't have another, more compelling reason for wanting the man dead. As we all know from many of our previous cases, appearances can be very deceptive."

"I'll nip along and see what I can find out. Someone who was at the engagement party ought to be out and about tomorrow," Wiggins said.

"And I'll see if I can find someone of my acquaintance that was a guest." Luty rubbed her hands together. "Surely someone I know was there that night."

"And I'll have a word at Howard's and see who might have had their rigs out that night," Smythe volunteered. "Coachmen and grooms see and hear plenty." He'd also make a quick stop at the Dirty Duck Pub. If anyone could find out if Osgood Parkington had a reason for wanting Sir Edmund dead, it was Blimpey Groggins.

"I'll put my sources onto it, as well," Mrs. Goodge added.

"Now that that is settled," Hatchet said. "I'd like to tell you what I found out today." Without revealing his source, he told them about his visit to Logan Fleming. "I know it doesn't give us any information about the night of the murder," he finished, "but it does speak directly to the question of both Sir Edmund's and his cousin's character."

"Sounds like Roland Leggett knows how to turn property into money," Mrs. Goodge said. "Seems like that's the way it always is, the ones that get the title and the estate are usually dumber than dirt while the one's that get the least turn it into the most."

Mrs. Jeffries didn't sleep very well. She spent most of the night trying not to think about their case, but of course, the harder she tried to put it out of her mind, the more the facts insisted on keeping her awake. She finally gave up and just lay there, letting the words and images come as they would.

She thought about Sarah Camden and whether or not the girl was telling the truth. Smythe had told them that the rooming house where Sarah stayed locked their doors early, but that hadn't stopped Sarah from following Sir Edmund to the party. It wasn't overly far-fetched to think the girl could have gone back to her lodging, gone to her room, and then climbed out a conveniently open window.

Mrs. Jeffries sighed heavily and turned onto her side. It was also quite possible that Beatrice Parkington and her American friend had planned to meet that night. Perhaps Sir Edmund had found out and followed them . . . oh bother, this was impossible. She simply didn't have enough facts to form any kind of reasonable idea about this case. She rolled onto her back and stared at the ceiling. They'd just have to keep at it, that was all there was to it.

She got up the next morning and hurried down to the kitchen to do the grocery list. The others were up early, as well. Everyone wanted to finish their chores so they could be out and about on the investigation.

As soon as breakfast was over and the clearing up done, Mrs. Goodge shooed them out of the kitchen. She wanted to get on with the serious business of baking for her sources. Mrs. Jeffries sent Wiggins off to the shops with the grocery list and dashed through the rest of her duties in record time.

Betsy swept the drawing room and dusted the furniture. When she'd finished, she hurried upstairs to her room. Mrs. Jeffries bedroom and sitting room were across the landing.

She stepped into the small room and closed the door. Inside was a single brass bed with a pale blue chenille bedcover and an oak chest of drawers with a blue-and-white hand basin and pitcher sitting on it. There was a nice mirror in a lovely wood frame on the wall next to the window and a tall wardrobe with a missing knob stood at the foot of the bed. Betsy hurried toward the wardrobe, opened it and yanked out her jacket. Yesterday it had gotten quite chilly and as she planned to be out most of the day, she wasn't taking any chances on getting cold.

There was a soft knock on the door.

"Come in," she called as she pulled on the lightweight wool garment.

Smythe stepped inside. "Are you ready to go?"

"Almost." She went to the dresser, opened the top drawer and scooped out some coins. She put them in the pocket of her jacket.

"Make sure you've enough to take a hansom home if it gets late," he warned.

Betsy laughed. "Don't worry, I've got plenty."

He smiled at her. "Sometimes I wish we were already married."

"Me, too." She took his arm. "But we both know we're not ready to give this up. Once we're wed, things will change."

He put his hand over hers. "It doesn't have to change. We could stay on here."

Betsy stared at him for a long moment. "You know that's not true. You know that you'd not want me working as a maid if I was your wife. I know you, Smythe. The minute we're married, you'll want to give me the world and that will change everything. I love you with all my heart and I know you love me, but I'm not ready to give this up. Not yet."

He sighed, knowing that she spoke the truth. Everything would change. He was rich, he was proud, and the minute he got that ring on her finger, he'd not be wanting her fetching and carrying for someone else, even someone as good as the inspector. "You're right, lass. I'm not ready to give this up yet, either. But come next June, you'll be walking down that aisle with me, no matter what."

"Of course I will," she promised as she tugged him toward the door. "Come on, then. Let's get going. We've got a lot to do if we're going to solve this case."

CHAPTER 7

A light mist softened the pale morning sunlight and wisps of fog drifted across the cobblestone road in front of Lord Keighley's Grecian-style house. The inspector leaned against a lamppost while he waited for Barnes to pay the cab driver. He was filled with resolve. During breakfast this morning, he'd suddenly realized he needed more information about the night Sir Edmund was murdered. He wanted to know more about what, if anything, had happened at the party proper and he wanted to speak at greater length to some of the guests that had been there that night. He also wanted a have a word with the servants. As Mrs. Jeffries had pointed out this morning, the staff frequently heard and saw much more than most people realized.

"Ready, sir?" Barnes asked.

"Absolutely," he replied. He started for the front door. "I feel as if I've been remiss in following up this line of inquiry. For all we know, it was something that happened at the party which precipitated the poor man's death."

"Not to worry, sir. We've already taken statements from most of the guests and none of them can remember anything unusual or sinister that involved Sir Edmund."

"But we didn't question the servants very carefully," the inspector replied. "At the time, I didn't think it was necessary. But I do now. To be honest, Constable, we're no closer to finding the killer now than we were three days ago."

"If we keep asking enough questions, something useful will turn up. It always does." Barnes reached for the knocker.

The butler opened the door and stared at them for a moment before he spoke. "May I help you?"

Barnes was having none of this. As Lord Keighley had been very cooperative, he wasn't going to put up with silly snobbery from a servant. "We'd like to speak to Lord or Lady Keighley, please."

"Lord Keighley is out," the butler sniffed disapprovingly. He was a tall fellow with thick white hair and spectacles. "Lady Keighley isn't receiving."

"This isn't a social call," the constable replied. "It's police business, and I'll thank you to tell the Lady we're here. We'll only take a moment of her time."

"We simply want her permission to question the staff," Witherspoon interjected gently.

The butler hesitated a fraction of a second and then pulled the door open and waved them inside. "Wait here," he instructed as soon as they'd stepped into the large, tiled foyer.

Barnes waited until the servant disappeared down the hallway next to the staircase before speaking. "I didn't mean to be rude to the fellow, sir, but sometimes it's the only way to get these people to cooperate."

"That's quite all right, Constable," Witherspoon replied.

He took his bowler off and wondered if he ought to put it on the marble-topped entry table by the front door or whether he ought to just hang on to it. "You do get results."

From down the hall, they heard a door open and then the low murmur of voices. A moment later, Lady Keighley, with the butler trailing her heels, appeared.

"You wanted to see me, Inspector?" She smiled and nodded politely at Barnes as she spoke. Lady Keighley was a thin-faced, middle-aged woman of medium height. She had light brown hair, blue eyes, and a very pale complexion.

"I'm sorry to disturb you, madam," the inspector replied. "But we've some more questions to ask."

"My husband isn't home just now," she replied. "You're welcome to question me, but I honestly don't know what else I can tell you about Sir Edmund."

"We'd like your permission to question your servants," Witherspoon said. "We think it's possible someone might have seen or heard something that night which might be of use to us."

"Of course, Inspector. You have my permission." She turned to the butler. "Foster, take the gentlemen down to the servants' hall and see that they have everything they need. Tell the staff they are to answer all their questions and cooperate fully."

"Yes madam," Foster replied. "If you'll come this way, gentlemen."

"Thank you, Lady Keighley," Witherspoon said. He was glad he'd hung on to his hat. "We appreciate your help."

Ten minutes later, Inspector Witherspoon was sitting at a table in the butler's pantry while Constable Barnes had a cozy nook set up in the servants' dining hall. The inspector was absolutely sure they'd find out something useful. Barnes was to interview the kitchen staff while the inspector would speak with the serving staff.

Witherspoon nodded politely to Foster as the butler pulled out a chair and sat down. The two men were face-to-face but despite Lady Keighley's instructions, Witherspoon could tell by the fellow's sour expression that he wasn't going to get a lot of cooperation from this one.

"Can you recall who arrived first on the night of the party?" Witherspoon knew that it was a silly question the moment it came out of his mouth, but he could hardly take it back.

"I've no idea," Foster replied. He flicked an imaginary piece of lint off his black coat sleeve. "The footman was opening the door. I was seeing to the liquor."

"You mean you were in the kitchen?"

Foster glared at him. "Certainly not, I was in Lord Keighley's study when the first guests arrived. I always make sure there's a full bottle of brandy available for the gentlemen."

"I see." Witherspoon decided to abandon that line of questioning. "Well, did you see anything unusual happen that night?"

"No."

"Did you happen to notice when Sir Edmund and Mr. Roland Leggett arrived."

"No. As I said, I was attending my duties, not watching the door."

Across the hall, Barnes wasn't doing much better than his superior. He smiled at the young kitchen maid sitting across from him and tried again. "Now Helen, are you sure you didn't see anything at all unusual that night?"

Helen flattened her mouth into a thin line and shook her head vehemently. "No sir, like I told you. I was busy running up and down them stairs with the food. I didn't have time to notice nothin'."

"Did you happen to notice if anyone spoke to Sir Edmund?" Perhaps being a bit more specific would help a little.

"Is he the one that was murdered?" The girl shook her head. "I didn't see anyone talking to anyone. All I ever notice is the ladies' dresses and the only one I noticed that night was Miss Parkington. She looked as plump as a Christmas goose in that gown she was wearin'."

Barnes sighed. This was the third girl he'd questioned and the only information he'd gotten so far was that a china platter had gone missing, someone had cracked the glass on one of the drawing room cabinets, and a window had been left open in the back sitting room. None of these items seemed particularly relevant, but Barnes had done his duty and duly noted all the facts in his little brown notebook. He hoped the inspector was having more luck than he was.

"Has Minnie gone blind?" Luty muttered to herself as she surveyed the drawing room. Brightly upholstered balloon-backed chairs were squeezed into corners beside tables loaded down with Dresden figurines, silver candlesticks, and intricately woven china baskets stuffed with silk flowers. The two tall windows were draped with heavy gold-fringed damask curtains and there were so many paintings crammed on the walls, it was difficult to even see the gold-and-white striped wallpaper. Three settees and six ottomans were grouped willy-nilly in the center of the huge room, and they were surrounded by tables, bookcases, and tallboys all covered with gauzy, fringed shawls of various colors. Every piece of furniture was cluttered with knick-knacks, carved boxes, oriental vases, and intricately framed pressed flowers. There wasn't enough free space on any surface to put so much as a teacup. Ye gods, it almost made her eyes hurt just to look at the place.

"How do you like it?" Minnie Sullivan, a short, fat woman dressed in an elegant pink day dress swept into the room and waved Luty toward a sapphire-blue settee. "I've had the whole room redone. When Horace and I moved in it was in horrible shape. Why, you could see the bare wood floors and the walls were covered in the most hideous paint."

"It looks real nice," Luty lied. She had to lie. Minnie was a sensitive soul and her feelings were easily hurt. Minnie Sullivan was a Canadian who, like Luty, had moved back to her husband's native country after they'd made a fortune. She was an old acquaintance of Luty's, and she'd been at Lord Keighley's the night Sir Edmund had been murdered. "Very lovely, Minnie. You've got wonderful taste."

Minnie's broad face beamed with pleasure. "Do you think so, really? Thank you. Horace claims I overdo it, but men don't have any sense of proportion whatsoever. I must say, it's nice to see you. I've not seen you since the Tarrington's Christmas ball."

"That's why I thought I'd drop by and have a visit," Luty replied. "What have you been doing lately, anything interesting?"

Minnie thought for a moment. "Not really, just the usual sort of thing."

Luty wanted to shake the woman. For goodness sake, she'd been at a party where murder had been done and the silly cow didn't find that interesting! But Luty forced herself to smile politely. She knew more than one way to skin a cat; not that she'd ever skinned a cat, she was actually quite fond of the creatures, but it was a good expression. "I've not done much lately either, nothing excitin' if you know what I mean. I did hear that Katherine Brighton was at a party the other night and one of the guests got murdered right before her very eyes. Now that's what I call excitin'."

"That's utter nonsense," Minnie snapped. "I was at the same party and it certainly didn't happen that way at all. That woman is a terrible liar."

"You mean there wasn't a murder?" Luty asked innocently. She had no idea whether or not Katherine Brighton had been at Lord Keighley's or not, but she did know that Minnie loathed the woman, and nothing got her tongue moving faster than Katherine Brighton.

"There was a murder all right, but it wasn't at Lord Keighley's party, it was afterward." She learned closer to Luty, "and not only that, but Katherine wasn't even there."

"I wonder why she said she was," Luty said conversationally. "Oh well, maybe I misunderstood her. Who was killed?"

Minnie snorted. "You didn't misunderstand her in the least. The woman's always claiming to know every single thing that happens in London society."

"Uh, who got killed?" Luty persisted. She wanted to get Minnie onto the murder and off Katherine Brighton.

"It's been in all the papers." Minnie waved her pudgy hand dismissively. "It was Sir Edmund Leggett. He was shot on his way home from the party. Pity, too, as he'd just announced his engagement to that mousy Parkington girl."

"Do they know who shot him?" Luty asked.

"Of course they don't," Minnie said. "It'll take the police ages to catch the killer, if they catch him at all. Of course, no one was very shocked when it happened. Edmund Leggett was the sort of man that got himself murdered, if you know what I mean."

"You mean he was a cad?" Luty said.

"Of the worst sort," Minnie continued gleefully. "Not that I'm condoning murder, of course. It's just that the man wasn't very discreet. I'm amazed that the Parkingtons wanted to have anything to do with him. But then again, Julia and Osgood Parkington are dreadful social climbers."

"You don't say," Luty prompted.

"Oh, but I do say." Minnie laughed. "Edmund Leggett was publicly flaunting his mistress while the marriage settlement was being negotiated. Disgraceful! Utterly disgraceful. Why, just two days before the engagement party, Edmund Leggett was seen at the theater with Harriet Wyndham-Jones."

"Perhaps he and this Miss Wyndham-Jones were just friends," Luty suggested. She couldn't believe her luck, her dry spell had finally ended. Minnie couldn't get the gossip out fast enough.

"Don't be naive," Minnie snorted delicately. "Harriet Wyndham-Jones wasn't the sort of woman to be friends with anyone, especially not with a rake like Sir Edmund. Why do you think he had to move so far beneath him to find a rich bride. Women of his own class wouldn't have anything to do with him."

Luty nodded encouragingly. "I take it the Parkingtons aren't old money."

"Osgood Parkington is the son of a Wiltshire farmer who used his wife's money to start out in business. He's done quite well for himself, but the gossip has it that it's Julia that has the head for business, not Osgood. Mind you, she'd come by it naturally; her people made all their money in textiles that they then sold all over the world. Not that there's any shame in coming from humble beginnings. But my point is that a generation ago, men like Sir Edmund would never have considered someone like Beatrice Parkington marriageable, no matter how much money she had."

Luty ducked her head to hide a smile. Minnie's own origins were pretty darned humble. Rumor had it she'd been born in a shack on the outskirts of Calgary. "I take it this Harriet Wyndham-Jones woman didn't have much money of her own."

"If that's what Katherine Brighton told you, then as usual, she's wrong!" Minnie retorted. "Harriet Wyndham-Jones is rich. But her money is all tied up in a trust. She's had her lawyers trying to break it ever since he died. Mind you, there's some that claim his death was a bit too convenient, if you know what I mean."

"Huh?" Luty didn't know what she meant at all. "What are you saying? Who's death?"

"William Wyndham-Jones, Harriet's first husband." Minnie grinned. "He died very conveniently for Harriet. The servants were all gone for the day, and when they returned, they found poor Mr. Wyndham-Jones lying at the foot of the staircase with a broken neck. Harriet supposedly had been out all afternoon shopping on Regent Street. But she didn't have any packages with her when she arrived home, and the next-door neighbors thought they'd heard her and William having a fierce argument that day."

"What did the police think?"

"Police?" Minnie shrugged. "I don't think there was much of an investigation at all. The magistrates' court ruled the death an accident and Harriet buried the poor old fellow. He was much older than she was, did I mention that? Oh, and another thing, William died just a few weeks after Harriet had met Sir Edmund Leggett."

Smythe opened the wooden door and stepped into Howard's, the stable where the inspector's horses and carriage were kept. Eddie James, the owner, poked his head out of a stall and called out. "Hello Smythe, you wantin' to take the rig out?"

"Not today," Smythe replied. He took a deep breath, filling his lungs with the scent of the stable. He didn't find the odor of horseflesh, hay, or manure in the least bit offensive. They were good, honest smells, and Eddie Howard ran the cleanest stable in all of London. "Actually, I've come for a quick word with you, if you're not too busy."

Eddie, a short man with bushy eyebrows and a head full of unruly brown curls, stared at him in surprise. He leaned the pitchfork he'd been using up against the wall. "Is somethin' wrong?"

"No, nothin' like that," Smythe said quickly. "I just need a bit of advice."

Eddie smiled in relief. "Is that it? Is it about the horses?"

"Not really. I'm lookin' to 'elp our inspector out a bit on this case 'e's workin' on." Smythe had decided to tell Eddie the truth, more or less. He knew that the odds of Eddie ever speaking to Inspector Witherspoon were very slight. "And I want to find out what other stables in London would be servicin' Belgravia or Mayfair?"

Eddie thought for a moment. "Well, there's Desmond's over on Parger Road. No, no, I tell a lie. They closed down last year. There's Wellington's over off Thornton Square, they're still in business. As a matter of fact, they're about the only ones left in that area. Stables don't do much business these days," he explained. "Not with the trains and trams and hansoms and all. It's hard to stay in business. Bloomin' expensive, if you know what I mean."

"You seem to do all right," Smythe said.

"Only because I own the land I'm on outright, a lot of other places weren't so lucky. Besides, you know as well as I do that it's gettin' harder and harder to keep horses in London. Just hauling their feed in costs the earth. But you didn't come here to hear me grousin' about the cost of doing business. If you're wanting to speak to one of the grooms or drivers about your inspector's case, you'd best try Wellington's."

"Thanks Eddie," Smythe replied. "I'd best go see Bow and Arrow, they'll be upset if I don't go give 'em a bit of attention while I'm 'ere."

"You goin' to take 'em out for a quick run?" Eddie asked. "They've not been out in a goodly while."

"Not today," Smythe said as he headed for the back of the stable. "I'm just goin' to pay my respects and be on my way. I'll come back next week and take them out for long one." He knew exactly what Eddie meant. Even for the very rich, keeping a horse and carriage was becoming a thing of the past. He wondered how much longer the inspector would want to keep Bow and Arrow in the stable.

"Hello boy." Smythe patted the big, black horse on the side of his head. Bow whined gently and bobbed his nose against Smythe's hand, hoping for some treat. Arrow, who was in the next stall, stuck his head out and snorted for attention. Smythe centered himself between the stalls so he could reach both animals and gently stroked Arrow's nose. The horses were notoriously jealous of one another so he gave each of them a bit of apple and patted them one last time. "Don't worry," he told them. "If the time comes that the inspector can't afford your keep, I'll take care of both of you." That was the nice thing about being rich, he thought as he left the stables, he didn't have to worry about the future of either the people or the animals he loved. He could afford to take care of all of them.

By the time Smythe got to Wellington's, he had a good story all ready. The stable was a long, one-story wooden building set back off the road behind a wooden fence. There was an old cobblestone courtyard and a large horse trough in front of the the double doors which led into the stable proper. He pushed open the gate and stepped into the courtyard just as a groom leading a big, gray horse came out into the yard. He stopped when he saw Smythe. "You lookin' for someone?" he asked politely.

Smythe pulled a couple of coins out of his pocket. "Actually, I'm lookin' to speak to anyone who was workin' a rig a couple of nights back."

"What do ya mean?" the groom asked, his gaze on the money in Smythe's hand.

"There was a party at Lord Keighley's . . ."

"I know the place. I worked a hired rig for that party," the groom said quickly. "You can talk to me." The horse whined gently and poked its nose on the lad's arm. "But I've got to walk Warrior here. You can walk with us if you like."

"I'll pay ya for your time," Smythe said. He hoped the boy had seen or heard something useful that night. There didn't look to be anyone else about and he was running short on time. He still had to get over and have a word with Blimpey. "Is there anyone else 'ere I might 'ave a word with? I mean, after I'm finished with you."

The groom shook his head. "Nah, Tommy and Mick are both out on runs and Mr. Wellington is home with a bad foot. Johnny's in the stable, but he can't help you. He wasn't workin' the night of the Keighley party."

"It looks like it'll be just you, then," Smythe murmured. "Aren't you curious as to why I'm wantin' to be askin' questions?" He liked to get that out in the open right away. It saved a lot of bother later.

"Not really, not if you're goin' to be payin' me for my time. I can use a bit of extra coin. Business is real bad and Mr. Wellington is probably goin' to have to let some of us go. Come along, then, let's not keep old Warrior waiting. He likes his exercise, he does."

Smythe fell into step beside the groom and the horse. "Well, then, let's hope you can 'elp me."

Mrs. Jeffries waited until the grocer's boy had left the kitchen, then she hurried down the stairs. Mrs. Goodge had gotten up and was heading toward the dry larder, a plate of buns in her hand. She stared at the housekeeper. "I thought you were out."

"No, actually, I was upstairs having a good think. Mrs. Goodge, I want to talk to you about what I've done."

The cook, looking slightly alarmed, stopped in her tracks. "What you've done? Gracious, Mrs. Jeffries, that sounds grim. What's wrong?"

Mrs. Jeffries laughed and waved the cook on toward the hall. "Oh dear, I didn't mean to frighten you, it's just that I've done something a bit . . . odd and I need your help in deciding what to do about it."

Looking relieved, Mrs. Goodge nodded and continued on toward the larder. A moment later, she slipped into the chair next to Mrs. Jeffries. "Now, what is it we need to talk about?"

Mrs. Jeffries pulled the list she'd made earlier that morning out of her pocket and set it on the table. "This is a list of the names of the guests who were at the Keighley's party. I copied it off the list the inspector had."

Mrs. Goodge raised her eyebrows but said nothing.

"Yes, I know it wasn't very nice, but honestly, Mrs. Goodge, I was desperate. I've got no feel for this case whatsoever."

The cook sighed. "I know what you mean. It's hard to even know what questions to ask people. What's more, no one seems to know much of anything when I can think of something to ask. I thought it was just me. On top of that, Letty Seabold, who's the biggest gossip in all of England, broke her ankle and couldn't come by today for tea. I don't know what I'll do if any of my other sources cancel. Frankly, Mrs. Jeffries, it's a bit of comfort to know you're having trouble, too."

"I think we all are," the housekeeper admitted. "Betsy looked so glum this morning she didn't even say where she was going, Wiggins tried to act cheerful, but he left with a long face, and even Smythe didn't seem his usual chipper self." She shook her head. "This must stop. We've got to set our sights on catching this killer and stay on course. That's all there is to it. Now, as I was saying, I copied this list of names and I think you and I ought to go over it carefully and decide if it's worth snooping about in that direction."

"But there's two dozen names here," the cook retorted. "We can't work on all of them."

"But you might recognize a name or two and you might know someone who was working for one of them."

"Of course, you're right," Mrs. Goodge pulled the list closer. "I'm bound to know someone in service to one of these people. That's one of the few advantages of getting old. You have a lot of sources to call upon. Now, let's see who we've got here."

"I've finished with the kitchen staff, sir," Barnes said to Witherspoon as he came into the butler's pantry.

"And I'm done here, as well," Witherspoon admitted as he got to his feet. "I don't know about you, Constable, but I'm very hungry. There's a café just off Eaton Place, let's go get some lunch."

The two men made their way upstairs. Witherspoon nodded at Foster as they reached the foyer. "We'll let ourselves out," he called to the butler. "Do thank Lady Keighley for us."

They went out into the tepid sunshine and crossed the street. Witherspoon shook his head ruefully. "I don't know that I've learned anything useful, though. No one seems to have heard or seen anything. Well, that's not quite true. Foster claims there was something odd with the brandy bottle."

"Odd in what way, sir?" Barnes asked.

"It was full and it shouldn't have been." Witherspoon sighed. "He said the gentlemen were all drinking that night and the bottle should have been half empty. But the next day, when he went to check the supply, he noticed it was as full as when he'd put it there the night before."

"The gentlemen were probably drinking whiskey," Barnes replied. "Not brandy. It sounds like you've heard the same sort of bits and pieces that I've found."

"Not had much luck?"

"Well, the scullery maid claims that someone's stolen a china platter and the tweeny insists that one of the guests broke the glass in the upstairs cupboard. Oh, and no one is admitting to leaving the window in the back sitting room open."

"So, in fact, neither of us learned much of anything." Witherspoon replied.

"Not that I can tell," Barnes said mournfully. "But we mustn't get discouraged, sir. We've still a lot of people to speak with. I've got the lads doing another set of house-to-house interviews at the murder scene. Perhaps something will turn up there."

"That's a good idea, Barnes. Let's get a couple of them working house-to-house here." He gestured back toward Lord Keighley. "Perhaps someone saw Sir Edmund being followed or something like that."

Barnes nodded. "I think whoever killed him must have followed him from the party."

"Really? Why?" Witherspoon asked.

"Because if we assume the murder was premeditated, then that means the killer would have had to have known that Sir Edmund would be walking home on his own that night, and no one could have known that in advance. Roland Leggett has told us that they decided against using the carriage at the last minute."

Witherspoon frowned thoughtfully. "Yes, I see what you mean. Of course, the murderer could have gotten lucky."

"You mean whoever killed Sir Edmund might have been wanting to do it for some time and saw their chance when he left the party on his own," Barnes said. They waited for a break in the traffic and then crossed the road to a small café. Barnes pulled open the door. "Then that lets out all the Parkingtons and Harriet Wyndham-Jones. None of them were at the Keighley's when Sir Edmund left. So they couldn't have followed him that night."

The café was crowded with people taking their mid-day meal. Office clerks, shop assistants, and even a housemaid or two filled the simple wooden tables. Barnes spotted an empty table in the corner and he moved toward it.

"They could have lain in wait," Witherspoon suggested as they pulled out their chairs and sat down. The inspector was oblivious to the curious stares he and the constable were getting from their fellow diners. "Whoever killed him might have simply been skulking about, waiting for their chance."

"True," Barnes replied. "But they'd have had to have the weapon with them. Which reminds me, sir. We've still had no luck tracing the young woman who'd been following Sir

Edmund. She wasn't staying at any of the lodging houses or hotels near Victoria Station."

"Have the lads keep checking," Witherspoon said. "Frankly, Constable, she's the only real suspect that we have."

A light rain had begun to fall by the late afternoon, and Betsy was the first to get back to Upper Edmonton Gardens. She came flying down the hall, shaking the water off her hat and cloak. "It's right miserable out there," she said. "I hope Smythe remembered to take his coat this morning. It's chilly."

"Have you had much luck today?" Mrs. Jeffries asked.

"Not really," Betsy replied. "I managed to get a bit of gossip out of a shop assistant. But it doesn't have anything to do with the murder."

"We've not had much luck, either," Mrs. Goodge complained. "But the tea is ready and it's nice and hot."

The others arrived within the next few minutes. As soon as everyone was dried off and sitting in their place, Mrs. Jeffries got the meeting started. "I hope you've had better luck than I did today, I've found out nothing. But I do have the list of names of the guests who were at the party the night Sir Edmund was murdered."

"Pinched it from the inspector, eh?" Smythe laughed.

"Don't be cheeky." Betsy playfully slapped his arm. "She didn't pinch it, she borrowed it."

Mrs. Jeffries smiled. "Thank you, Betsy. But I'm afraid Smythe is correct. I pinched it, not that I think it's going to do us much good. But it does give us more names to look at if we can't make any headway with our current group of suspects."

"I've got some sources that work for some of these people," Mrs. Goodge volunteered. "I've already sent messages around to several of them. So, perhaps in the next day or two, we'll learn something useful. God knows I've not learned much today. No one knows much of anything except that Sir Edmund was being hounded by Sarah Camden, and we're fairly sure she isn't the killer."

"Don't feel bad Mrs. Goodge," Hatchet said mournfully. "I found out very little today. I did manage to speak to an acquaintance whose wife had gone to school with one of the suspects. But the only thing I heard was that Julia Parkington was good at grouse hunting and mathematics."

"And that doesn't sound like it's got anything to do with the murder," Luty said gleefully. "Well, not to blow my own horn."

"Humph." Hatchet gave a derisive snort.

Luty shot him a sly grin and then went on talking. "But as I was saying, not to blow my own horn, but I did find out something useful today. I think that we'd best take a closer look at Harriet Wyndham-Jones. Her first husband died in very mysterious circumstances, and what's more, he died shortly after Mrs. Wyndham-Jones had met Sir Edmund Leggett. By the way, she was besotted with the fellow from the minute she laid eyes on him."

"How did he die?" Betsy asked.

"It was supposedly an accident," Luty said. "He was found at the foot of the stairs with a broken neck and it was assumed he'd fallen down the stairs. But none of the servants was home and it was his wife who found him."

"All the servants were gone?" Smythe asked.

"That's right." Luty nodded. "And that smells fishy to me right there. We're talking about rich people and they don't fend for themselves unless they have to."

"Didn't the police investigate?" Wiggins asked.

"Not if the coroner ruled the death an accident and there was no reason to suspect foul play," Mrs. Jeffries replied. She gave Luty an admiring smile. "You've done very well. Let's do take another look at Mrs. Wyndham-Jones."

"More importantly, let's get the inspector to take another look at the woman," Hatchet said. "I'll bet he's no idea how her first husband died."

"I'll put a flea in his ear about it this evening," Mrs. Jeffries replied. "And I'll try to find out which of the guests that were at the party have already been interviewed. Now, who would like to go next?"

"I had a chat with some of the drivers," Smythe said. "But I didn't hear much of anything. I found one groom that remembered seeing Sir Edmund leave Lord Keighley's that night, but he didn't see anyone following him."

"And he was sure it was Sir Edmund he saw leave?' Mrs. Jeffries clarified. This might be important. If no one followed Sir Edmund from the party, then that might mean that none of their current suspects had anything to do with the murder.

Of course, there was a good chance that all of their current suspects were innocent. Sir Edmund Leggett was the sort of person who had a long history of hurting other people. Perhaps someone had finally had a chance to even the score a bit, so to speak.

"He was certain," Smythe replied. "I made sure of that. I knew it was important. We've had the idea that someone followed Sir Edmund from the party that night, but now I'm thinkin' we're wrong. Could be that someone who hated him just got lucky that night."

"You mean one of his enemies just happened to run into him in the middle of the night?" Hatchet said, his expression incredulous.

"And they'd have had to have been armed," Betsy added. "No, that doesn't make sense. Even if he weren't followed from the party, someone had decided to kill him that night. I don't know how they could have known he was walking home . . ."

"Everyone knew he was walkin'," Smythe shot back. "He'd not used his carriage in ages. He'd been planning on using it that night, he actually sent word to the stables that he wanted to rent a couple of their horses, but he changed his mind. His carriage is as old as the hills and keeps losing wheels. It wasn't safe."

"How did he get about then?" Wiggins asked.

"He took a hansom, walked, or got rides with his friends when he went out," Smythe explained. "That was common knowledge amongst his crowd."

"So anyone could have known he might be walking home alone that night," Mrs. Jeffries replied. "Frankly, that does rather cast the events of the evening in a different light."

"I don't see how," Wiggins said. "Even if he didn't use his own carriage, he might have gotten a ride home with the Parkingtons or taken a hansom. The killer still couldn't have known he'd be walking and even if they did think he might be on is own, he might just as easily have walked home with his cousin."

Mrs Jeffries thought for a moment. "Then perhaps the killer would have shot them both," she said softly. "You know, perhaps we ought to find out who inherits the title and the estate if both the Leggetts are dead. After all, our killer came prepared. Sir Edmund was shot three times." She broke off as a loud, impatient knocking came from the back door.

Fred started barking and charged down the back hall. Smythe got to his feet before any of the others. "I'll get it. Whoever it is seems in an almighty state about something," he said as he disappeared into the dark hallway. "It's alright, Fred. Don't fret so."

They heard the back door open and a murmur of voices. Then Smythe and Fred came back and they had a teenage boy walking between them. The dark-haired lad had a small red cloth bundle in his hands.

"Jon." Hatchet got to his feet first. "What on earth are you doing here?"

"What's wrong," Luty cried. "Are you all right, boy?"

"I'm fine, Mrs. Crookshank," Jon said quickly. "But I wasn't sure what to do. You told me to watch her and I tried my best, but she's run for it, she has. Sarah's gone."

"What happened?" Luty demanded.

Jon came over to the table, his eyes on his employer. "I think it was my fault. You see, I noticed that instead of putting her bundle of things in that little trunk at the foot of her bed, she kept it in the back of the dress cupboard." He paused and looked down at the table-top.

"Go on, Jon," Hatchet said kindly. "We'll not be angry with you, just tell us what happened."

"When Sarah was in the kitchen, I snuck into her room and had a look in her bundle. I saw that she kept goin' back to her room, checkin' like to make sure it was still there. But there's no thieves in the household, so like I said, I got curious so I went and 'ad a look."

He put the bundle on the table in front of Luty and tossed back the heavy fabric. "I found this." He pulled out a pistol. "Sarah saw me. The next thing I knew, she'd taken off out the back door."

CHAPTER 8

———◦◦◦◦◦———

"I tried to follow her," Jon explained. He looked at Luty, his expression worried. "I really did. I ran as fast as I could, but she moved like the wind."

"Don't fret, Jon." Luty very gently took the gun from him. "You did your best. You did the right thing by comin' to us as quick as you did."

"You certainly did, Jon," Hatchet added. "About how long ago did she uh . . . see you checking her bundle?" He wanted to see how much of a head start the woman had on them.

"It's been about an hour," Jon said cheerfully. "I grabbed the bundle and come right 'ere as soon as I realized what she was doing. But I wasn't sure of exactly how to get here and I was on foot. I got lost once and that put me back a bit. But then I remembered the inspector lived off the Holland Park Road and I asked a cabbie and he showed me the way."

Smythe, who'd sat back down, got up again. He gave Betsy a quick smile and then turned his attention to Mrs. Jeffries. "I'm going to 'ave a go at trackin' 'er. I've got a feelin' we oughtn't to lose any time gettin' after the girl."

"But it's getting dark," Betsy protested. "You'll never find her tonight."

Smythe put his hand on her shoulder. "I know that, lass. But I can check a few places where a young woman might go if she was in a bit of a state." He hesitated, not certain if he should tell them that he knew one person in London who might be able to find the girl very quickly. Perhaps it was just as well that Blimpey hadn't been at the Dirty Duck when he'd stopped by this afternoon. Now he could see him this evening and kill two birds with one stone. He still had to ask Blimpey about Osgood Parkington.

Hatchet got up as well. "I ought to go with you."

That was the last thing Smythe wanted. "Why don't you see if the girl's gone back to Lorna McKay's lodging house? People tend to go to familiar places when they're in a state."

He nodded. "That's a good idea."

"I don't know, Smythe, perhaps we ought to wait until tomorrow," Mrs. Jeffries murmured. "Betsy's right. It's getting late."

He decided there was no harm in letting them know he had a few sources he could call upon in a crisis. "Don't worry, I'm not going to be gone long. But the girl had a gun." He nodded at the weapon which Luty had now laid on the table. "And Sir Edmund was shot. I think that means we need to find her quickly. I know someone who can 'elp do that. He's reliable, I've used him a number of times before, and he knows how to keep his mouth closed." That was as far as he'd go in telling them about his sources.

"Then you ought to get moving," Mrs. Jeffries said briskly. "We all have our sources and if you know someone that can assist us, all the better." She turned to Hatchet. "If Luty's willing, she and Jon can stay here with us until you return."

"That's fine by me," Luty said softly. "I'd just as soon stay until these two get back so I know what's what."

"Excellent decision, madam," Hatchet said. "It shouldn't take me long to ascertain if our young miscreant has taken refuge at her former abode."

"And I'll not be gone long, either." Smythe looked at Betsy. "I promise."

The inspector came home a bit earlier than was his usual habit when he was on a case. Mrs. Jeffries, looking a tad flustered, hurried to greet him as he was hanging his coat and hat up.

"You're home a bit early, sir," she said brightly. "I'm afraid dinner isn't quite ready."

"That's quite all right," he replied. "I could do with a glass of sherry first."

"Of course, sir." They made their way to the drawing room and soon the inspector was ensconced in his favorite chair. Mrs. Jeffries handed him a glass of Harveys and poured one for herself. "How is the case going, sir? Any new details come to light?"

Witherspoon took a sip of sherry and sighed in pleasure. He told her about the events of the day. It was always such a relief to talk with his housekeeper. He felt so much better afterward.

Mrs. Jeffries listened carefully and occasionally asked a question. He had a substantial amount of information to add to what they already knew, but in truth, nothing he mentioned made her feel they were getting any closer to the truth.

"Tomorrow we're going to go back to the Parkington house." He took a quick sip from his drink. "We simply ran out of time today, and of course, I do want to ask Mr. Parkington why he didn't mention that his daughter hadn't come home with them on the night of the murder, and why he didn't tell us he'd gone back out himself." Mystified, he shook his head. "People must think us fools. Didn't he know we'd find out."

"People often get confused, sir," she said softly. "They get afraid that the truth will trap them rather than set them free."

"If they're innocent, they've nothing to fear from telling us the truth," he declared.

"Then we're going back to question Harriet Wyndham-Jones again."

"Really, sir," Mrs. Jeffries murmured. She was glad he'd mentioned Leggett's mistress. After what they'd heard from Luty, she wanted to give the inspector a nudge in that direction. "As a matter of fact, I heard some gossip about her first husband." She paused as if she were trying to remember something she'd heard. "Oh dear, I can't quite recall what it was. It was all very vague, sir. I'm sure a few discreet inquiries on your part will elicit any useful information there might be about the subject." She didn't want to have to come right out and tell him, it was always so much better when he discovered valuable information on his own.

"Well, it's good policy to do a bit of checking when one hears things," he replied. "Her first husband, was it?" Witherspoon made a mental note to be sure and follow up that line of inquiry.

"Yes, sir, I do wish I could recall what it was, but I simply can't." She smiled. "Would you care for another sherry, sir?" She was trying to stall him as much as possible. With the events of the afternoon and the unexpected arrival of Jon, dinner was late.

"No, this one is all I need." He smiled self-consciously. "One doesn't want to depend on alcohol. It's the sort of habit that could be quite destructive."

"I hardly think you're in danger of drinking to excess, sir," she said quickly.

"But these things can creep up on a person, especially when things aren't going well." He sighed again. "And I will admit, this case is frustrating."

"But you've got the Parkingtons to interview again," she pointed out. "As you said, they were both out on the night of the murder."

"Yes, but Mr. Parkington appears to have no reason to want Sir Edmund dead and I'm sure Miss Parkington didn't take a firearm with her to her engagement party."

"Perhaps she had an accomplice," Mrs. Jeffries suggested. She held her breath, hoping he'd take the hint. "And you've still got that mysterious man who was at Sir Edmund's funeral. Perhaps he had something to do with the murder."

Witherspoon stared at her over the top of his spectacles. "You know, I do believe you're correct. There are a number of inquires left for us to pursue. Frankly, I was afraid we'd run out of useful areas to investigate. The house-to-house near the death scene hasn't revealed any additional clues and we've not seen hide nor hair of the young woman who was stalking the victim since the night he was killed. But your words have made me see things differently, Mrs. Jeffries. I do feel so much better when I talk to you about my cases. I must make it a point to do it more often."

"Thank you, sir. I'm flattered that my suggestions are useful to you." Mrs. Jeffries looked down at the floor. She felt terrible. Sarah Camden was gone and they'd deliberately kept the girl hidden from the inspector. But just because the girl had run, didn't mean she was the killer. Luty had sniffed the barrel of Sarah's gun and had stated that the gun hadn't been fired recently. But Mrs. Jeffries didn't think one could ascertain such a fact by waving the tip of a gun under one's nose. Especially when one was Luty's age, and one's sense of smell wasn't quite what it used to be.

She didn't really know what to think about Sarah Camden, she just knew she felt guilty and frustrated that they hadn't handed the girl over to the inspector when they had the chance. But, as Luty had rather colorfully put it, "ain't no use cryin' over spilt milk." Their task now was to find Sarah and solve this murder as quickly as possible.

"They're very useful, Mrs. Jeffries, and of course, it's absurd to think that it was a robber that killed Sir Edmund," Witherspoon continued.

"Yes, of course it is, sir," she agreed quickly. "A robber wouldn't have left his jewelry or ah . . . ah . . ."

"Or the money he was carrying," Witherspoon added. "I told the chief inspector that I was certain it wasn't a robbery, no matter what Inspector Nivens says."

"Inspector Nivens!" Mrs. Jeffries exclaimed. "What's he got to do with the case?" Inspector Nivens was a horrid little man who was constantly undermining Witherspoon. He was an inept policeman who was, unfortunately, very well connected politically. He'd been a rising star on the force until Witherspoon, with his impressive record of solving homicides had come along. Nivens was always trying to horn in on their cases. The Witherspoon household loathed the man.

"Oh, nothing, really. He was simply asking Chief Inspector Barrows if perhaps Sir Edmund's murder might not be a robbery gone bad."

"That's nonsense, sir." Mrs. Jeffries gave a rather unlady—like snort of derision. "Utter nonsense."

It was dark by the time Smythe made it to the Dirty Duck Pub. He pulled the door open and stepped inside, grateful to be out of the chilly wind blowing off the Thames. He moved to one side as he surveyed the crowded room, looking for his quarry.

"Over 'ere," Blimpey called. He was sitting at his usual table in front of the fireplace.

Smythe pushed his way through the crowd. The noise level was fierce, but he reckoned he could talk loud enough to make himself understood. He pulled out the stool and sat down. "Evenin' Blimpey. You 'ave time for a quick word?"

"That's what I'm 'ere for. You want beer or something stronger?" Blimpey raised his hand and signaled the barmaid.

"Beer's fine," Smythe replied. "I've got a real problem tonight and I'll need ya to get on it quick."

Blimpey raised an eyebrow but said nothing.

"Sarah Camden's scarpered," he continued. "And what's more, she's 'ad a gun with her all along." He broke off as the barmaid brought their drinks.

"Ta, Jess," Blimpey said, giving the woman a bright smile. He waited until she left before turning his attention back to his companion. "That's a surprise. She looked too green to be armed. When did you find this out?"

"Late this afternoon," Smythe took a quick sip of beer. "One of the other servants at the place where we had her stayin' got curious as to why she was always goin' to check on her little bundle of personal bits. She caught him havin' a snoop and realized he'd seen the weapon. Before he had time to say anything, she was out the back door. I need you to find her for me fast."

"What's the rush?" Blimpey asked. "She didn't strike me as a killer. Besides, she were tucked up good and proper at Lorna McKay's lodgings on the night of the murder."

"A lodging house isn't a prison. She could have climbed out a window," Smythe said. "And whether you think she's a murderer or not, she's got a gun and Sir Edmund was shot three times in the chest. To my mind, that means she needs to be found and quickly."

"That's goin' to cost you." Blimpey leaned toward him. "Take my word for it, the girl scarpered home. A quick telegram to the local police constabulary will probably find her back where she came from. If I set my lads out to lookin' tonight, it'll cost you an arm and a leg. Frankly, you're a good customer and I don't want you thinkin' I'm out to gouge you. But getting' lads on her tonight will cost me a pretty penny and I've got to pass the expense along to you."

"Don't worry about it," Smythe said. "I just want her found."

"Right then." Blimpey got to his feet. "I'll be back in a few minutes. Don't leave, I've got some other information for ya." He sauntered toward the bar, slipped behind the counter and then a moment later, disappeared through a door.

Smythe sipped his beer while he waited. After ten minutes, Blimpey was back at the table. "The lads are on it," he said as he slipped into his seat. "I'll have something for you by tomorrow morning."

"That's awfully fast," Smythe retorted.

"I'm awfully good." Blimpey cackled at his own joke. "That's why you keep comin' back. Anyway, my friend, onto that other matter I mentioned. I've found out a bit about your Mr. Roland Leggett."

"That's what I was hopin'."

"Sir Edmund might have got the title," Blimpey said. "But Roland Leggett is the one with the brains. He's got plenty of money and he got most of it because he's smart. Not like your murder victim, who, I believe had a bundle left to him and managed to piss most of it away on gamblin', women, and very slow horses."

"Sir Edmund played the ponies?"

"Often and not very well," Blimpey replied. "But that's by the by. He didn't have any punters out after him. I know that for a fact. The creditors on his back were the real legitimate ones, you know, the banker, the grocer, and the tax man. But as I said, it's Roland you want to know about."

Smythe nodded and said nothing. He didn't mind finding out a few more bits about Sir Edmund.

"Roland inherited a bit of property from his mother. He took it and went into partnership with the Merriton Brothers. They're builders, and they built a whole heap of houses on Roland's property, making him a very rich man in the process."

"So he wouldn't need Sir Edmund's money," Smythe mused.

"Sir Edmund had no money," Blimpey reminded him. "Fellow was up to his arse in debt. That fancy house is mortgaged to the hilt, the estate's not bringing in any income, and Roland paid the grocery bill last month."

"Seems like a bit of a decent sort," Smythe said softly.

"Seems like it," Blimpey continued. "He's cleaned up more than one of Sir Edmund's messes. By that, I mean he's used his own money to pay off the occasional irate father or brother."

"I suppose that now that he's going to be lord of the manor, he'll feel obligated to clean up all of Edmund's mistakes," Smythe mused thoughtfully. "Maybe he'll do right by the Camden family."

"Maybe," Blimpey replied. "But I don't think he'll be playing lord of the manor. You mark my words, he's going to sell off most of that moldy old estate and slap up a heap of houses and whatnot! By this time next year, he'll be a lot richer than he is now."

Hatchet made it back to Upper Edmonton Gardens only moments before Smythe walked in the back door. Everyone except Jon, who was asleep in Mrs. Goodge's room, was sitting at the table.

"Sorry it took so long," the coachman said as he took his spot next to Betsy.

"That's all right," Mrs. Jeffries replied. "The inspector came home unexpectedly early for dinner. So we had to take time to get him fed. Was your source able to help us any?"

"I should know something by tomorrow morning," he replied. "And we ought to send off a telegram to her home, she might have just gotten on a train and gone home."

"We've already done that," Luty declared. "We sent Wiggins off to the telegraph office as soon as you two left."

"And I almost run smack into the inspector when I was comin' down Holland Park Road," Wiggins added. "Fancy 'im comin' in so early!"

"Yes," Mrs. Jeffries murmured. "Luckily, he didn't take it into his head to come downstairs. We would have had a difficult time explaining why there were so many people sitting around the kitchen table. But he did give me some interesting information and as you're all here, I'll give a full report as soon as Hatchet has told us what he's learned."

"Sarah hasn't gone back to Lorna McKay's lodging house," Hatchet said. "They haven't seen her since she came here. But my trip wasn't completely wasted. I did have a good look at the establishment." He grinned. "The windows on the ground floor aren't locked, so even if Sarah had gone in at dark on the night of Sir Edmund's murder, she could easily have climbed out a window. Apparently at the McKay establishment, payment is always done in advance so the landlady isn't overly concerned about her customers slipping out a window and disappearing into the night without paying their bill."

"I wonder where she's gone," Luty muttered.

"I expect we'll find out soon enough," Mrs. Jeffries said. "Now, let me tell you what I found out from Inspector Witherspoon." She told them everything she'd learned and she also mentioned that she'd put a flea in the inspector's ear about Harriet Wyndham-Jones' first husband.

"But you didn't tell him anything about how the fellow died, did you?" Hatchet asked.

"No, I thought he ought to find that out for himself. If he

doesn't follow up on the inquiry, I'll have a quick word with Constable Barnes."

"This case is sure gettin' muddled." Wiggins shook his head. "I can't keep it all straight."

"It'll all come out right in the end," Betsy said cheerfully. "It always does. What I find hard to credit is that Osgood Parkington hired his butler just because he'd worked for an aristocrat. That's the silliest thing I've ever heard."

"People do things like that all the time," Luty added. "They're called social climbers and it seems the Parkingtons are the worst. It's strange, too, because Julia Parkington seems to be seein' her doctor a lot these days. You'd think if there was something really wrong with her health, she'd stay home instead of sashayin' all over London trying to be the queen bee of the social set."

Everyone looked at her. Mrs. Jeffries voiced what they were all thinking. "Uh, Luty, did you find this out recently."

Luty's hand flew to her mouth as she realized she'd committed the most cardinal of sins. She hadn't told them everything. "Oh, Nellie's whiskers," she exclaimed. "I'm so sorry. Minnie was tellin' me this information as I was leavin' and it just now come to me. I'm so sorry."

"It's not like you to forget to tell us something," Mrs. Goodge said. "But then again, we've all done it."

"There's no excuse for me forgettin'." Luty banged her hand against the table.

"Don't worry about it, Luty," Mrs. Jeffries said kindly. "As Mrs. Goodge has pointed out, we've all probably forgotten a detail or two when we give our reports. There's no harm done."

"It's not really relevant information anyway," Hatchet said kindly. "Most women of Mrs. Parkington's class tend to be a bit hysterical about their health. She's probably no different than any of her friends."

"Well, it's right nice of all of you to be so kind about

this," Luty said. "I'll try harder in the future to remember everything."

"There's something else I don't understand," Wiggins said. "On the night of the engagement party, the butler claims he heard Mrs. Parkington telling Miss Beatrice she wouldn't 'ave to marry Sir Edmund. That doesn't sound right. She's the one that's been pushin' the girl to marry 'im all along."

"And she was still wanting the girl to marry him," Mrs. Goodge snorted. "Mark my words. She'd not changed her mind. I've seen it happen before. The girl starts to balk at being forced into marriage, especially right before the engagement is to be announced, and the parents will lie their heads off to get her to go along and not make a scene." The cook's lip curled in disgust. "Thirty years ago, when I worked for the Fanninghams, the very same thing happened. Their daughter didn't want to marry either, and was going to make a right ugly scene at the engagement party. The mother lied to her and said she'd not have to go through with it and that she'd get her out of it later. Just go along for tonight and everything will be all right. But of course, it wasn't. The poor girl was harassed into marrying the man and a year later she was dead in childbirth."

"I'm inclined to agree with Mrs. Goodge," Mrs. Jeffries said. "It's simply too convenient that the butler overheard such a conversation the day the engagement was to be announced."

Mrs. Jeffries made sure the house was locked up tight before going upstairs that night. She wasn't sure she could sleep. She picked up the lantern and went quietly up the back stairs to her rooms. She stepped inside the small sitting room and put the lantern on her desk. Then she lighted two other lamps, placed one on the bookcase by the window and the other on the side of the desk.

Sitting down, she started to reach for a sheet of notepaper and then changed her mind and opened the top drawer. Reaching inside, she pulled out the heavy ledger she used for the household accounts, opened it, and turned to the back. She stared at the page for a moment, deciding that the heavy lines across the top and the neat columns were precisely what she needed. She ripped out the last page, closed the book and shoved it back in the drawer. Then she got busy.

An hour later, she looked at her handiwork and nodded in satisfaction. Along the top of the page, she'd drawn a line and inked in a rather nice time sequence of events. More importantly, she'd written where each of the suspects claimed to be at any given moment on the night of the murder. Underneath the time sequence she wrote the names of the suspects. Roland Leggett, Sarah Camden, Beatrice Parkington, William Carter, Harriet Wyndham-Jones, and even the three Parkingtons had their own columns. Every column was filled with the details she knew about each and every suspect. She only hoped she hadn't missed anything. At the bottom of the page, she'd written what could be the possible motive each of these people had for murdering Sir Edmund Leggett. The only two that didn't have a motive at the bottom of their columns were the Parkingtons. Mrs. Jeffries stared at their names and debated taking them off the sheet altogether. Then she decided against it. The elder Parkingtons might not have wanted Sir Edmund dead, but they did have quite a bit of useful information about the situation in their columns.

She sat back and examined her handiwork closely, hoping that some sort of idea or pattern would be evident. For a long time, she studied the time sequence, reread everyone's motive, and went over all the individual information in each column. But there was nothing that leapt out at her.

Her gaze went back to Beatrice's column again. The girl hated her fiancé, had no real alibi for the murder, and was probably in love with another man. She was the perfect suspect, except for one detail. Beatrice had jumped out of the carriage on the way home. So unless she'd taken a gun with her to her own engagement party, she couldn't have done it.

Her eyes shifted to William Carter's column. He was out alone that night, as well, and quite conceivably did have a gun. Mrs. Jeffries leaned back in her chair, wondering if it was possible that Carter and Beatrice had planned the murder together. She blinked, shifted her eyes to Harriet Wyndham-Jones' column and then realized she could say the very same thing about her. She was just as likely a suspect as Beatrice. She really did have grounds for hating Sir Edmund. He'd seduced and discarded her in the cruelest manner possible.

Mrs. Jeffries was suddenly very tired. It was impossible at this point to say who was or wasn't the killer. She simply didn't have enough information. Perhaps tomorrow they could learn more.

Inspector Witherspoon put the file down on the desk and shook his head. "I simply don't understand why there wasn't more of an investigation into this man's death."

He and Constable Barnes were in a storage room at the Marylebone High Street Police Station. The walls were covered with shelves containing old files, ledgers, and boxes of police reports. The inspector had decided to come along and have a look at the file on the death of Harriet Wyndham-Jones' first husband, Louis Wyndham-Jones.

"Apparently the local police felt there was no need to dig any deeper." Barnes nodded at the file. "And the magistrate ruled it an accident."

"He ruled it an accident based on shoddy police work." Witherspoon pursed his lips. He didn't wish to cast aspersions on the habits of his fellow police officers, but the cursory investigation into what was a very suspicious death was a genuine travesty. "For goodness sake, they didn't even bother to ask any decent questions."

"You mean why all the servants had been given the day off by Mrs. Wyndham-Jones," Barnes replied. "That alone should have made the investigating officers suspicious."

The door opened and a police constable stuck his head inside the door. "Are you all right, then?" he said to Witherspoon. He was a balding, portly man with a ruddy complexion and a cheerful grin. "Is there anything else you need, sir?"

"Actually, there is something." Witherspoon flipped open the police report and gave it a quick look. "Is Constable Gallagher still at this station?"

"No, sir," the constable replied. "He's left the force. He emigrated to New Zealand a year ago."

"How convenient," Witherspoon murmured.

The constable frowned slightly. "Convenient, sir? I don't understand."

"Is Inspector Quinn still here?" Witherspoon asked as he put the file down.

"No, sir, he's dead. He passed away last March." He glanced at the file on the desk and then back at Witherspoon. The name of the deceased was written in bold, block letters on the front of the file and was clearly readable from where the constable stood. "If you're wantin' to speak to someone about that, sir, you'd best talk to me. I'm the only one here who had anything to do with that case."

"Your name isn't mentioned in the report," Barnes said softly.

"I was working the front desk," he replied. "And I was never happy with the way that whole thing was swept under the carpet. Neither was Constable Gallagher. He kept pressin' Inspector Quinn to ask a few more questions. But the inspector wasn't havin' it and he weren't one to be crossed. Said that there was no need to be upsettin' the widow with a lot of questions when it was obvious it was an accident." He broke off and sighed. "I'm not one to be speakin' ill of the dead, Inspector Quinn was a good copper. But he'd lost his wife the year before and he was real lonely and a bit lost-like. He was easy prey for someone like the Wyndham-Jones woman. He'd started to do a thorough investigation of the circumstances, had Constable Gallagher talking to the servants and findin' out what was what, when all of a sudden, he decided there weren't no need to do anything more. Mind you, that was right after the widow started having him 'round for tea every afternoon. Truth to tell, Inspector Quinn made a right old cockup of that case."

"Tell me something," Barnes said, "Just between us coppers, what do you think happened to William Wyndham-Jones?"

The constable didn't hesitate. "I think she pushed him, sir. I think she got the servants out of the house, and then walked up behind that poor old man and shoved him down the stairs, and then I think the widow batted her eyelashes at Inspector Quinn and got him to look the other way." He grinned broadly. "And that's why I was so glad when you and the inspector showed up this morning and started askin' questions about Mrs. Wyndham-Jones."

Witherspoon picked up the file and handed it to the constable. "Thank you, Constable. You've been most helpful. We'd be most obliged if you'd keep this file available for a while. We might need it a bit later." He started toward the door.

"I'll keep it at the front desk, sir. Will you be reopening the case?" the constable asked as he followed them out into the hallway.

"We're looking into the matter," the inspector replied. He and Barnes nodded respectfully at the officers as they moved through the foyer and toward the front door.

Barnes waited till they were outside before he spoke.

"What do you make of it, sir?" He was very glad that Mrs. Jeffries had nudged the inspector in this direction.

"I think the situation and the woman certainly are worth another look. I only wish I'd been a bit more aggressive in my questioning of Mrs. Wyndham-Jones the first time we saw her."

"You couldn't have known there was any mystery to her first husband's death," Barnes replied as he pointed across the busy street. "It's just up that road, sir." The police station they'd just left was less than a quarter mile from Harriet Wyndham-Jones' home. They were walking there instead of taking a cab. "And what's more, sir, she was in no fit state to be questioned. Those hysterics were real," he added.

"Let's hope she doesn't have them again," the inspector replied.

A few minutes later they were escorted into the Wyndham-Jones' drawing room and told to have a seat.

"At least this time we can see," Barnes murmured as he sat down on an elegant red-and-white striped settee.

Witherspoon sat down on an uncomfortable-looking empire chair. He glanced around the room, noting that it was furnished in the old French style that had gone out of fashion during the Napoleonic wars. The door opened and Mrs. Wyndham Jones stepped into the room. She was still dressed in black, but the dress was form fitting and quite low-cut for a day dress. The veil was gone, too.

Both men got to their feet. "Good day, Mrs. Wyndham-Jones," the inspector said. "I'm sorry to bother you, but we do need to speak to you about Sir Edmund Leggett."

"Please sit down," she said. She moved gracefully toward them and sat down on a red silk upholstered chair opposite the inspector. "I don't know what it is you want me to tell you, Inspector, I don't know anything about Edmund's death."

Witherspoon said, "First of all, we'd like your permission to question your staff."

"I wasn't aware you needed my permission to speak to them," she replied, her expression amused.

"We don't, ma'am," he replied. "I was simply being courteous."

Barnes got to his feet and started toward the drawing room door. "I'll go and have a word with your housekeeper," he said.

Witherspoon nodded at him and then turned his attention back to Harriet Wyndham-Jones. He wasn't sure what to ask. Would it be best to ascertain her whereabouts on the night of Sir Edmund's murder, or should he just plunge straight in and ask a few questions about her first husband's death?

"I was out on the night Sir Edmund was killed," she said. "I was going to meet some friends for an early supper and then we were going on to the theater. But I was still so upset over his betrayal that I sent them a note begging off and went for a long walk instead."

Witherspoon sighed inwardly. Half of London appeared to have gone for a walk that night. "Where did you walk?"

She shrugged. "Oh, here and there, around the neighborhood. You must understand, I was very upset."

"Did you see anyone you know?"

"You mean anyone who can vouch for my whereabouts?" She smiled sadly and shook her head. "If anyone saw me, I was too upset to notice them."

"What time did you come home?" he asked. These questions were tedious, but very necessary.

"I'm not sure," she said, her expression thoughtful. "I was out for quite a long time, I know that because my shoes were very dirty and I was very tired. I'm sure your man will ask my housekeeper . . . oh dear, that won't work. She was already in bed when I arrived home." She smiled at him. "I don't expect my servants to wait up for me when I'm out."

Witherspoon was sure she was lying. Perhaps it was the coquettish way she looked at him as she spoke or perhaps his impression of her was colored by what he'd heard at the police station, but in either case, he knew that she hadn't gone for a walk that night. "That's very good of you," he said. "Your servants must appreciate that very much. I understand you'd also given them the day off when your first husband died."

She drew back in surprise, her expression stunned. "How dare you."

"I'm only stating a fact, madam," he said calmly. "Now, we can either sit here for a number of hours discussing both cases or you can tell me what you really did on the night Sir Edmund was murdered." He'd no idea where those words had come from but once they'd popped out of his mouth, he was sure he was on to something.

She eyed him suspiciously and then shrugged. "I didn't kill him," she said. "I wanted to, but I didn't. Have you ever been in love, Inspector?"

Witherspoon thought of Lady Cannonberry, his lovely widowed neighbor. She was forever going off to take care of one of her late husband's legion of sick relations. He missed her most dreadfully. "I don't think that is particularly relevant," he said softly.

She gave a sad little shrug. "For the first time in my life, I was madly and deeply in love. Don't be shocked, Inspector. I didn't love my first husband but I didn't murder him either. All in all, we had quite a good marriage, and I was truly devastated when he died. But I was passionately devoted to Edmund."

"He apparently didn't share your devotion," the inspector said. "I'm not trying to hurt you, ma'am, but I do need you to tell me precisely what happened that night."

"But of course, Inspector, I was getting to it. I knew where he was going to be that evening. Edmund made no secret of it. He could be quite a vicious man, you know. Do you know what's so interesting about London, Inspector? If you dress the part, you can get in anywhere."

It took a moment before Witherspoon understood what she meant. "Er . . . uh . . . what are you saying? Did you try to go to his engagement party?"

She laughed. "I didn't just try, Inspector. I walked right in the front door and was accepted as an invited guest. When you're wearing as many jewels as I was, very few servants have the nerve to ask to see your invitation."

CHAPTER 9

⸻◦◦◦◦⸻

Wiggins pulled his jacket tighter against the morning chill as he walked past the Parkington house for the second time. It might be spring, but the wind still had some bite. He got to the end of the street, looked over his shoulder to make sure no one was watching him, and then crossed the road and started back in the direction he'd just come. So far, no one had appeared to notice him, but he knew he couldn't spend too much more time trying to find someone who'd talk to him. This was a posh neighborhood and eventually, some nosy Parker would be on to him.

Wiggins didn't think there was much left to learn here, but as Betsy was off to have a go at the Leggett house, he'd decided to have another try at the Parkingtons. But he was beginning to think he ought to have gone with Betsy and tried to have another conversation with Jasper, the elderly footman from across the road from the Leggett house. Or

perhaps he ought to have tracked down William Carter
again and had a chat with him. This was certainly turning
into a waste of time, and it was wearing on his nerves to
keep watching out for the inspector and Constable Barnes.
Mrs. Jeffries had said they were coming back this morning
to talk to the Parkingtons again.

He made his way slowly up the road, keeping his eyes
on the pavement as though he were trying to find something. That was his story. If anyone asked him what he was
doing, he'd simply say he'd dropped a shilling and was determined to find it. A shilling was a lot of money. Wiggins
had just reached the front of the Parkington house when
the door on the lower level opened and a girl came out. She
was a housemaid, he could tell because she had on the
same kind of pale lavender dress that Betsy usually wore.
She also had on a short, gray wool jacket with the collar
turned up against the wind. She climbed the short flight of
stairs to the street level and hurried off down the road. Wiggins took off behind her.

He waited till they were out of sight of the house before
he caught up with her. "Excuse me, Miss," he said. He
quickly took off his cap in a gesture of respect. "But I was
wonderin' if you'd let me walk with you?"

She stopped, her brown eyes widening at the boldness
of his request. The girl was on the plump side with black
hair, pale skin, a round face, and a turned up nose.

"I'm not bein' forward, Miss, I was hopin' you could
'elp me. I'm lookin' for a position and I've had the worst
luck. I saw you come out of that grand 'ouse and I was
hopin' you could tell me if they've any positions available."
He'd come up with this excuse earlier this morning. He
hoped his plea was the right combination of boldness and
humility. If he was lucky, the girl would be the sympathetic
sort.

"You're welcome to come along," she said brusquely.

He smiled in relief. "I don't want to be a nuisance if it's your day out," he began.

"It's not my day out," she interrupted. She pulled an envelope out of her pocket and waved it at him. "I'm runnin' an errand for the mistress of the house."

"Thanks ever so much," he said as he fell into step next to her. "I'll not be any trouble, I'll just walk along with you for a bit and you can tell me what's what where you work."

"You'd better walk fast, then," she said, quickening her steps. "I've got to get back right quick. The mistress doesn't want anyone else in the house to know I'm gone. I'm taking a note to Mrs. Parkington's doctor. Like I said, you're welcome to come along but it'll not do you much good. There's no positions open at the household."

"Oh, that's too bad," he replied. "Do you think there might be one in the future? I'm a trained footman and I can also drive a coach." Both of these statements were out-and-out lies but as he wasn't really interested in getting a position, he didn't think that it counted as a genuine falsehood. "My name's Hector Jones."

"I'm Nancy Pierce," she replied with a shrug. "There might be some openings soon. But they'll want someone who's more a jack of all trades rather than a proper footman. They think they're real posh, but they're not. Mrs. Parkington and the young mistress are both nice, but the old man's a nasty snob. Gives himself airs, if you know what I mean."

"Right now I'm so desperate for work, I'd do most anything." He took her elbow as they came to the corner and escorted her safely through the heavy traffic.

"Why? There's plenty of situations available," she retorted. "My cousin just got a position with a doctor in Islington and he's not got any training or any manners. You've got both."

He shrugged. "Well, the last person I worked for got

himself murdered," he said. He watched her out of the corner of his eye, hoping his tale would get him the response he wanted. "And frankly, people don't want to know you if you've been around a house where murder's been done."

Nancy's eyes opened wider. "You don't say. I've been close to a murder, too."

Wiggins stopped in his tracks, pretending to be deeply shocked. "Are you 'aving me on? This is a joke, right? Because if it isn't, then I'm not interested. I'll not go back to another house where there's been murder."

"The murder weren't done at the Parkington house," she said quickly. "It were done at Lord Keighley's, but it was the young mistress' fiancé that got himself done in."

"Cor blimey, there must be a bloomin' rash of these things," he exclaimed. "Your young mistress must be ever so upset."

"Not really." Nancy giggled. "She wasn't all that happy with the idea of getting married. Now that her fiancé's dead, she thought she'd be able to do what she likes, but the staff can already see that her old father has his eye on another match for the poor girl. He's already invited Mr. Roland over for dinner." She shook her head. "You know, I used to envy the rich until I saw how miserable that poor Miss Beatrice is."

"Did you say the father has his eye on someone else for the girl?" Again, Wiggins pretended to be shocked. He wanted to find out more about this dinner that Roland Leggett was invited to attend. Did it mean anything?

"Oh yes, why even Mrs. Parkington was stunned at the master's lack of feeling. They had a right old row over the situation just last night. I heard her screaming at him that trying to marry Miss Beatrice off so soon after Sir Edmund's death would ruin them in London society."

"I don't know much about society," Wiggins replied. "But I expect most people would think it's not very nice to marry right after a death like that."

"He don't care whether it's nice or not," Nancy snorted delicately. "All he wants is to get her married off to an aristocrat. Now that Mr. Roland's going to inherit Sir Edmund's title he's got his eye on Mr. Roland. The young mistress is very upset. She'd hoped that now that Sir Edmund was dead, she might have a chance with her young American friend. Mr. Carter's a nice one, he is, even Mrs. Parkington likes him. I know because I overheard her telling Miss Beatrice to be patient, that everything would work out nicely for her." She stopped and pointed to a discreet sign for a doctor's surgery in the window of a two-story red brick house. "This is where I've got to go, but I'll just be a minute if you'd like to wait for me."

Wiggins couldn't believe his luck. "I'll be here, Miss. I'd be pleased to walk you back."

"We might have to stop at the chemist's on the way," she warned as she turned and dashed up the steps. "Sometimes he doesn't come, sometimes he just writes out a prescription."

"I'll be 'ere, miss," he promised. "You can count on it."

"Well, sir, she's got nerve," Barnes said as they settled back in a hansom. "She was there that night and we've not heard nary a word about it. Either we're talking to the wrong people or she took some pains to keep out of sight once she got into the party."

"I find it difficult to believe that Lord Keighley or one of Sir Edmund's friends didn't spot her that night. Perhaps we'd better have another word with them. If she was truly there, as she claims, someone must have seen her." Witherspoon shook his head in disbelief.

Barnes grabbed the handhold as the hansom hit a pothole. "I'll warrant that at least one of his friends saw her but decided against telling us. Do you believe her story, that she confronted him and then left before dinner was served?"

"I don't know," he admitted honestly. "If she was telling the truth, then she left hours before the murder."

"But she could have lain in wait for him," Barnes pointed out. "And she would have had plenty of time to go home and get a gun. It's not that far from the Keighley's to her house."

"Have the lads check with the hansom cabbies who were working the area that night," the inspector said. "She claims she left the party and then walked for hours. She was formally dressed and wearing jewels, surely if she was out and about, someone must have seen her. We'll check with the local constables as well, perhaps one of them saw her." He looked out the window and sighed. The more he learned about this case, the more confusing it became. "Now, who is this Mr. William Carter?"

"I suspect he's the fellow that we chased at Sir Edmund's funeral," Barnes replied. "My informant only said he was someone we ought to question."

"But your informant knew where the man was staying?" Witherspoon pressed. He wished he had the kind of information sources the constable had, but then again, the constable had spent many years working the streets.

"Yes, sir, and that he's an American."

"And your informant is reliable?"

Barnes turned and looked out the window to hide a smile. Mrs. Jeffries had waylaid him for a quick cup of tea in the kitchen early this morning while the inspector was finishing his breakfast. "Most reliable, sir."

"Good, now let's just hope Mr. William Carter is at his lodging house. So far, we're one for two, Constable. I'm amazed that Osgood Parkington was already gone when we got to his house this morning."

"As was Miss Beatrice Parkington," Barnes muttered. "I wonder where she went so bright and early?"

"According to the butler, she went for her morning constitutional. Apparently, she goes out every morning. I do hope Mr. Carter is available. I don't fancy wasting a lot of time tracking him down all over London."

"We'll know soon, sir," Barnes replied as the cab pulled up in front of a three-story gray brick house.

A few moments later, they were standing on the front steps of the lodging house. Barnes knocked and the door opened immediately.

A fat, red-haired woman wearing a white apron, stuck her head out. "Yes, what do you want?" Her gaze flicked over the two policemen and then swept up and down the street. "This is a decent house. We've nothing to do with the police."

"I'm sure that's true, madam," Witherspoon said politely. "It's one of your lodgers we've come to see. Do you have a Mr. William Carter staying here?"

"The American? I knew I shouldn't have let the room to him. They're always trouble." She sighed deeply. "What's he done?"

"He's done nothing," Barnes replied quickly. He rather liked Americans and felt it wrong to condemn the whole lot of them for no good reason. "We'd simply like to speak with him, if we may."

"Well, I suppose if you must." She stepped back and opened the door wider. "Go on in to the parlor." She jerked her head to the right, indicating they should go in that direction. "I'll go up and get him. Mind you wipe your feet, please, I've just had the rugs cleaned."

"Yes, of course." The inspector dutifully wiped his feet and stepped inside. Barnes followed suit.

"She's a bit of a tartar," Barnes said to Witherspoon as they went into the parlor. The room was neatly furnished with a pale gray three-piece suite, lace curtains, and potted ferns.

They heard footsteps on the stairs and a moment later, a tall, dark-haired man stepped into the room. They both recognized him immediately.

Witherspoon looked at Barnes. "You were right," he commented. "It is our fellow from the funeral."

"I'm William Carter, and I understand you wish to speak to me." He drew himself up ramrod straight and stared the inspector directly in the eye.

"We would indeed, sir," Witherspoon replied. "I'm Inspector Gerald Witherspoon and this is Constable Barnes. We've a few questions we'd like to ask you." He noticed the landlady was hovering by the open door. "Could you please close the door and give us some privacy," he called to her.

She frowned and opened her mouth as though to argue, then she clamped her lips shut and pulled the door shut. A second later they heard her stomping down the hallway.

"Do I need to contact my solicitor?" Carter asked.

"You may if you'd like," Witherspoon replied. "But honestly, all we're going to do is ask you some questions. You're not under arrest. Why don't we sit down?"

Barnes sat down at the end of the settee and took out his notebook, Carter took the overstuffed chair, and Witherspoon sat down on the other chair. "Mr. Carter," he began, "can you explain to us why you ran the other day?"

"Why do people usually run, Inspector?" Carter swallowed heavily. "I was frightened. I knew Sir Edmund had been murdered and when I saw you coming after me, I lost my head."

"Why would seeing us cause you to panic?" Witherspoon asked softly.

"Isn't it obvious?" Carter replied. "I'm the perfect suspect."

"How so, sir?"

"I'm a foreigner, I've no alibi, and I loathed Sir Edmund Leggett."

Witherspoon was so surprised to get so much information from one short question that he wasn't certain what to ask next. "Why did you dislike Sir Edmund?" That seemed a safe enough inquiry. He didn't want the fellow to go mute on him.

"I disliked the kind of person he was," Carter replied. "Like so many of your aristocrats, he was a decadent, pathetic excuse for a human being. He was born to wealth and privilege. Yet, instead of using his position and good fortune for the betterment of his fellow man, he spent his life drinking to excess, gambling the family fortune away, and ruining the lives of young women whom he seduced and abandoned with no thought to the misery he inflicted upon them. What was there about the man to like? On top of that, he was quite stupid. He had a fine education and it was completely wasted on the fellow. He knew nothing about the natural world, literature, world affairs, or science. In other words, gentlemen, he was a stupid, rich dolt that was probably murdered by someone he'd wronged. But, as he'd never wronged me personally, I didn't kill him."

Witherspoon looked over his spectacles at Carter. There were dozens of questions he wanted to ask. He started with the simplest one. "Where were you on the night Sir Edmund was killed?"

Carter hesitated. "I've already told you I've no alibi for that night. The truth is, I went out to have a look at the heavens. But the soot and the filth was so bad, I couldn't see a thing."

"I see." The inspector nodded. "Did your landlady see you leave?"

"No." Carter grimaced. "She locks this place up tighter than a bank vault as soon as the sun sets. I climbed out a window."

"You climbed out a window?" Barnes repeated. "Why didn't you just ask the woman for a key?"

"She wouldn't give me one," Carter replied. "I asked for one, I even offered to put down a deposit, but she wouldn't have it. She claimed that decent people didn't need to be out after dark. For goodness sake, I'm an astronomer, I do my work at night."

"Why didn't you go elsewhere? There are dozens of lodging houses in London," Witherspoon said. He watched Carter closely, hoping he could tell if the man was lying.

"Inspector, I came to London to settle my cousin's estate and collect an inheritance. My solictor made the arrangements for my lodging before I set foot in your country," Carter said. "I'm not a poor man, sir, especially now. But I don't believe in wasting money, and the lodgings, difficult as the landlady might be, were already paid for. Frankly, it was easier to climb out a window than it would be to get a refund out of the woman."

"So you made it a habit to climb out the window in the evenings," Witherspoon pressed. "That's an odd way to run a lodging house."

"Not really." Carter shrugged. "Most of the other tenants are elderly ladies who simply don't go out at night."

"But you did?" the inspector clarified.

"Of course," he replied. "London is a wonderful city. Aside from the fact that my work is done at night, there are concerts and lectures and exhibitions. I wasn't going to miss any of it."

"Were you personally acquainted with Sir Edmund?" Barnes looked up from his notebook.

Carter hesitated. "I met him once. I was walking in the park with a mutual acquaintance and she introduced us."

"Was the mutual acquaintance Miss Beatrice Parkington?" Barnes asked.

Carter nodded. "Yes."

"How are you and Miss Parkington acquainted?" Witherspoon asked.

"Miss Parkington is an amateur astronomer," he said. "Several years ago, she read an article I'd written and wrote to me with a question. We've corresponded regularly ever since. When I came to England, I took the opportunity to make her acquaintance in person. I called upon her when I arrived."

"You met her at her home?" Witherspoon asked curiously.

"Yes. She invited me for tea and I accepted."

Witherspoon was puzzled. "Did you meet her parents?" He was certain the Parkingtons wouldn't have taken kindly to a scholarly, untitled American showing up on their doorstep.

"Only her mother," Carter replied.

"Mrs. Parkington knew you and her daughter were friends?" Barnes pressed.

"Yes, she knew about our correspondence. She's quite interested in natural history. In Beatrice's letters, she'd frequently ask questions for her mother about the variety of wildlife we have in America."

"Mrs. Parkington had no objection to your friendship with her daughter?" Witherspoon asked.

"Not that I knew about. I only met her twice, but she was always very kind to me."

"When did you find out Miss Parkington was to marry Sir Edmund?" Barnes looked up from his notebook again.

"The day of the party. She slipped out after tea and met me in the park. She told me her engagement was going to be announced that night," Carter said. "But she didn't intend to go through with the wedding."

Barnes flicked the inspector a quick glance and then said. "How did she plan to avoid it?"

"She was going to leave," Carter replied. "Look, I know this sounds bad, but Miss Parkington had no intention of ever marrying Sir Edmund Leggett."

"How do you know?" Barnes prodded.

"Because she was going to marry me," Carter exclaimed.

Mrs. Goodge smiled at Edna Thomas and pushed the plate of currant buns closer. "Do have another bun, Edna, you've hardly eaten anything." So far, Edna was the third person she'd seen today and she'd gotten no information about the murder whatsoever. She hated the thought of showing up for their evening meeting with no information at all. Again.

"Ta." Edna picked a bun out and plopped it on her plate. "I'm right peckish today. It must be the weather. I was ever so surprised when I got that note from you, it's been ages since we've had any contact."

"I know." Mrs. Goodge clucked her tongue. "And that's very unfortunate. You and I worked together for a long time. It's sinful the way we've lost touch with each other." She and Edna had worked together for less than two years and that had been ages ago! But as Edna now worked for Lord Drummond and Drummond's name had been on the list of guests at Lord Keighley's, Mrs. Goodge had invited her old acquaintance around. Things, however, weren't progressing as she'd hoped. Edna wasn't much of a talker.

"You're right," Edna sniffed primly. "It's wrong to lose the acquaintance of old friends."

"How do you like your present position?" Mrs. Goodge asked.

Edna shrugged. "It's a good house. Not like the old days, though. These young ones have it too easy. They give you sass when you tell them to peel a potato or two. I tell you, Mrs. Goodge, it's not like when we entered service. We knew how to work in those days. Seven days a week it was, with maybe an afternoon to yourself if all the work was done. We treated our housekeepers and cooks and butlers with respect. None of this flippancy and demanding time out and more wages for us," Edna said stoutly. "We knew our place."

"And exactly what was our place?" Mrs. Goodge stared at her old friend sadly. If she'd not been lucky and gotten fired from her last position for being old, she'd never have come to work for the inspector. She'd never have been exposed to new ideas and more important, to new ways of thinking about society. She'd have ended up exactly like Edna; old, alone, sad, and hankering for a past that had never existed in the first place. "We frequently served people who were stupider, meaner, and often had no character whatsoever. We were paid a pittance and worked as slaves. We were kept in our place by a silly set of rules made up to keep the ones at the top on top and the ones on the bottom hoping to claw their way to the top." She shook her head. "I'm sorry, Edna, but I don't agree with you. I wish our generation had been able to ask more questions and throw some of them silly rules about how one was to behave right out the window. But we couldn't. It was a different time and a different world and I, for one, am glad it's changed."

Edna's jaw dropped in shock. "Gracious, Mrs. Goodge, you've given me a shock. You used to be a right old snob. Always going on about one's place in the household and how one ought to behave to their betters."

"I was wrong. Everyone's got a right to askin' for proper wages and being treated with respect. We're all God's children and equal in his eyes." Mrs. Goodge echoed the sentiments she'd picked up from Mrs. Jeffries and Lady Cannonberry. "Now, tell me again how you like your position."

"I hate the place." Edna sighed. "The Drummonds are cheap as sin and complain about every bite the servants put in their mouths. The servants' hall is cold as ice, the kitchen smells because it's old and needs to be redone, and frankly, if I could afford to, I'd leave in a heartbeat. But I'm too old for factory work and too old to emigrate."

"Don't despair," Mrs. Goodge said kindly, "You can always come down in the world a bit and try to get a job with a professional person like my inspector. They're often decent to their servants. Besides, it's ever so excitin' working for a police inspector. We get to hear about all his murders." She felt bad for Edna but she did need to bring the conversation around to their case.

"Well, I get to hear a bit about murder, too," Edna replied. "The mistress was at the party where one of the guests was murdered on his way home."

"How excitin'," Mrs. Goodge said eagerly. "Do you know anything? I mean, did your mistress or master hear or see anything to do with the murder?"

"He didn't," Edna snorted. "That's for sure. He passed out drunk in Lord Keighley's study. I know because Lady Drummond was furious at him for making her go home alone in the carriage. She said he put her in an awful position." She broke off and laughed. "Mind you, I thought it was very funny, but Lady Drummond doesn't have much of a sense of humor."

"Gracious, what on earth happened?" Mrs. Goodge asked. She was pleased as punch that Edna had finally started to talk.

"Well, it seems that just before Sir Edmund, he's the one that was murdered, went into the study to drink himself into a stupor, he stopped to say a word to Mrs. Parkington. She's the one whose daughter was going to marry Sir Edmund. Anyway, Lady Drummond had just gone out front to get her carriage when she heard Sir Edmund talking to Mrs. Parkington. She said it was so embarrassing because Sir Edmund was quite rude. He told her that if she went through with it, he'd go to his solicitors. Then he noticed Lady Drummond standing there and shut up tighter than a butler's cupboard."

"Do you know what he meant?" Mrs. Goodge asked.

Edna shook her head. "No. All I heard Lady Drummond say was that she thought they ought to tell the police, but Lord Drummond told her they shouldn't. He said it would only cause trouble and for them to mind their own business."

"I suppose it could mean that the Parkingtons might be having second thoughts about the settlement," Mrs. Goodge mused.

"Can I help myself?" Edna reached for the teapot and poured herself another cup. "You're probably right, the rich are a tight-fisted lot, that's why they're rich, I suppose. Though I've never heard that Osgood Parkington was particularly cheap, he's probably just like all the rest. He'd wait until after the engagement was officially announced before he'd start haggling over the price."

"But don't they have to sign some papers in a marriage settlement?" Mrs. Goodge murmured.

"They can sign all the papers they want," Edna declared. "But when it comes to money, nothing's written in stone."

They had lunch before they went back to the Parkington house. Witherspoon stepped down from the hansom and stared at the large, gracious home. The white window frames were painted perfectly, the brass lamps were polished to a high shine and the front steps were so clean one could probably eat off them. Osgood Parkington wasn't stingy when it came to the upkeep of his property. "I do hope someone is in."

"So do I, sir," Barnes muttered.

Luckily, all the Parkingtons were home. Witherspoon paced in the drawing room as he waited for the butler to fetch Miss Beatrice Parkington. He'd decided, for no very good reason, to speak to her first.

"Here she is, sir," Barnes said softly as the young woman entered the room and closed the door behind her.

Beatrice Parkington no longer dressed in mourning. She wore a dark blue day dress with white lace at the collar and cuffs. "Good day, gentlemen," she said. "Please sit down. I understand you wish to speak to me."

Witherspoon and Barnes each took a seat. "Thank you for coming so promptly, Miss Parkington," the inspector began. He hesitated, not sure how to start the questioning. Should he mention that they'd interviewed William Carter, or start off with the fact that they knew she'd jumped out of the carriage on the night of the murder.

"I expect you want to know where I went when I got out of our carriage that night." She sighed. "I don't suppose you'd believe me if I told you that I simply walked for ages."

"It's not a matter of what I'll believe or disbelieve," the inspector replied. "What matters is that you tell us the truth. If you were walking about, then someone will have seen you and remembered you."

"I was walking, sir. I was trying to decide what to do, you see." She shrugged. "And people did see me. There was a policeman on the Brompton Road who stared at me for quite a long while and a doorman at a hotel I passed. I'm sure they'll remember me. I don't suppose one often sees a weeping woman walking the streets of London. But then again, perhaps it's quite a common sight."

"You were crying, miss?" Barnes asked.

"Oh yes, my father had just told me that I was an ungrateful chit who was going to be the death of him. He threatened to toss me out on my ear without a penny if I didn't marry Sir Edmund. You see, I'd just told him I wasn't going through with the marriage and there wasn't anything he could do to force me."

"Is that why you jumped out of the carriage?" Witherspoon asked. "You were upset?"

"I jumped out of the carriage because I was afraid he'd try to hit me again and that my mother would try to stop him," she retorted.

"Your father got violent?" Barnes asked softly.

"Yes. When I said I wouldn't marry Sir Edmund, he'd slapped my face and told me to do as I was told. That's when I'd told him there was nothing he could do to force me. I know the law, Inspector. These days the courts and the church won't force women to marry against their will. Father really lost his temper then. I wasn't that frightened for myself, you see. But when he struck me, my mother tried to slap his hand down and he'd pushed her back against the seat. I was quite shocked. I'm used to my father losing his temper, but my mother never does. But she did that night."

"Your mother was upset?" the inspector pressed. He knew that was a silly thing to say, but he wanted to keep her talking.

"More upset than I've ever seen her." Beatrice nodded. "I've never seen her so angry. Though Father was still furious, I could tell he was stunned by her actions. I was afraid if I stayed in the carriage, he'd try to hit me again and she'd try to stop him. I didn't want him to do her violence, so I got out."

"How dare you," Osgood Parkington stood in the open doorway and glared at his daughter. "How dare you air our dirty linen in public!"

"We're not the public, sir," Witherspoon said. "We're the police."

Parkington slammed the door shut and stormed toward his daughter. Witherspoon got to his feet, as did Barnes. But Beatrice didn't so much as flinch. She simply stared at him as he charged toward her.

"Mr. Parkington." Witherspoon leapt in front of Beatrice Parkington's chair. "Please calm yourself. You'll have an opportunity to tell us your version of the evening's events."

Parkington skidded to a halt a few feet away from the inspector. "I can't believe this, my own daughter telling everyone that I'm an ogre."

"I didn't say you were an ogre, father," Beatrice said calmly. "I simply told them the truth about what happened that night." She started to rise and Witherspoon stepped back to give her room. "I suggest you do the same," she said to her father. Then she looked back at the inspector. "I'll be in the back parlor if you'd like to ask me more questions."

"Thank you, Miss Parkington," Witherspoon said. "We'll speak to you later." As soon as she left, he turned to her father.

Osgood Parkington was glaring at the door his daughter had just closed. "Children today have no sense of duty. But I don't care what kind of airs she wants to give herself, she'll do just as she's told if she wants to keep a roof over her head."

"Why don't you sit down, sir?" the inspector suggested. "Then you can tell us what happened that night."

Parkington gave a little shake and then plopped down in the chair his daughter had just vacated. "I don't know what there is to tell, sir. My daughter had a temper tantrum and jumped out of the carriage. That's all there was to it."

Witherspoon sighed inwardly. Honestly, he was so tired of people thinking the police were fools. "Mr. Parkington, we know that your daughter got out of the carriage. We also know that you came home and went back out to look for her."

"Of course, despite what my daughter thinks, I'm not a monster. She's my only child, I wasn't going to let her wander the streets all night. There are ruffians, thieves, and all manner of disreputable persons about. It's not safe for a young woman to wander around." He flicked a piece of lint off his sleeve.

"Is that why you went into your study and got the gun, sir?" Barnes asked. "Because it wasn't safe out on the streets?"

CHAPTER 10

For once, they were all on time for their afternoon meeting. "Let's get this moving along, then," Mrs. Goodge said as she set a platter of buttered brown bread on the table. "I've a feeling we've got a lot to report."

"Aren't there any currant buns left?" Wiggins asked. He stared glumly at the bread. "I was lookin' forward to 'avin' a nice bun."

"Sorry," the cook replied as she sat down in her usual spot. "But they've all been eaten."

"What about that nice seed cake you were bakin' this mornin'?" Wiggins asked, his expression hopeful. "Is that gone, too."

"I'm saving that for tomorrow," Mrs. Goodge retorted. "It takes a lot of food to keep my sources talking, and when I've so many comin' in for a chat and a sit down, it's hard to keep up with my baking. I've got to dole it out a bit, so to speak. I had a lot of people through my kitchen today."

"Then I'll bet you've got a lot to tell us," Luty said as she helped herself to a slice of bread.

"Not as much as you'd think," Mrs. Goodge muttered.

"Would you like to go first." Mrs. Jeffries poured herself a cup of tea and took her seat.

"It isn't exactly exciting news, but it is better than nothing, I suppose. As I said, a goodly number of people were through the kitchen today, but most of them were fairly useless." She paused, pursed her lips and shook her head. "It's downright sad how few people there are that take an interest in someone else's business."

"I know just what you mean," Wiggins agreed.

"Yes, I'm sure we all do," Mrs. Jeffries said quickly. "Please, Mrs. Goodge, do go on."

"I'm not sure how to say this."

"Just tell it straight out," Mrs. Jeffries advised. "That's usually the easiest way."

"I'm not tryin' to be difficult, it's just that I'm not sure what my information means." The cook hesitated briefly and then plunged ahead. "Edna Thomas came 'round today, and she works for Lord and Lady Drummond. They were at Lord Keighley's on the night Sir Edmund was murdered."

"Is this the Alex Drummond who was supposedly in Keighley's study after most of the other guests had left?" Betsy asked. She wanted to make sure she had all her facts correct. One day, she hoped to be able to put the pieces of the puzzle together just the way Mrs. Jeffries did. She didn't think she'd ever be as good as the housekeeper was at it, but she was determined to try. She'd noticed that Mrs. Jeffries always got the facts right.

Mrs. Goodge nodded eagerly. "That's him all right, and it was because he was stayin' behind to drink himself into a stupor that Edna found out her little bit. Mind you, like I said, she's no idea it was anything important." She told them all the details she'd learned from her old friend. She took great care to tell them everything, as she didn't want to make the same mistake that poor Luty had made the other day and leave out any useful information. When she was finished, she leaned back in her chair and picked up her teacup. "So that's it, then. I don't know what it means. Edna and I thought that maybe the Parkingtons were startin' to haggle over the cost of the marriage settlement."

"But the settlement papers had already been signed," Betsy pointed out. "I don't think you can do that."

"I would think a marriage settlement is some sort of a contract," Mrs. Jeffries mused, "but frankly, I don't know for certain."

"Neither do any of the rest of us," Smythe said glumly. "But even if the settlement agreement is or was a contract, it'd mean nothing unless the marriage actually took place. Which it didn't because Sir Edmund was murdered."

Hatchet added. "But that certainly puts the events of the evening in a different light. Apparently, all wasn't sweetness and harmony between the Parkingtons and Sir Edmund. Perhaps we ought to have another look at Osgood Parkington. He was out that night and he had a weapon."

"Perhaps we should," the housekeeper replied.

"It's a bit vague, I know, but that's all I managed to get out of anyone." Mrs. Goodge looked at the others and shrugged apologetically.

"Your information might turn out to be quite important," Mrs. Jeffries said kindly. She didn't want Mrs. Goodge to feel badly about her contribution. The poor woman had spent hours on her feet baking for her sources and she'd learned very little for all her fine efforts. The cook was correct in one sense, her information was so imprecise it could have any number of meanings. "Hatchet, why don't you go next?"

"Thank you, madam, I shall be happy to oblige. As we discussed at our last meeting, we all agreed it would be prudent to know who would have inherited if both Sir Edmund and Roland Leggett had been shot that night," Hatchet began.

Luty rolled her eyes. "Get on with it, man. We remember what we discussed. It was only yesterday."

Hatchet shot his employer a disapproving look and then continued speaking. "According to my source, and by the way, it's quite a reliable source, if both the Leggetts had died that night, the title and the estate would go to an elderly cousin currently living in Kent."

"You know this feller's name?" Luty demanded. She'd planned on harassing her lawyers into finding out this information, but drat, that darned Hatchet had beaten her to it.

"Of course, madam. The gentleman's name is John Reginald Bartholomew Leggett," Hatchet replied. "And he's plenty of money of his own. So I don't think he had anything to do with Sir Edmund's murder."

"But we don't know that for certain," Luty retorted. "He might have planned on killing both Roland and Sir Edmund that night. But as he's old and crotchety, when he saw it was just Sir Edmund, he pumped him full of lead in a fit of rage. Old people can get right cranky, you know."

Hatchet looked at her pityingly. "Really, madam, is that the best you can offer? If he'd been planning on doing both of them in, he'd have killed Sir Edmund and then had a go at Mr. Roland Leggett. But as Roland Leggett is still in remarkably good health . . ."

"He is," Betsy interrupted. "I saw him today when I was at the Leggett house."

"Then I think it safe to cross this elderly Leggett cousin off our list of suspects," Hatchet finished smoothly.

"I agree," Mrs. Jeffries said quickly. She gave the elderly American a fleeting smile and then looked back at the butler. "But Luty does have an interesting point. Do you have anything else for us?"

He bowed his head slightly. "I've finished. Though I do

expect to hear some interesting tidbits about Osgood Parkington tomorrow."

"Can I go next?" Betsy asked. "I didn't learn all that much, but I did see Roland Leggett. I saw Osgood Parkington, as well."

"By all means," Mrs. Jeffries said. She helped herself to a slice of bread.

"When I got to the Leggett house, I noticed that there was workmen out front sprucing the place up a bit," Betsy said. "I wasn't sure if I ought to hang about and try to have a word with one of them or not. I'd just about made up my mind to leave when the front door opened and out comes Roland Leggett and a young serving girl. He was carrying this great big tray with a huge teapot and some cups on it. The maid was pushing a trolley."

"What kind of a trolley?" Wiggins asked curiously.

"It was like a tea trolley, but it wasn't fancy," she replied. "It was made of metal but it had a flat top and was pushed along on wheels. But that's not important. Roland Leggett called to the workmen to come have some tea, and then he put the tray down on top of the trolley. Then he started helping the girl pour the men tea!"

"Roland Leggett was serving tea to his workmen?" Mrs. Goodge asked incredulously. "That's amazing." In her day, a nobleman would no more have served a workman than he would have sprouted wings and flown to the moon.

Betsy nodded. "I couldn't believe my eyes! Honestly, I don't want to think that he's our killer, he seems such a decent sort."

"He certainly does," Mrs. Jeffries murmured. But she knew that appearances could be deceptive. She also knew that if Roland Leggett was as smart as they'd heard, he could very well have thought the police might be keeping an eye on him. They too would have been favorably impressed if he was seen to serve tea to his workers. "When did you see Osgood Parkington?"

"He came just as they were all having their tea," Betsy continued. "Thank goodness there's that garden in the middle of the square. I managed to hang about by pretending I was interested in the plants along the edge of the wrought iron fence."

"That's very clever of you," Smythe told her.

"I had to do something." She gave him a quick, pleased smile. "I couldn't stand about staring at the house with all of them outside. Anyway, they were having their tea when all of a sudden a brougham pulled up and out steps Osgood Parkington."

"How close to them were you?" Mrs. Jeffries asked.

"Close enough to hear some of what was being said," she replied. "By this time I'd managed to work my way around to the front of the house. I was still some distance away, but Osgood Parkington has a powerfully loud voice. I overheard every word he said."

"And what did he say?" Mrs. Jeffries pressed.

"About what we'd expect," Betsy said. "He's a dreadful snob. He made some comment about how it didn't look good to be drinking tea with the hired help, and then he invited Roland Leggett to a late breakfast the next day. He said he had something very important he wanted to speak to him about."

"What was Leggett's answer?" Mrs. Goodge asked.

"That's just it." Betsy sighed. "I couldn't hear. Roland Leggett doesn't have a loud voice, and by this time, pretending I was interested in the bushes and shrubs was starting to wear thin. Several of the workmen were starting to stare at me, so I had to leave. I'm sorry, I wish I could have stayed longer, but I couldn't. I know it's not much, but it was the best I could do today. I tried asking some questions with the local shopkeepers again, but the only thing I found out was that Osgood Parkington likes codfish and that Miss Parkington won't wear a tight corset."

"You've done very well, Betsy," Mrs. Jeffries replied. "You've reported on an incident that gives us quite a bit of insight in Roland Leggett's character."

"And we know that Osgood Parkington was wantin' him to come for a meal," Smythe added. "Which fits with what I 'eard about the fellow. Except I heard he was invitin' Leggett to dinner."

"Maybe he did invite him to dinner and he couldn't come, so Parkington then invited him to a late breakfast," Betsy suggested.

"I suppose that's possible." Smythe took a quick sip of tea. "But that's not all I 'eard. According to my source, Osgood Parkington is obsessed with the aristocracy."

"Obsessed?" Mrs. Goodge repeated. "You mean like he spent all his time wantin' to be one of them•or tryin' to meet them? Is that what you mean?"

"That's right." Smythe grinned. "I wasn't sure what it meant myself until my source explained it." He'd known perfectly well what the word meant, but he didn't want the cook to be embarrassed by her ignorance. "Parkington didn't just happen to meet Sir Edmund Leggett, he hunted the fellow down and then bribed him to come to dinner."

"Do you mean that literally?" Hatchet asked.

Smythe nodded. "Parkington actually made Leggett's acquaintance by forgiving him a debt. Leggett did some business with Parkington's firm last year and, of course, he didn't pay what he owed. Parkington arranged to meet Leggett and told him if he'd come to dinner, the debt would be forgotten. Leggett came to dinner, took one look at the goods that Parkington was trying to sell, and knew he'd found a way out of his financial troubles. My source claims Parkington made it obvious from the first that his daughter was on the block to someone with a title."

"You mean he made it clear that he'd settle a great deal of money on any titled man who married his daughter," Mrs. Jeffries clarified.

"That's right." Smythe glanced at Betsy and wondered how anyone could marry for any reason other than love.

"Cor blimey, that's right cold-hearted," Wiggins exclaimed. "Surely he must have 'ad some feelings for her? Miss Beatrice seems a right nice young lady. She don't deserve to be treated like that."

"No woman deserves to be treated like goods on the auction block," Betsy muttered darkly. One part of her was beginning to think that Sir Edmund might have gotten what he deserved.

"I hate to ruin your illusions, Wiggins, but Sir Edmund had no more feelings for Miss Parkington than he had for the lady on the Cadbury's cocoa tin." Smythe smiled sadly. "Some men are just plain fools, and it seems Sir Edmund was one of them. I also found out where Sarah Camden went. She went home."

Mrs. Jeffries sighed heavily. "Yes, I know. Earlier this afternoon, I got a reply to my telegram to the police in Bristol."

"That doesn't sound good," Luty said. "I was hopin' they'd tell us they'd not seen hide nor hair of the girl."

"Miss Camden has turned out to be quite a problem for us." Mrs. Jeffries looked around the table at the others, making sure they all understood what she was saying. "If we say nothing to the inspector and she turns out to be the killer, we'll have helped her to escape."

"But if we do tell the inspector, and he talks to her, it'll be obvious we've been helping with his cases," Betsy said glumly.

From the expressions on their faces, Mrs. Jeffries knew they all appreciated the gravity of their dilemma.

"Sarah will give the game away, won't she?" Betsy said to Mrs. Jeffries.

"I'm afraid so." The housekeeper shrugged faintly. "But it can't be helped. We did what we thought was the right thing to do at the time. Perhaps we should never have sent the girl to Luty's. But we did, so we'll have to deal with the consequences if they arise."

"I don't think Sarah is the killer," Luty declared. "When she saw Jon snoopin' with her little bundle of things, she got scared and run."

"But she had a gun," Mrs. Goodge pointed out.

"So do I," Luty argued. "But that don't make me a killer. She was a green girl all alone in a big, strange city. She probably brought the gun with her for protection."

Mrs. Jeffries cleared her throat. "I'm inclined to agree with Luty. For the present, let's go on the assumption that Sarah is innocent. We say nothing to the inspector unless it becomes apparent she's our killer. In which case, I'll confess everything and take full responsibility for our actions."

Everyone began to protest, but the Mrs. Jeffries waved her hand for silence. "Let's hope that Sarah isn't our killer and that I don't have to say a word to the inspector. Of course, when I sent the telegram to the Bristol police, I used the inspector's name, so let's also hope he doesn't have a reason to contact them. Now, who would like to go next."

They spent the remainder of their meeting hearing the rest of the reports and then going over the new information they'd acquired.

But no matter how many facts she had or how much they talked about the case, it was still a puzzle to Mrs. Jeffries. By the time the last slice of bread disappeared and the last drop of tea drunk, she was nearing panic, but she took great pains to keep her expression from showing her true feelings.

She reached for the empty teapot just as Luty and Hatchet got up to leave. "We'll meet here tomorrow morning," she said. "That way I can let everyone know what I get out of the inspector this evening."

There was a loud knocking on the back door and then a second later, a woman's voice called out, "Yoo hoo, may I come in?"

"It's Lady Cannonberry." Wiggins leapt to his feet and raced off down the hall to greet her. Fred, who'd been sound asleep in front of the cooker, jumped up and ran after him.

Ruth Cannonberry was their neighbor and the widow of a lord. But she'd been born the daughter of a vicar and had very advanced ideas about social justice, women's rights, and the Irish question. She believed in the equality of all souls and insisted that everyone in the Witherspoon household call her by her Christian name. The household considered her a good friend and confidant.

"We're ever so glad to see you back," Wiggins said to the middle-aged, slender, blonde woman he escorted into the kitchen. "It's ever so excitin'. We've got us a right nice murder."

"Oh, excellent," she replied. "Then I'm just in time. Hello everyone. I do hope I'm not intruding, but I got home late this afternoon and I couldn't wait to see everyone. Luty, Hatchet, I'm so happy you're here as well."

"We're glad to see you, too." Luty grinned. She put her purple parasol back down on the table and took her seat again. Hatchet remained standing.

"Hello, Ruth," Mrs. Jeffries said. "Of course you're not intruding. You're always welcome. Do sit down. Would you like tea?"

"I had tea on the train," she replied as she sat down next to Wiggins. "Now, if you've time, do tell me all about your murder."

Hatchet nodded at Ruth. "It's good to see you ma'am. Perhaps the others can give you all the details, but we really must be going."

"Why do we have to leave?" Luty demanded. "I ain't seen Ruth in a month of Sundays. . . ."

"The reception at Viscount Lumley's, remember? We might pick up some valuable information about our case."

"Well, Nellie's whiskers." Luty reluctantly got up. "Much as it pains me to say it, Hatchet's right. We can't afford not to go. Half the people at the viscount's reception will probably have been at Keighley's the night of the murder. I'm real sorry to have to go, Ruth, but it can't be helped. We'll have to catch up later. You take care now and I'm glad you're home."

"You must come to tea soon," Ruth replied. "I've ever so much to tell you."

Luty and Hatchet said goodby to the others and then disappeared down the back hall.

Ruth turned to Mrs. Jeffries. "What's happened? Who was murdered?"

Mrs. Jeffries glanced at the carriage clock on the sideboard to make sure it wasn't getting too terribly late. She didn't want the inspector to come home whilst she was in the midst of telling everything. But it was a good hour before the inspector was due and the household was in good order. "Several nights ago, Sir Edmund Leggett was shot on his way home from his engagement party."

"Sir Edmund Leggett?" Ruth repeated. "I've never heard of him."

"I'm not surprised you'd not heard of him, Sir Edmund wasn't in the least interested in social justice, public health, or women's rights." Mrs. Jeffries spent the next half hour telling Ruth what they knew thus far. When she was finished, she sat back in her chair and asked, "I don't suppose you know any of these other people, do you?"

Ruth shook her head. "No, I'm afraid not . . . wait, I tell a lie, I have seen one of the Parkington women. She's come to several of my women's suffrage meetings. She always comes in late and slips into the back row, almost as if she doesn't want to be noticed."

"Women's meetings?" Smythe prodded. "You mean the

ones where they're wantin' women to get the right to vote?"

"What's wrong with that?" Betsy demanded.

"Nothing, luv, I'm all for women voting. Probably be a better world if women had more say in running it," he said quickly.

"I'm not surprised that Beatrice Parkington believes in women's suffrage," Mrs. Jeffries replied. "But I am surprised she works so hard not to be noticed."

"Oh, it's not Beatrice," Ruth replied. "It's Julia Parkington who comes to our meetings. I know that for a fact because one of the other women on the committee lives just across the road from her. I expect Mrs. Parkington tries to be discreet because of her husband. From what I hear, he's a domineering sort of person."

"I tell you Mrs. Jeffries, this case has me completely baffled." Inspector Witherspoon sighed deeply and took a quick sip of his sherry. "Just when I think we might have a decent suspect, something comes along to ruin my theory."

Mrs. Jeffries was completely baffled herself, but she could hardly say so. She also knew she needed to keep his confidence up. "I'm sure you'll catch the killer, sir," she replied. "You always do."

"But perhaps this will be the time that I don't," he said glumly.

"Nonsense, sir. You must listen to your 'inner voice,' sir. It's never failed you yet."

"I'm trying to, Mrs. Jeffries, I really am. But so far, my 'inner voice' isn't saying a ruddy thing. It's gone horribly quiet." He shifted his weight in the chair. "I'm flummoxed. Completely flummoxed."

"Don't despair, sir, you're simply tired. That's all."

"I thought perhaps Mr. Roland Leggett might be the killer." He took another sip of sherry. "But the evidence against him is very circumstantial."

"What evidence?" She didn't recall any real evidence against Roland Leggett. "I thought he had an alibi. Wasn't he asleep in Lord Keighley's study with several other men."

"But they were asleep as well," Witherspoon pointed out. "So he could have come and gone as he pleased and they'd be none the wiser, and there's some evidence that the bottle of whiskey in the room was tampered with."

"Bottle of whiskey," she repeated.

He made a face. "Oh dear, I'm not telling this very well, but my idea was that Roland Leggett knew the men would all end up in Keighley's study for a nightcap. Apparently, that happens quite frequently. Leggett puts a sleeping draught in the whiskey and the men all drink it and fall asleep. He then nips out the window in the back parlor, follows his cousin and kills him with three shots to the man's chest, and then nips back to Lord Keighley's."

"That's a very interesting theory, sir," she said slowly. She couldn't believe that he'd come up with the idea. It was actually very plausible.

"We know that a window was open," Witherspoon said, warming to his subject, "because all of the staff were insisting they'd not done it. We also know that the next day, the butler claimed the whiskey bottle should have been half empty but, instead, the bottle was full. Well, of course, if Roland is our killer, he wouldn't have left the drugged bottle of whiskey at the Keighley house for us to find, so he'd have tossed it in the river and substituted a full bottle."

"So, you're thinking he knew his cousin would leave early and walk home," she began.

"That's where my theory breaks down," the inspector admitted. "We've no evidence he had any idea that Edmund would leave early. Nor is there any evidence he brought a bottle of whiskey with him and hid it somewhere until it was needed."

"It's still a fairly good theory, sir," she was impressed.

Perhaps the inspector didn't need quite as much help as they thought. "How did the rest of your day go, sir?"

"I'm not sure," he replied. "No one confessed, which is most unfortunate. It would certainly make my life easier if someone did." He gave her the remaining details of his day, finding that as he spoke, his spirits began to lift. By the time he'd finished telling her about his meeting with William Carter, the Parkingtons, and everything else that had happened, he was feeling ever so much better.

"You sound as if you've had a most enlightening day, sir," she said as she got up. "I'm sure you're going to solve this one. Are you hungry yet?"

"Actually, I'm quite famished."

"I'll just go see if dinner is ready. Oh, by the way, Lady Cannonberry is home. She stopped by late this afternoon. She wanted to know if you'd come see her after you've eaten."

"I should be delighted," he exclaimed. "I wasn't expecting her home for another week."

Mrs. Jeffries started for the door. "Go on into the dining room, sir. I'll bring your dinner tray straight up. Then you can go right on over."

The inspector ate quickly, gave Fred a perfunctory pat on the head, and then raced out the back door.

Mrs. Goodge, Betsy, and Mrs. Jeffries did the washing up, Wiggins took Fred for his evening walk, and Smythe went over to Howard's to give the horses a quick treat. By the time everyone was back and the kitchen in good order, the inspector still hadn't returned from his visit across the garden.

"Did he take his key?" Smythe asked. He fought back a yawn.

"I don't believe he did," Mrs. Jeffries murmured. That meant someone would need to wait up and let him in the back door. She gazed at the others. Wiggins was openly yawning, Mrs. Goodge had dark circles under her eyes,

Betsy's shoulders were drooping with fatigue, and Smythe looked like he was half-asleep on his feet. Even Fred had flopped down on the rug and put his head down. Everyone loved their investigations, but all the activity on top of their normal chores could lead to exhaustion. "But all of you go on to bed, I'll wait up for him. I'm not tired yet."

"Are you sure?" Wiggins asked as he headed for the back stairs. Fred got up and trotted after him.

"I'm dead tired," Mrs. Goodge muttered. "I'm for my bed. 'N all."

"I can stay up." Smythe tried to stifle another yawn, but couldn't quite do it.

"Go on, all of you, I'll be fine." It took a few more minutes, but she finally got everyone off to bed. She sat down in the quiet kitchen and listened to the faint ticking of the carriage clock.

She jumped as a loud knock sounded on the back door. "I'm coming," she called. But when she opened the back door, she started in surprise. "Gracious, Dr. Bosworth, I wasn't expecting you."

"I'm sorry, I hope I'm not disturbing you." He smiled sheepishly. "I saw your lights on, and well, frankly, I was hoping to beg a cup of tea."

"Of course, Doctor, do come in," she held the door open and motioned him inside. "Go right on in. I was just going to make myself a cup."

"I got called out on an emergency," he explained as they went to the kitchen, "and I've not had a bite to eat or drink in hours."

"Then you've come to the right place. We've plenty." She was pleased he was comfortable enough with them to drop by unannounced. "Go sit down." She motioned him toward the kitchen. "I'll just stop off in the larder and get a few things for you to eat."

"That would be heavenly. Shall I put the kettle on?" he asked.

"Of course," she replied. By the time she returned to the kitchen carrying a tray of food, Dr. Bosworth had the kettle on the boil. "I'm afraid it's not very elegant," she said as she put the food down on the table. "But I've some pickled eggs and onions, brown bread, gooseberry jam, and a nice seed cake. There's a bit of roast chicken, as well. Will this do for you?" She silently prayed that Mrs. Goodge would understand about the seed cake.

"This is a feast, Mrs. Jeffries." He licked his lips hungrily, pulled out a chair, and sat down.

Dr. Bosworth was a tall man with dark red hair, pale skin, and a sharp, bony face that reminded Mrs. Jeffries of President Abraham Lincoln.

"I'm being dreadfully rude, I know," he said with a shrug. "But all the cafés are closed and my landlady will be tucked safely in bed by now, and I'm genuinely starved."

"Nonsense, Dr. Bosworth, we're old friends. You're not at all rude." She put the plate of roast chicken down in front of him and then ladled a pickled egg out of the small crock. "You've certainly done us favors when we've needed help with one of the inspector's cases."

"You're being kind, Mrs. Jeffries." He laughed and speared a piece of chicken. "And I thank you."

She sliced a piece of the cake, slapped it on a plate, and put it next to his dinner plate. Then she made his tea while he ate his meal.

"Thank you," he murmured as she put the mug down next to him.

She remained silent while he finished his food. Then she said. "You were out on an emergency, you say?"

He nodded and took a quick sip of the hot tea. "I got called out to the hospital in Hammersmith. There was a nasty accident between two fully-occupied omnibuses. I've been in surgery for what seems hours." He pushed his empty plate away and reached for the seed cake. "This looks wonderful. How is your case going?"

"Not all that well, I'm sorry to say." She glanced at his empty plate. "Do help yourself to more food, Doctor," she urged. "We've plenty." Hopefully, Mrs. Goodge wouldn't have too many people coming through tomorrow. Perhaps she'd not care that a goodly-sized hunk of her cake was gone.

"No, this is more than enough." He took a bite of cake and sighed in pleasure. "Oh . . . it is wonderful. Please give Mrs. Goodge my compliments."

"I will," Mrs. Jeffries replied. "She'll be pleased you enjoyed her food." She hoped the inspector stayed at Lady Cannonberry's for a while longer. Explaining the doctor's presence might be a bit difficult. After all, she could hardly admit that the doctor had become a friend of the household because he was always helping them.

"I'm sorry the case isn't going well," he said. He shoveled another bite into his mouth. "But you'll sort it out, you always do."

"I'm not so sure," she admitted honestly. "This time, we've a huge number of suspects, no one has an alibi, and the victim was universally loathed. Frankly, Doctor, I'm not sure this case is going to get solved at all."

He gazed at her sympathetically. "Oh well, there's no rush, not unless your primary suspect is Julia Parkington, and I don't think that's likely. She's desperate to see her daughter happily married."

"What do you mean?"

Bosworth flushed. "Well, surely you knew about her condition? She's got stomach cancer. She's not expected to live much longer."

"You're her doctor?"

"No, but the doctor I was working with today is her physician, and he asked me about drug dosages. He's quite a young man and not very experienced. Her name came up and he told me her condition had worsened to the point where she was taking so much laudanum that he was getting concerned it wasn't providing her with any pain relief. He said she was asking for morphine."

"Morphine? That's stronger than laudanum?" Mrs. Jeffries felt a great surge of pity for the woman. She must be in dreadful pain.

"They're both made from the same source," he said. "But morphine is much purer and stronger. In cases like Mrs. Parkington's, it's to be recommended for pain relief. Dr. Marks was concerned, but I asked him what difference it made if she was dying anyway."

•"We didn't know about Mrs. Parkington's condition," Mrs. Jeffries admitted. "Which is odd, because we've found out a lot of information about the family. But not this."

"Frankly, I was a bit shocked when Marks mentioned her. The Parkingtons are wealthy. I'd have thought they would go to one of the fancy men on Harley Street. I asked him how long he'd been the family doctor and he admitted, he wasn't. He was her doctor." Bosworth shook his head. "Dr. Marks doesn't think she's told her family of her condition. As a matter of fact, he's sure of it. That's probably why you didn't come across the information."

"Gracious, if she's dying, why wouldn't she tell them the truth?"

"I don't know." Bosworth glanced at the clock. "Egads, Mrs. Jeffries, it's terribly late. You must be exhausted. I'd better let you get to bed."

She had dozens more questions she wanted to ask, but she didn't want the inspector to arrive home while the good doctor was still here. "You must be tired, too, Doctor."

"Let me help you tidy up." He got up.

"No, please, let me do it. You go on home, I can manage."

She managed to get him out the back door and make it back to the kitchen a few minutes before the inspector arrived home. She'd gotten most of the food cleared up but the seed cake was still sitting on the table.

"I'm sorry you had to wait up for me," Witherspoon apologized. "I say, that cake looks jolly good."

"Yes, I was a bit peckish," she replied. "Would you like a slice, sir?" Silently, she prayed he'd decline.

"Well, I really oughtn't to, but, oh, all right. Let's us have a slice. I'm sure Mrs. Goodge won't mind."

CHAPTER 11

———◦≫◦≪◦———

Despite being exhausted, Mrs. Jeffries couldn't fall asleep. She lay flat on her back and took long, deep breaths for a good ten minutes. But it didn't work; she was still wide awake and staring at the ceiling. It was almost as if her mind was trying to tell her something, trying to force her to see what was right under her nose. Or perhaps that was just wishful thinking. Perhaps she couldn't sleep because she felt they'd failed on this case. No, that couldn't be right. She rolled over onto her side and punched the pillow. Because when she closed her eyes, she couldn't stop thinking about the murder or their suspects. Images, ideas, and bits of phrases repeated themselves one after the other in her mind.

Roland Leggett seemed a decent man, yet of all their suspects, he was the one who actually gained something by Sir Edmund's death. He got the title. Perhaps that was his motive. England was a country where class was important. There were many who would kill to have a "Sir" affixed to the front of their names. But was Roland desperate to be a nobleman? Did it matter enough to him to kill for it?

Sarah Camden claimed that Sir Edmund was more use to her alive than dead, yet she'd been stalking the man for weeks and had gained nothing for her efforts. When his engagement had been announced, maybe she'd given into her rage and decided to extract a little vengeance for what he'd done to her family. Circumstances certainly pointed to her as the likely killer; and she'd run when they'd discovered she had a gun.

Mrs. Jeffries rolled onto her back and tried staring at the ceiling again. William Carter and Beatrice Parkington were obviously in love with one another. Both of them were very intelligent and very capable of conspiring to commit murder. But to what end? Murdering Sir Edmund wouldn't have solved their problem. Osgood Parkington would simply have gone on the hunt for another impoverished nobleman for his daughter. No, there was no genuine reason for those two to have committed the crime. It would have been far easier for the two lovers to simply run off. Especially now that it appeared William Carter wasn't an impoverished academic, but had come into an inheritance.

And what of Osgood Parkington? Perhaps they ought to take a closer look at him. He certainly seemed to have been delighted to be bringing Sir Edmund into the family fold, but Mrs. Jeffries had observed that what people *said* often obscured their true motives in life. It was far better to watch what people actually did rather than pay attention to the words that came out of their mouths. Perhaps Osgood Parkington had only used marrying his daughter off to the man as a ruse to get close to him. Perhaps Parkington had an old grudge against Sir Edmund? Or perhaps, he'd gotten fed up with Sir Edmund's demands. She rolled back over onto her side. Yes, perhaps they ought to have a closer look

at Mr. Parkington. The man had a dreadful temper and he
may have shot Sir Edmund in a fit of anger. Sir Edmund
had been heard to threaten Mrs. Parkington with his solic-
tors; perhaps he had been demanding a larger settlement.
From what they knew of the man's character, that was certainly well within the bounds of possibility. When Parkington went out looking for his daughter that night, he might
have stumbled upon Sir Edmund, who then drunkenly repeated his demands for more money. Parkington could
have become furious, lost his temper, and shot the man.

She sighed and sat up. There was no point in lying here
speculating about the identity of the killer. For all she
knew, they were completely wrong and the murderer might
well be someone from Sir Edmund's past.

Mrs. Jeffries tossed the covers off and got up. She
lighted the lamp, sat down at her desk, and picked up her
list of suspects. Then she began to study the clues written
in the columns under each name. If nothing else, the exercise might make her sleepy.

The sun was shining brightly when Mrs. Jeffries walked
into the kitchen the next morning. "Good morning, all,"
she said.

"You don't look well, Mrs. Jeffries," Betsy said. She
was laying the table for their breakfast. "Are you feeling all
right?"

"I'm fine, dear. I just didn't sleep very well last night.
That always puts dark circles under my eyes." Mrs. Jeffries
knew she looked a bit haggard, but in truth, she felt quite
good. She was fairly certain she knew who their killer
might be. "Where's Wiggins and Smythe?"

"Wiggins has nipped out on some mysterious errand of
his own," the cook replied as she lifted a strip of bacon
onto a plate of brown paper to drain.

"Smythe's gone upstairs to change his shirt," Betsy
added. "He keeps losing buttons."

"Not to worry," the coachman said cheerfully as he reappeared in the kitchen. "I've got you to sew them on for me now. Good morning, Mrs. Jeffries. Cor blimey, are you all right?"

"I'm fine, Smythe," she replied. "I just didn't sleep very well."

"Let's get breakfast on, then," the cook said. She pushed the bacon strips onto a platter of fried eggs and picked it up. "I've some sources coming in this morning and I want you lot out of here."

"Oh dear, I do wish Wiggins was back," Mrs. Jeffries murmured as she took her place at the table.

"Is there something you wanted him to do?" Smythe eyed her speculatively.

"No, not really." She took a deep breath and plunged ahead. "But it would be better if he was here so I don't have to repeat myself. I'm not certain that I'm right, but well, actually, I was up most of the night thinking about this case and I've come to a conclusion about who our killer might be."

"Might be?" Betsy prodded. She wasn't sure she liked the sound of that. In the past, Mrs. Jeffries had often said she wasn't sure about the identity of the killer, but there had been something about her person that always convinced the others she knew exactly what she was doing. This time, Betsy could see that the housekeeper's uneasiness was real.

Just then, Wiggins raced into the kitchen. "Morning all," he said. "Cor blimey, just in time. I didn't want to be late for breakfast. I'm really 'ungry this mornin'."

"When are you not hungry?" the cook muttered as she gave him a good glare. "Someone helped themselves to two huge pieces of my seed cake and everyone knew I was saving it for today!"

"It wasn't me," Wiggins protested. "It'd be more than my life's worth to touch a cake you were savin' for your sources."

"He didn't eat your cake, Mrs. Goodge," Mrs. Jeffries said. "It was Dr. Bosworth and the inspector. I'm sorry, I know it was to be saved for today, but I had no choice."

"Dr. Bosworth?" Mrs. Goodge repeated. "He was here?"

"He dropped by late last night after everyone had gone to bed," she explained. "And the information he gave me is one of the reasons I think I might know the identity of our killer. But first, I'd like to know where Wiggins has been."

"I had a quick run over to the Parkington house," Wiggins replied.

"Why?" Mrs. Jeffries asked curiously. She picked up the serving spatula and began flipping fried eggs and bacon onto the plates.

"Because last night I couldn't sleep."

"Sounds like there's a rash of that goin' round," Smythe said softly.

"And I kept askin' myself what 'ad changed in Sir Edmund's life right before 'e were killed." Wiggins nodded his thanks as Mrs. Jeffries handed him his plate. "Seems to me that it's lookin' at what changes in a victim's life that might be a clue to why they end up dead."

Mrs. Jeffries paused momentarily and then slipped the last egg onto her own plate. Wiggins reasoning was quite impressive. It often was a change in a victim's circumstance that was the reason for their murder. "That's often quite true."

"Ta, Mrs. Jeffries." He grinned happily. "Anyways, I realized the only thing that 'ad really changed for Sir Edmund was 'im gettin' engaged. And the engagement involved the Parkingtons and their money. So I went along to 'ave a quick look this morning just in case something might be goin' on. You never know what's what until you 'ave a good look."

"Well," Betsy demanded. "Was anything happening?"

"I'm not sure," he admitted. He reached for the pot of

gooseberry jam. "But I saw Mr. Parkington leave and then a few minutes later, Mrs. and Miss Parkington come out and walked to the end of the street. I got up fairly close behind them. I 'eard everything Mrs. Parkington said to her daughter."

"They didn't notice you followin' them?" Smythe commented.

"They was too busy gettin' the hansom to notice anythin' and she kept lookin' around, like she was watchin' for him to come back," he replied.

"You mean Mr. Parkington?" Mrs. Goodge asked. She hated it when things weren't clear.

"That's right," he replied. "I saw her peekin' out the front window as 'e was leavin'. I think she was waitin' for 'im to go before she and her daughter come out to get their hansom. What she said was right strange, I don't know what to make of it." He stopped and took a bite of bacon, oblivious to the fact that the others were staring at him.

"What did you hear?" Mrs. Jeffries prodded.

"Well—" he swallowed his food—"Mrs. Parkington told Miss Parkington not to come back no matter what 'appened. She repeated it twice, she told 'er not to come back no matter what. I think she was tossin' Miss Parkington out of the 'ouse. Which is funny when you think of it, it were always Mr. Parkington who were threatenin' to toss the girl out on 'er ear. That's why I wasn't sure what to make of the whole business. Her words sounded right harsh, but she kept strokin' Miss Parkington's arm and kissin' her cheek."

Mrs. Jeffries went absolutely still. Then she pushed away from the table and leapt to her feet. "There's not a moment to lose. Wiggins, hurry along to the end of the road and waylay Constable Barnes. He's got to get the inspector to the Parkington house right away."

Inspector Witherspoon was a bit confused, but he trusted his constable's judgement. "Are you sure that Miss Parkington has gone?" he asked again. "Your informant is absolutely certain?"

Barnes silently prayed that Mrs. Jeffries was right. If she wasn't, there would be red faces all around, and his would be the reddest. "Yes, sir, my informant saw Mrs. Parkington put the girl in a hansom this morning. It appears as if she's trying to get away."

They turned the corner and started up the street to the Parkington house.

"And your informant is equally sure that Miss Parkington's departure has something to do with Sir Edmund's murder?" Witherspoon pressed. He wanted to make certain he understood the underlying reasoning for the constable's actions.

"That's what he said, sir. He told me to, 'Get along to the Parkington house. The girl's made a run for it.'" As Barnes was making this up as he went along, he didn't want to say too much. The inspector's memory was odd, sometimes he could remember the most amazing details, while at other times, he could barely remember who they spoke to half an hour ago. "I doubt that it's anything, sir. But I thought it worth going along to have a look."

"Of course, Constable." Witherspoon nodded approvingly. "If one of our suspects engages in any kind of unusual activity, we must go and see what it's all about. It was very clever of you to have one of your street informants keep an eye on the place," Witherspoon shot the constable an admiring glance. "I wish I'd have thought of that."

Barnes looked away as guilt flooded him. He'd done no such thing, of course. But he'd had to come up with some excuse as to how he was getting all his information. "I had a lot of years on the street, sir. You learn a few tricks here and there."

They were almost to the Parkington house when the front door flew open and Roland Leggett rushed out. His eyes were wide and his mouth open as he charged toward the policeman.

"Oh my God," Leggett screamed. "She's insane. She's mad. She's going to kill everyone."

Barnes, who was intensely relieved that something, even a hysterical madman had appeared, grabbed Leggett by the shoulders and gave him a shake. "Get a hold of yourself, sir. What's happened? What's wrong?"

"What's wrong?" Roland cried. "I'll tell you what's wrong." He pointed to the Parkington house. "She's crazy. She's stark raving mad. I was invited for breakfast, and even though I've no interest in his damned daughter, I didn't wish to be rude so I accepted. But I'm not used to being greeted at the front door with a pistol in my face." He pulled away from the constable's grip and began backing away down the road, his gaze on the Parkington's front door. "I'm getting out of here. I want nothing to do with those insane people."

"But sir," Witherspoon protested. "We'll need you to make a statement."

"Damn your statement, man. You can come and see me later." Leggett turned and raced up the road, trying to put as much distance between himself and the house as possible.

"Gracious, Constable. This seems a very odd business." Witherspoon said. "We'd best go along and see what's . . ." he broke off as a loud, sharp shot rang out.

"That's gunfire," Barnes cried as he ran up the walkway with Witherspoon right on his heels. Leggett hadn't closed the front door all the way so Barnes pushed it open and the two men burst into the house.

They sped into the drawing room and then skidded to a halt at the peculiar scene in front of them.

Osgood Parkington was sitting in the middle of the settee. His mouth gaped open, his face was white, and his expression was one of horrified disbelief. Blood was seeping through his trouser leg. He'd been shot in the thigh.

Julia Parkington was standing in front of her husband. She had a pistol leveled at his head. "Don't come any closer, Inspector," she said softly as she cast a quick glance at the policemen. "Otherwise, I'll kill him right now."

Witherspoon forced himself to stay calm. "Mrs. Parkington, please put the gun down. You don't want to hurt anyone."

"But I do," she replied. She was wearing a white tea gown of French silk which draped softly about her person. Her hair was tucked loosely up in a chignon and a few curls had escaped to frame her face. Her expression was placid, even peaceful. She shifted her position slightly, so that she could see both her husband and the two policemen. "And I assure you, I'm quite a good shot. No matter what you do, I'll be able to kill him."

"Why do you want to murder your husband?" the inspector asked politely. He wasn't sure what to do next. She was quite correct, even if they tackled her, she'd be able to get a shot off. But, egads, he couldn't stand by and let a man be murdered in cold blood.

"Why else, Inspector," she replied. "I want him dead before he can ruin my daughter's life. He won't give up, you see. He's obsessed with getting a damned title. So obsessed he no longer even sees Beatrice as a human being; she's merely an instrument to be used for his own social ambitions."

"That's not true, Julia," Osgood said pityingly. "You don't understand. You don't know what it's like to grow up poor and be treated like dirt. I wanted our daughter to have a good life, I never wanted anyone to look down on her. I love our daughter. I only want her happiness."

"Liar," she hissed. "You want your own happiness. You forget, Osgood, I know you. I know what a stupid, shallow, fool of a man you are. You weren't treated badly when you were a youth and you weren't that poor. It was your own pride that made you take umbrage at every little slight.

Well you've ruined my life, but I'm not going to let you ruin hers."

"Did you kill Sir Edmund," Barnes asked. It never hurt to get a confession and like the inspector, he was at a loss as to what to do next. He'd decided to keep her talking as long as possible.

"Of course." She laughed. "I saw him cooing with his mistress at my daughter's engagement party. Can you believe that? He was such a monster he didn't care one whit that my daughter was being publicly humiliated. As soon as the whore had left, I confronted him. I told him I wasn't having it, that I was going to break the engagement and make sure she never married a useless fool such as he. I know all about being married to a fool, Constable. I've been married to one for thirty years."

"Oh God, Julia, you can't mean this." Parkington groaned softly and began to cry.

"But my miserable marriage isn't important," she continued. "He caught me in the foyer as I was leaving and told me that if I ended the engagement, he'd sue me."

"So you shot him?" Witherspoon pressed.

"Yes. When Beatrice jumped out of the carriage, I saw my chance and I took it. When we got home, I forced Osgood to go out looking for her. Then I took one of his guns from the study, wrapped myself in the housekeepers cloak, and went out hunting. I knew all about that girl that had been stalking him. Everyone in London knew about her, so I knew no one would suspect me as the killer."

"How did you know where to find him?" Barnes asked. "Did you go back to the party."

"That's right." Her hand began to shake a bit. "I knew he'd walked to the party with his cousin. I was fairly certain they'd walk home together, so I hid in a darkened doorway and waited for them to come out."

"Were you going to kill Roland Leggett as well?" The inspector edged closer to the woman.

"No, I was just going to cosh him on the head. But God was on my side and Sir Edmund came out alone. I know this neighborhood very well, Inspector, so I was fairly certain of the route he'd take home. I got ahead of him and when he was close enough, I stepped out in front of him." She laughed. "You should have seen his face when he saw the gun in my hand. I shot him three times in the chest. He looked ever so surprised."

From the corner of his eye, Witherspoon saw Barnes had taken another step closer to Mrs. Parkington. "Yes, I expect Sir Edmund was quite surprised."

Julia smiled sadly. "But I'd shot the wrong man, you see." She waved the gun at her husband. "I should have shot him. Good Lord, he couldn't even wait a decent amount of time before he was trying to sell our daughter off to the man's cousin." She leaned closer to the settee. "But you can't touch her now. I've given her lots of money and sent her off to the man she really loves. By now, she and William Carter will be on a ship sailing for America."

Osgood wiped the tears from his cheek and stared at her for a long moment. Then he straightened up as best he could. "You don't love me at all, do you?"

"Love you? I wanted to, I really did. But now I don't know," she replied. "You made it so difficult."

The room was deathly quiet. Witherspoon could hear his own breathing and the thump of his heartbeat roaring in his ears. He wondered if the others could hear it, as well. He inched closer to Mrs. Parkington.

The clock struck the hour and the most peculiar thing happened. Julia Parkington's shoulders relaxed and she smiled at her husband. "It's eleven o'clock. She's gone by now. She's out of your reach."

She stepped to one side and put the gun down on the top of a table that was between the settee and a chair. There was a cup of tea on the table. She picked up the cup of tea, flopped down in the chair, and drained the teacup.

"Mrs. Parkington," Witherspoon said. "You're under arrest for the murder of Sir Edmund Leggett and the attempted murder of Osgood Parkington."

"I won't be pressing charges," Osgood said quickly. "No matter what she might think of me, she's my wife." His voice broke but he managed to get hold of himself. "And I love her."

"I suppose you might," she replied. Then she smiled at the inspector. "I'll never stand trial, sir. I won't live long enough for the magistrate to charge me. I've got cancer, you see." She raised her empty teacup. "But it's almost over. My daughter is safe and going to a country where a woman can do what she likes."

Osgood started to sob. He shifted on the settee, trying to get closer to her. "Oh God, Julia, what have you done?"

She slumped against the back of the chair. "I've done what's best for all of us. You'll be free now, as well." Her eyes began to close but she struggled for a moment and forced them open. She reached out a hand to him and he grimaced in pain but managed to lean close enough to grasp her finger.

"I do love you," she whispered. "I just didn't love your ambition. Promise me you'll be a decent father to Beatrice and bless her marriage to William Carter. He's a good man. He'll make her happy."

"I promise." Osgood sobbed. "Oh God, Julia, how could it all go so wrong."

But Julia Parkington didn't answer him. Her eyes had closed for the final time.

Mrs. Jeffries was getting worried. It was hours since Smythe and Wiggins had gone off to the Parkington house to see what, if anything, might be happening. "I think I've made a dreadful mistake."

"You think she's not the killer?" Mrs. Goodge asked bluntly. "She's as good a suspect as any of them and Wig-

gins did say there was some strange goings-on there today." But the cook wondered if maybe this time, Mrs. Jeffries was wrong. The evidence against Mrs. Parkington
wasn't very good at all. But she wasn't going to say that out
loud. She could see by the expression in the housekeeper's
eyes that she was afraid she'd sent everyone off on a wild
goose chase. Oh well, she couldn't be expected to be right
all of the time. Everyone was entitled to the occasional
mistake.

"I don't know," Mrs. Jeffries replied. "It's been hours.
Why hasn't someone come back yet?"

"Maybe nothing's happened yet," Betsy suggested. But
like the cook, she wondered if Mrs. Jeffries was wide of
the mark this time. "Maybe Smythe and Wiggins have
found something and they're off on the hunt."

"Maybe nothing's happened because Mrs. Parkington is
completely innocent and I got it wrong."

"You didn't get it wrong," Luty said. "It's just maybe
takin' a bit longer than we thought." She looked at Hatchet.
But he was no comfort, he looked as anxious as she felt.
"Let's give it a few more minutes. If one of them ain't back
then, I say we send Hatchet over the Parkington house."

"That's an excellent idea, madam." Hatchet agreed.

But he didn't have to go anywhere as both Smythe and
Wiggins came in a few minutes later.

"You was right." Wiggins grinned at the housekeeper.
"You must be like one of them gypsy fortune-tellers, Mrs.
Jeffries. One of them people that can see what's goin' to
'appen before it does."

"I take it something happened?" Mrs. Jeffries held her
breath, hoping that she'd been correct.

"You can say that again," Smythe pulled out his chair
and sat down. "Julia Parkington is dead. She tried to kill
her husband."

"Cor blimey, it were something," Wiggins added excitedly as he sat down. "Roland Leggett come runnin' out like

the 'ounds of 'ell were after 'im, and then we 'eard the gun shot, and the inspector and Constable Barnes went runnin' inside. We didn't know what to do!"

"There was a gunshot!" Betsy looked at Smythe in alarm.

"And the inspector and Barnes charged in with no thought to their own safety," Wiggins said. "Smythe and I was standing a ways off out of their line of sight and we didn't know what to do after the inspector run into the house. So we just stood there, waitin' and hopin' that it'd all turn out all right. Which it did, more or less. 'Course I felt bad when they hauled poor Mrs. Parkington's body out."

"I'll give you the quick version of events," Smythe said. He looked toward the door. "I've a feeling that the inspector will be here soon and he'll want to 'ave his say." He told them what they'd seen as they stood outside the Parkington house. When he'd finished, he sighed and shook his head. "We knew everything was going to be all right when Barnes came out and blew his police whistle. We'd not heard any more shots so we were fairly sure the inspector was all right. I still don't know how you figured it out, Mrs. Jeffries. She was the one person who didn't seem to have a motive for wanting Sir Edmund dead."

"I wasn't even certain myself," the housekeeper admitted. "But when Wiggins told us what he'd seen this morning, I thought my suspicions might be correct." She reached into her apron pocket and pulled out her suspect list. Unfolding the paper, she pointed at the names and the information written underneath each one. "You see, if you'll look under her name, the bits and pieces we learned about her didn't make sense if we assumed she was as socially ambitious as her husband. These clues show a woman of great intelligence and character. Yet she appeared to be going along with her husband's ambitions for her daughter. But if you'll look closely, she obviously didn't want the girl to marry Sir Edmund."

Betsy studied the paper. "How did you come to that conclusion?"

"I didn't until I went over the list again early this morning, well, actually, in the wee hours of the night. When I put that together with what Dr. Bosworth told me last night, it all seemed to make a sort of horrible sense. Look here," she pointed to an item at the top of the list. "It says here that she was the one who bought her daughter the telescope and here it says she knew about Beatrice's correspondence with William Carter. A socially ambitious woman doesn't deliberately turn her daughter into an unmarriageable bluestocking."

"And Carter told the inspector that Mrs. Parkington was always nice to 'im," Wiggins added. "Why would she be nice to 'im if she wanted to scare 'im off her daughter. We all should 'ave seen that one."

Betsy scanned the list of clues. "You're right, if you look at that list, it's obvious that Julia Parkington was very different from her husband. But why did you think she was the killer? Why not just insist the engagement be broken if she didn't want her daughter to marry Sir Edmund."

"Because Sir Edmund threatened to sue them," Mrs. Jeffries replied. "That's why she had to kill him."

"That's what Edna overheard her mistress telling Lord Drummond," Mrs. Goodge exclaimed. "Sir Edmund wasn't wanting to haggle over the price of the marriage settlement, he was threatening her with the law if they tried to back out of it."

"Right," Mrs. Jeffries nodded. "And knowing her husband as she did, she knew he'd never call the wedding off if he was going to be sued, so she decided to take matters into her own hands. We know she could shoot a gun . . ."

"That's right. My source told us that," Hatchet interjected. "When she was a schoolgirl, she was good at grouse hunting and mathematics."

"And we also know that when Osgood went out looking

for Beatrice that night, the maid overheard Julia Parkington go into Osgood's study. She did go into the study, but it wasn't to wait for her husband, it was to get one of his guns. Then she crept out the back door and went off to find her victim . . ." She broke off as they heard the front door open upstairs. "That'll be the inspector."

They heard his footsteps come down the length of the hallway. "Yoo hoo, are you all in the kitchen?" Witherspoon called out as he came down the stairs.

"Yes sir, Mrs. Crookshank and Hatchet have dropped by for a cup of tea. Do join us."

"Mrs. Crookshank, Mr. Hatchet, how very nice to see you." He smiled at their guests. "This looks very nice. I believe I will have a cup of tea and a slice of that wonderful-looking seed cake. I had a nice slice last night and it's excellent, Mrs. Goodge, really excellent."

"Thank you, sir." Mrs. Goodge smiled proudly.

Mrs. Jeffries got up to get a cup. "Do sit down, sir. How goes the case?"

Witherspoon sat down next to Luty. Mrs. Goodge handed him a slice of cake. "We've made an arrest. Well, that's not really the truth. The case is over and we would have made an arrest but our murderer took a massive dose of what we think is morphine. We won't know what she took until after the postmortem is complete. But the doctor was fairly sure it was an opiate of some kind."

"Gracious, sir, what happened?" Mrs. Jeffries put his tea down next to his cake.

Witherspoon sighed deeply and then told them everything that had happened. Despite watching Julia Parkington die, he was delighted the case was finally over. Her fate had been very sad, but at least she wasn't suffering anymore, and frankly, Sir Edmund Leggett had been a fairly sorry excuse for a human being.

Everyone listened closely, occasionally looking at one another as he related a detail that fit in with the information they'd all help gather. But they were careful not to give the game away by reacting too vividly to his comments. They were all very fond of their inspector.

When he'd finished, he shook his head. "I don't quite know what to make of the whole matter."

"In what sense, sir?" Mrs. Jeffries asked. "It seems to me you put everything together quite nicely and probably saved Mr. Parkington's life. It's not your fault that your murderer took her own life."

"I don't think she'd have killed him," he replied. "I think she simply wanted to hold him at bay until the girl reached the ship."

"Has she left the country, then, sir?" Smythe asked.

Witherspoon tapped his finger against the side of his cup. "Actually she hasn't. The eleven o'clock time that Mrs. Parkington reacted to was the time that the train left Victoria Station for Southampton. The ship isn't sailing until this evening. Osgood Parkington, to his credit, didn't want us to send for the girl. He wants her out of the country when the whole ugly incident hits the newspapers."

"But won't she have to testify?" Hatchet asked. "I mean, they'll be an inquest, won't there?"

"Oh yes, but as Mrs. Parkington confessed in front of two policemen, her husband, and several servants who were hiding behind the door, we don't think her testimony will be needed." He shrugged sadly. "I almost felt sorry for the poor woman. Of course, that's no excuse for committing murder, but well, it's really very sad. She simply wanted her child to be happy. She didn't want her to endure the same kind of marriage that she'd had."

"Why didn't she leave him?" Betsy asked softly. "I know divorce isn't very nice, but it's better than killing someone."

"That's a solution that women of Mrs. Parkington's generation wouldn't consider," Mrs. Jeffries said. She looked at the inspector. "Thank goodness you and the constable went over there today. Otherwise, there might have been more deaths. You must be exhausted, sir."

"I am tired and I'm glad this case is over." Again, he shook his head. "But not all the questions have been answered. I'd still like to know what happened to that young woman who was stalking Sir Edmund."

"Perhaps she went 'ome, sir," Wiggins suggested. "She must 'ave come from somewhere."

"Yes, well, I expect you're right. But honestly, it seems as if the world is full of disappearing women."

"Disappearing women?" Hatchet repeated.

"But of course," Witherspoon exclaimed. "First there was Edith Durant and now we've got this young woman disappearing into thin air."

"At least this one isn't a murdereress," Smythe said.

"That's some comfort, I suppose."

"You'll find Edith Durant eventually," Mrs. Jeffries assured the inspector. "You always get your suspect, sir, one way or another."

"Thank you, Mrs. Jeffries." Witherspoon smiled at them and got to his feet. "I do hope you'll forgive me, but I think I'll go and lie down for a while before dinner. I am suddenly so tired I can't keep my eyes open."

"You go on, Inspector," Luty said. "Seems like you've had a right full day."